Winnifred Cottage

Jennie Alexander

www.JennieAlexander.biz

JennieAlexander@hotmail.co.uk

For Mum and Dad
With Love

Chapter One

Abigail Morgan hurried along the hospital corridor in her pink fluffy slippers relieved to see the phone was free at last. It was late, and she was dreading this, but it was important. She tapped in the number and waited, impatient for her sister to answer.

'Come on Jilly,' she muttered, anxious to get the call over with.

'Hello?'

'Hi, it's me. Listen, it's just a quick call, I've been thinking, and I've changed my mind. I've decided not to sell Gran's place after all. I just wanted to let you know.'

'What do you mean, you're not selling? I thought it was all decided. What's changed your mind?'

'Well, for one thing my house burnt down a few hours ago - remember? Abbie noticed a couple of nurses looking at her and quietened her voice. She knew this wasn't going to be an easy conversation. 'Jilly, I need somewhere to live.'

'So you're just going to up sticks from Dorset and move three hundred miles away?'

'The Lake District is a beautiful place to live. And anyway, I've nowhere else to go. And, you know, this just seems the obvious answer.'

1

'But you haven't seen the cottage in years; it could be a complete wreck.'

'It can't be that bad. Hopefully it'll be a fresh start for me.'

'So you're definitely finishing with Jack then?'

It felt like an accusation. 'It wasn't me who messed things up.' Abbie could hear her sister sighing on the other end of the phone. She knew it wasn't a sigh of compassion.

'You don't know for sure that he was doing anything wrong.'

'I know enough. I'm not going to hang around for the gory details.'

'For goodness sake Abbie, why do you always give up so easily? As soon as you have something to deal with, a bit of life in the real world, and you're off.'

'What do you know of life in the real world?' snapped Abbie, her voice rising again. Thoughts of Jilly's beautiful home, her large family and adoring husband rattled her. 'What have you ever had to deal with?' Abbie stopped abruptly, cringing at the thought that she could so easily say too much. 'Look, I have to go, someone else is waiting for the phone.'

'You could always stay with us for a while, until you get yourself sorted.'

Abbie smiled sardonically but said nothing. The silence between them said it all as far as she was concerned. They said their good-byes and then she walked back to the ward where the other patients were settling down for the night.

Despite the icy March rain hammering the windows, it was oppressively hot inside the hospital and Abbie kicked off the ridiculous fluffy slippers and tossed the equally fluffy dressing gown onto the chair at the side of her bed. Typical of Jilly to bring pink of all colours – the last thing Abbie would have chosen for herself. She lay on top of her bed and gently touched the stitches across her temple, feeling along to the bruised and tender brow bone. She stared ahead, not really seeing the stranger in the opposite bed and reflected on the last few hours in which her entire life had been turned upside down.

First, there was this bang to the head. Nothing heroic or glamorous. She had merely slipped on a wet floor while giving an evening art class at the local college. She had fallen sideways, whacking her head on the corner of a table before landing clumsily on the floor. Dazed and struggling to get up, Abbie had felt silly and conspicuous as people rushed to help. They insisted her head injury should be treated in hospital and finally managed to persuade her to go although she convinced them she was OK to drive.

Abbie remembered sitting in her car in the college car park phoning Jack. She wanted to tell him not to bother cooking the Chilli Con Carne for dinner which would be dried up and inedible after the inevitable hours of waiting in casualty. Jack would insist on going with her to the hospital, which is what she wanted, but as it was, he didn't even answer his phone. She decided to stop off anyway to change out of her jeans which now had a very obvious wet patch on the backside.

From there on, Abbie's recollection of events got a little jumbled. So much had happened in such a short space of time, it was difficult keeping it all in order. She remembered the ominous sight of blue flashing lights as she turned into her road and the increasing feeling of dread in her stomach as she drove slowly, getting closer and closer, finally realising that the police car was positioned directly outside her house and the hoses from the fire engine had been aimed at where her bedroom window used to be.

Looking up at her house and anxiously trying to decide where to park, Abbie scuffed the tyres on the kerb, parking close behind Jack's van. She got out of the car, dizzy and unsteady on her feet, not sure whether it was due to the scene before her or the knock to her head which was now beginning to throb.

There were firemen everywhere, walking around calmly now, gathering up their equipment. The worst was done. Abbie looked up at her home helplessly, thinking if she'd got there sooner, she might have been able to do something to prevent it.

Two firemen were coming out of her front door and in a haze of confusion she wondered if they had wiped their feet before going in. She spotted Jack talking to a policeman and at the same time they began walking towards her. She wanted to speak to him, but he was hanging back and the policeman got to her first.

'Are you Abigail Morgan, owner of this property?'

'Yes.' She felt giddy again, aware that she was swaying slightly.

'Steady there. Are you OK?' The policeman held her arm gently and then squinted in the darkness at the gash on her head.

'How did that happen?' he asked, thinking he'd stumbled on something juicy.

Abbie touched her temple, still wet and sticky with blood. 'It's nothing.'

'That's a serious wound there. I wouldn't call it nothing.' The policeman's words caught Jack's attention and he moved in a little closer, peering down at Abbie.

'Bloody hell Abbie, what's happened?'

'Nothing!' she snapped. 'I think this is more important.' She jerked her chin in the direction of her burnt-out home. 'Can someone just tell me what's happened? How bad is it?'

'Fortunately, the damage seems to be limited mostly to the one room,' said the PC.

'Thank God,' muttered Abbie looking up at her bedroom and shuddering at what she might have lost if it had spread further. 'Can I go inside?'

'I'm afraid not,' said the constable. 'Not tonight anyway.'

'Oh God. What am I supposed to do?'

'You need to get to a hospital and get that wound looked at before anything else. Would you like to tell me how you got it?' The constable was reaching for his notebook, in investigative mode now.

'No, I wouldn't.' At last she caught Jack's eye. 'What happened, how did it start?' she asked, impatient for the answers that for some reason weren't forthcoming. What was the matter with him? Why wasn't he reassuring her and telling her everything would be alright?

'I don't know how it started,' he said. A little too emphatically thought Abbie, confused by his behaviour.

After a few seconds of telling silence, the PC proceeded to fill in the blanks. 'It's not conclusive and the final investigative report will give the full details but initially it seems that it was started by a stray cigarette butt.'

Abbie shook her head trying to make sense of things. She didn't smoke. And neither did Jack. She looked at him, imploring him to speak. He looked lost in the darkness, the red and blue flashing lights striking hypnotically across his pale face.

The PC cleared his throat as if to give importance to his final delivery. 'It seems that the fire started in the bedroom.' Abbie half expected him to take a bow. She glared at him and he took the hint and moved away. Abbie could feel herself swaying again but was determined not to pass out in front of Jack.

'Who's been smoking in our bedroom?' she asked, quietly now, all energy draining from her body.

'No-one. Abbie, I swear. They've got it wrong.'

'Yeah, of course they have.' Abbie turned, shaking all over from the cold and everything else. She headed back to her car.

'More like it's me who got it wrong,' she shouted back over her shoulder.

'Where are you going?' Jack followed her to her car.

'To the hospital.'

'I'll come with you.'

'No.'

'Abbie let me come with you. Then we need to find somewhere to stay for the night. We could go to Jilly's?'

'Hardly!' How could he be so stupid as to even think that?

'Or Pete's then?'

'You go where you want. I'll sort myself out.' Abbie almost fell into the car seat. She could feel fresh blood trickling down the side of her face and straightened up to look at herself in the rear-view mirror. The side of her face was caked in blood which was congealing messily in her shoulder-length hair. She noticed it needed re-highlighting and then she saw the anxiety in her blue-grey eyes; she looked tired and scared.

On auto pilot Abbie drove to the hospital, parked and made her way to the emergency department. She had to have five stitches and because of the concussion they kept her in overnight, for which she was bizarrely grateful. That was one problem solved.

Later that evening Jilly had appeared – flapping and fussing around. Jack must have phoned her. Fortunately, there was only half an hour of visiting time left. Abbie didn't feel like talking and just gave a brief account of what had happened that evening although she became more animated when it came to her own interpretations and assumptions of what Jack was up to. Typical of Jilly not to see her side of things.

That was all a few hours ago and since then Abbie had lay there in the hospital bed thinking about her uncertain future. Finally, she reached a decision – not to sell the cottage in the Lake District that she had recently inherited from her gran. It seemed an obvious answer to all her problems right now. And Jilly had reacted to her change of heart with predictable negativity.

Abbie couldn't settle for the night. Her thoughts were circling round and round on a never-ending loop. She lay awake for hours, aware of the silence which was eerie in a place with so many people in it. Just before dawn she heard the low rumble of an aeroplane, like thunder, the warning of an impending storm and finally fell into a deep sleep.

The early morning start on the ward jolted her awake. Immediately thoughts of yesterday filled her head. There was so much to think about and so many decisions to make but instead she lay there watching passively as nurses and patients did what they needed to do. She waited obediently for instructions and for the doctor to arrive to tell her if she was allowed home. To where, she didn't know.

It wasn't until the afternoon that Abbie was given the all clear to leave the hospital. She was bundling her few things together when Jack appeared at the foot of the bed. He looked surprised to see her dressed and ready to go.

'Hi, how are you feeling today?'

Abbie thought he would have visited before now but wasn't about to let her disappointment show.

'I'm OK,' she said, noticing he looked tired. he was still gorgeous, even with sleepy eyes and in need of a shave. She loved his big brown eyes and long eyelashes, his sharp closely cropped hair with just a fine hint of grey beginning to show.

Abbie turned away from him and fussed with her handbag. It didn't matter how gorgeous he was, he'd let her down. And she had been here before, in other relationships, too many times. But it had felt so right with Jack. Or maybe she just wanted it to be right. At thirty-four she wanted some stability in her life, something to build on that was constant and reassuringly safe.

And yet here she was, being forced to move home, to another part of the country and on her own. Not part of the plan. And it was all his fault. She turned back to him.

'What did you want?' The directness and harshness of the question startled him. He was hoping Abbie would have got over the worst of the shock by now and be more willing to talk and listen and of course to believe him. But now he didn't feel very optimistic.

'I just wanted to make sure you were OK. Jilly said you had concussion. I didn't think you'd be getting out just yet.'

'Yeah, I'm getting out, in more ways than one.'

'Eh?'

'Oh, nothing. It doesn't matter.'

'Abbie, we need to talk. I honestly don't know what started the fire. Why don't you believe me? The cigarette thing is only a theory, they don't know the truth yet.'

9

'I've been here before Jack. And you've been found out, whatever the report says.'

'Look, not all men are the same. You can't judge everyone by your past mistakes.'

Abbie shot him a look.

'I'm sorry, I didn't mean it like that.' Jack hated them arguing. 'OK, I'll leave you to it for now. Where are you going to be staying?'

Abbie paused.

'Look, I'm not going to follow you. If you want some time, that's fine, OK?'

'I'm staying with Luisa.'

'In her one bedroom flat? That'll be cosy.'

'Aaron's in Finland - she's happy to have me!'

'You could do worse than staying with Jilly, you know. She's OK, really.'

The glare from Abbie told him it was time to leave.

'OK, I'm going. And by the way, you're allowed back into the house, if you want to collect some things. I'll call you later, if that's OK?'

Abbie didn't answer but continued to fuss with the contents of her bag. She didn't look up until she knew Jack was walking away and then sadly she watched him as he went out of the ward and along the long corridor towards the exit and out of sight.

Chapter Two

'Where did they come from?' demanded Eva as she
poked her bony finger in the direction of a pretty
china jug full of golden daffodils.

'From the garden of course,' replied Lilleth, calm
and patient as always.

'Taken from my flowerbeds I suppose?'

Lilleth rolled her eyes, mentally counting to ten
but saying nothing. Her sister's claim to the
flowerbeds was merely based on the fact that she
tended them. Gordon Cottage, in the heart of the
Lake District, belonged to Lilleth. It was tiny and
ancient but cosy, a single storey dwelling with two
bedrooms. Lilleth had taken Eva into her home two
years ago after she'd fallen and injured her hip. What
actually happened was that Eva came to stay while
she recuperated, and never went home again.

Lilleth smiled as she warmed the old brown
teapot, refusing to be rattled. 'I took them from the
side of the shed where they can't be seen anyway.
They'll be much more appreciated in here.'

Eva wandered outside mumbling something to
herself that was not meant to be heard, so Lilleth
didn't ask. The tea made, Lilleth carried the tray
outside and placed it on the wooden table; well worn,

11

rickety and bleached by the sun, as were the two Delaney sisters, both in their mid-seventies.

'Tea's ready,' called out Lilleth. Eva pretended not to hear. Lilleth knew she had and waited, well acquainted with her attention tactics. Eventually, Eva stopped pretending she was doing something useful over by the shed and went to sit with her sister. She sniffed the frosty air.

'It doesn't look like anyone's been inside the place yet. It still looks undisturbed. I wonder if we'll ever get to meet this great-niece of ours, not that she's ever bothered with us over the years.'

Lilleth shook her head, just a fraction, as she poured the tea. 'I'm sure we shall meet her eventually.'

'I don't want to wait for eventually. I'd like to see her right now. Tell her what I think. Up front.'

'Calm down Eva. She hasn't done anything wrong. It's strange to think she was probably at Anna's funeral – sad that we didn't know who each other was.'

'Well, it isn't right. That much I do know. It should stay in the family.'

'She is family too, Eva.'

'Yes, but why to her?'

'Why not? She is Anna's grand-daughter. Mind you, Anna was a dark horse, I'll give you that. All these years and we didn't even know she owned the place. Such a darling little cottage; I've often passed it and wondered why it hadn't been snapped up by one of those building refurbishers. It's all a bit of a mystery.'

'It's more than a mystery – there's definitely something fishy about all this if you ask me.'

Lilleth sighed. 'Well, I'm not asking you. It's none of our business,' she said decisively. Eva sniffed again, a look of distaste in her eyes. Both women looked away from each other, avoiding eye contact that might expose their own secrets.

Eva took a sip of tea and pulled a face that looked as if she was about to spit it out. 'This tea's disgusting. What have you done to it?'

Lilleth sighed again. 'I haven't done anything to it. If you don't like it, don't drink it.'

They were silent for a few seconds and then in a slightly less caustic tone, Eva spoke. 'It just needs a little something.' They turned to face each other and started to grin, their eyes twinkling.

'Come on then,' said Lilleth, picking up her cup and saucer. 'Bring the tray – it's too cold out here anyway.'

In the kitchen the sisters stood side by side; Eva was the tallest and slim in a straight up and down way with her grey hair cut stylishly if a little severe. Lilleth was shorter but shapelier and her fine white hair was regularly trimmed in a soft feminine style. Lilleth took a half-full bottle of brandy from a low cupboard and poured a generous measure into each cup before topping up with tea. Eva cupped hers in both hands and took a sip. 'Mm, much better,' she smiled.

They took their teacups, the teapot and brandy bottle, leaving ceremony and the saucers behind and pulled two chairs away from the kitchen table sitting as close as possible to the Aga, in companionable silence, drinking away the afternoon with their brandy tea.

Chapter Three

Abbie drove from the hospital straight to her house but waited in the car until Luisa arrived. The afternoon light was fading, and it was grey and miserable, not that any amount of sunshine would have lifted her mood. She looked out the window at her once lovely home, now with its ugly black scar spreading out at all angles from the upstairs window. She wondered how long it would take to put right - ages probably, taking into account all the insurance paperwork and getting quotes and everything. It was totally depressing.

Abbie thought back to when Jack had moved in with her, eighteen months ago. It had been such a happy time. She had met him six months before that at a vintage car exhibition that actually neither of them had an interest in but had been invited there by their respective friends. Their eyes met over a bright orange MG Midget, attracted by mutual boredom. And they were even more attracted when they discovered shared interests in other things such as art and photography.

Jack was a successful freelance photographer, temporarily but gratefully staying with his brother while he house-hunted after a speedy divorce. It wasn't long before he was spending most of his time at Abbie's house, but it was still such a wonderful feeling when he moved all his clothes and framed prints and photographic equipment in.

A loud rapping on the car window made Abbie jump in her seat. She turned to see Luisa standing outside, smiling in at her, tall and elegant in a long fawn coloured coat. Together with her height, her soft brown eyes and long black hair, she had a striking appearance. Abbie got out of her car and Luisa's smile faded fast.

'You were miles away. Are you OK?'

'Mm, a bit deep in thought that's all. I'm dreading this.'

'Come on, it'll be OK.' Luisa wrapped her arm around Abbie's shoulders, towering protectively above her as they walked to the house.

Inside the hallway the smell of smoke and stale water hit them immediately – Abbie felt sick and wasn't sure she wanted to continue. Luisa suddenly realised the enormity of what had happened to her friend's home. She wouldn't be able to joke her out of this one.

'Abbie, I think your clothes and things may be ruined,' she said gently.

'I know, I was just thinking the same thing. It's all going to stink, isn't it? You won't want anything from here in your flat.'

'I wasn't thinking about that. Let's just get back to mine, I can lend you some things.'

Abbie moved towards the stairs. 'I'd just like to take a quick look upstairs. Do you mind?'

'No, of course not. Do you want me to come up?'

Abbie paused on the first stair. 'Yeah, please.'

The bedroom was black; the walls, the ceiling, the furniture but almost worse was the subsequent water damage which had left everything soggy and sodden, a pathetic dirty mess.

Abbie stood in the doorway, scanning the room. She had quickly taken in the state of the place, but she wasn't really looking at that now. She was searching for signs. Who had been here last night? She tried to imagine a woman here in her bedroom - with her boyfriend. She'd been smoking a cigarette – was that before or after? There was no evidence; no wine glasses, no stray saucer used as an ashtray. Nothing. She looked at the carpet, searching for a patch that was particularly burnt, trying to see whatever it was the firemen saw that enabled them to reach their conclusion.

Luisa was close behind Abbie and peered over her into the bedroom, just as keen to make some relevant observation.

'Shall we go Abbie? Maybe this wasn't such a good idea.'

'Yes, you're right. Let's go. Sorry to drag you here for nothing. I really didn't expect it to be this bad.'

'Don't be silly. It had to be done. I understand.'

Luisa headed for the stairs while Abbie dashed into the spare bedroom which she and Jack shared as a workroom. Despite being told the fire damage was mostly in the main bedroom, she was still relieved to see all their equipment had survived.

'I just need to get something,' she called out. Abbie went to a chest of drawers and opened the bottom one. She lifted out a small wooden box, grateful beyond measure that it was safe.

Back outside they both took deep breaths of cold fresh air, relieved to be out of the house and its rotten stink; bitter and mouldy.

'Are you OK to drive?' Luisa could see Abbie was rather shaken.

'Yes, I'm fine. I'll follow you but if you go racing off, I'm not even attempting to keep up with you.'

'I'll put the kettle on and have a nice cup of tea ready for you.' Normally Luisa would have continued the joke, teasing Abbie about her slow, safe driving and how she would have a three-course meal ready by the time Abbie arrived but this afternoon, it didn't seem appropriate to even try to be so jolly.

She fussed her friend into her car then ran back to her own and quickly pulled off, leading the way to her home, constantly checking her rear-view mirror to make sure Abbie was still close behind.

Luisa's welcoming flat was elegant and cosy. Sophisticated shades of cream and warm honey were used to perfection in the converted Victorian house. As Abbie stepped over the threshold, the first things she noticed were the incredible warmth and the delicate scent of fragranced candles – it was pure luxury. Suddenly, she was full of despair, wondering when she would ever feel such comfort in a home of her own. She stood in the hall, immobilised, feeling needy and useless, unable to think what to do next or how to behave in this situation. She held onto the box, clutching it to her chest like a child clinging to a favourite toy.

Luisa took the lead. 'Give me your coat Abbie. I'll hang it up.'

Luisa helped Abbie off with her coat and hung it in the hall cupboard before gently steering Abbie up a few stairs and into the small lounge. The developer had cleverly managed to create six flats in the property and the project was nicely done. The higgledy-piggledy layout adding to the charm of the original features. She settled Abbie in front of the fire, carefully positioned a few logs and soon had it blazing nicely. While she was busy in the kitchen preparing something to eat, she periodically peeked her head round the door to check on Abbie and noticed she'd dozed off a couple of times. She had to wake her to eat and instead of talking until the early hours, as expected, Abbie slept for most of the evening until Luisa woke her again, to go to bed.

The next morning Luisa had already left for work by the time Abbie got up. She had slept on the settee and must have been in a deep sleep not to have heard her go. She was reminded of Christmas mornings as a child, amazed at how Father Christmas could have come into her bedroom and arranged a whole pile of presents without even disturbing her. On the chair to the side of her, Luisa had left a pile of clothes for her to borrow.

After washing and dressing and several cups of coffee, Abbie sat down to write a list, but her mind was so full, she didn't know where to begin. And she still felt tired. It was probably the shock of it all finally sinking in. After some further attempts at list-making, she dozed on and off all afternoon but every time she woke, thoughts of everything that had happened came flooding back.

When Abbie came to again later in the afternoon, it was dark and she went around the flat closing the curtains on the winter evening outside. Luisa wasn't due home for at least a couple of hours and Abbie searched the kitchen cupboards for ingredients to cook a special thank-you meal. There was an impressive selection, plenty of inspiration for her to prepare a feast for when Luisa arrived home.

Less than two hours later, Abbie had prepared a vegetable soup; perfectly warming for a winter's evening, followed by her own adaptation of chicken chasseur with tomatoes and mixed olives and finished with a rich cheese topping cooked until lightly brown and bubbling under the grill. And finally, Abbie made a raspberry cheesecake, not particularly wintry fare, but Luisa's absolute favourite and so a definite must for a thank-you meal.

'Oh crikey, how am I going to put up with you staying here?' said Luisa lying flat out on the sofa, stroking her over-full belly. 'If you keep cooking like that, there won't be enough room for two people here! It was all absolutely delicious.'

'It's just my way of saying thank-you for helping me out. I'm so grateful for this Lou.'

Luisa waved her hand in the air dismissively. 'No need, honestly.' Luisa sat up, still rubbing her tummy. 'You look better anyway, now you're washed and fed.' Luisa was grinning; she had a stunning smile with toothpaste advert perfect teeth.

'Thanks, you make me sound like a waif, off the streets.'

'Well, you are, sort of.'

'Mm, I suppose I am.'

'So, what are your plans? And let's get one thing clear, you can stay here as long as you want. You know that. Cordon Bleu cookery or not.'

'Thanks Luisa. Honestly, you don't know how much I appreciate this.'

'I think I do. You're homeless and have no-where else to go apart from your dreadful sister's house!'

'Thank you, I feel a lot better for that! Actually, I do feel better. I hardly slept at the hospital but now I've had a good night's sleep and a nap this afternoon I feel more human. My plans? Well, you know I've decided to keep my inheritance. I told Jilly I wouldn't be selling, not at the moment anyway.'

'What did she say?'

'She wasn't very pleased. We didn't talk for long but I'm sure she'll have more to say.'

Luisa smiled, understanding. She had been friends with Abbie for fifteen years and never known her to get along with her sister although she didn't really know why. Jilly seemed OK to her.

'So, tell me properly about this inheritance. Everything's happened so quick and we've hardly had a chance to talk about it all.'

'I know – the last couple of weeks have been totally crazy. Well, Gran died a few weeks ago, as you know.'

'Yeah.' Luisa knew how much Abbie adored her grandmother.

'Her name was Annaliese – pretty, eh?' Abbie smiled and gave a little laugh. 'We used to call her Granna-liese. She always thought that was funny. And then, a letter arrived out of the blue - from some solicitors, saying I'd inherited this cottage in the Lake District that belonged to my gran.'

'Fantastic. And so, you know the place?'

'Yeah, I've been there loads of times. When I was a little girl I used to visit whenever I could, in all the school holidays – any excuse to get to The Lakes. Every year we took a cruise on Windermere and always went somewhere new as well – I remember Lake Derwent, in Keswick I think, that was amazing.'

'And what's the cottage like?'

'Lovely – from what I can remember.' Abbie stared into the flames of the open fire, warm with happy memories. 'It's big for a cottage; lots of windows so it's bright and sunny in the summer. But in winter, the weather can be wild – torrential rain and really strong winds. I remember being frightened one night and Gran letting me stay up late. We toasted bread over the fire – a huge inglenook – I used to sit inside it.'

'And now it's all yours. What about Jilly – was she left anything?'

'No, nothing, which kind of makes it awkward. I was always Gran's favourite. Maybe because I was the youngest, or because I loved visiting her and the whole place, I don't really know.'

'Maybe she left it to you because she thought you needed it more. Jilly's set up, has a family and everything.'

'Mm, maybe. And then I went and opened my stupid mouth and said I would sell the place and give her some of the proceeds.'

'It was a nice gesture. And surely she understands why you've changed your mind?'

'I'd like to think so, but she didn't sound too pleased.'

'She'll come around – eventually. It'll take a little time for her to get used to the fact that she had a little windfall – and then she didn't.'

'She doesn't need a windfall,' mumbled Abbie.

'So, is there any other family?' Luisa asked gently. Annaliese's daughter - Abbie's mother - had spent the last two years in a care home. She had dementia, unaware of herself or her surroundings or even that her mother had recently died. Abbie's father had died three years ago after a short illness and Abbie had always been convinced it was the shock of losing her devoted husband that had been the catalyst to her mother beginning to lose her mind.

'Not really; Mum was an only child and then there's just me and Jilly. Gran still has some family in the Lake District I think - a couple of sisters. I tried picking them out at the funeral but there were so many people there. I was a bit lost; Jack was booked on a photo shoot, so I was on my own. I just stayed for the service and got the train straight back.'

'I wonder how they feel about you inheriting the cottage. Perhaps they got some jewellery or her extensive art collection,' said Luisa, grinning.

'I don't know about any of that. I don't think they were close which is probably why Gran hardly ever mentioned them. But I did get this as well.' Abbie gestured towards the wooden box which was on the floor, tucked in close to her chair.

'Oh yes, I was going to ask you about that. It's a pretty box.'

'Yes it is, isn't it? This is so typical of my gran – she loved pretty things.'

'What's inside?'

Abbie bent over the arm of the chair and carefully hauled the wooden box up onto her lap. The top and sides were decorated with violets and primroses; simply painted and with a thin layer of protective varnish which had almost worn away by decades of having been lovingly polished. Abbie released the delicate latch and lifted the hinged lid to reveal an interior lined with green silk. Inside was an eclectic store of personal treasures.

Luisa leant over for a closer look as Abbie held up an art deco perfume bottle before carefully replacing it back in the box. And then she flipped open a small velvet box containing a dainty heart pendant necklace. Abbie was familiar with all of the contents although she didn't have a clue as to the significance of the collection.

Luisa looked puzzled. 'Did your gran leave this to you in her will?'

'No, she gave it to me – a few months back. She was ill and getting weaker; I reckon she knew she

24

didn't have much time left. I think it was a real wrench for her, you know, to part with it.'

'What's the little package, all wrapped up?'

Abbie picked it up and unwrapped it to reveal a small watercolour painting of a village scene – a stile in the middle of a field of sheep. The subject matter wasn't particularly striking, but the style of the artist's brushwork was. He obviously had a delicate hand; tiny strokes with the finest brush produced a scene of almost photographic quality but it was the use of colour and light that gave the painting an ethereal feel.

'Mm, interesting. It's rather nice,' said Luisa, noting that it wasn't to her liking but not wanting to say anything unkind.

Abbie knew the painting wasn't in keeping with Luisa's sharp sense of style, but she loved it herself and didn't want to get into a critical debate. There was something magical about it and most importantly, it obviously held a special significance for her gran. She began to wrap it up again.

'Hang on - what's that on the back? Is it an inscription?'

'Oh yes,' said Abbie, pulling the paper back again. 'This is interesting; 'To my dearest Anna, my inspiration for everything I do, GT.' And then the date 1958.'

'Ooh, who's GT? Your grandfather, I take it?'
'No.'

They looked at each other, all eyebrows raised.
'No?'

'No, I don't know who GT is. I tried asking Gran about it but she was always vague and she deteriorated so quickly in the end - she didn't even know who I was.'

'That's sad. So, you didn't manage to get any information?'

'Just bits and pieces – if they're to be believed. She used to say he was a *real* artist and she always kept the painting close by, on her bedside table for the last few years.'

'It obviously meant a lot to her.'

'Mm. And changing the subject somewhat; what I'm planning to do, hopefully, is to convert her cottage into an art gallery/studio, something along those lines. What do you think?'

'Wow, that's ambitious. But yeah, it sounds like a great idea.'

'It's the perfect place for it. Like I said, it's spacious and bright and from what I can remember, it's all higgledy-piggledy, with lots of odd extensions obviously added on over the years. I could have a dedicated teaching room, a dark room and still have plenty of room for displaying. I'm actually getting quite excited about it,' Abbie said enthusiastically.

'So I see.' Luisa smiled, delighted to see her friend happy again but she was inwardly cautious too. Abbie was pinning a lot of hopes and dreams on a place that she hadn't even seen in years.

Chapter Four

Neither of them said anything but both Eva and Lilleth noticed that each had made a particular effort that afternoon. It happened almost every time they had a certain visitor.

Jed Tobin smiled as he pushed open the gate. It was late afternoon and the light was fading but the curtains hadn't yet been drawn and Jed could see the two ladies flitting about the kitchen. He gave a courteous knock before letting himself in, ducking as his large frame filled the doorway. The smell of baking and the warmth of the kitchen welcomed him as he stepped inside out of the freezing early spring rain. He'd been away for a few weeks and it felt good to be back.

'Afternoon ladies.'

'Ah Jed. It's lovely to see you,' said Lilleth. 'Come on in and warm yourself.'

Eva was already at his side, linking her arm through his and leading him into the room. 'Yes, it most certainly is lovely to see you. And it's been far too long. You're not to go off like that again. We've been inconsolable haven't we Lilleth?'

Lilleth was making tea, cringing at her sister's over-the-top nonsense even though she had missed Jed's company herself. She brought the teapot over to the table, but Eva was already leading Jed into the other room.

'We'll have tea in the lounge Lily, in front of the fire.'

Lilleth was left to load the tea things onto a tray, trying to keep calm at being spoken to like a skivvy. And at being called Lily. Eva knew she hated it. Lilleth took a fruit loaf out of the oven and turned it out onto a plate. She banged the tin into the sink hoping Eva would take the hint and come to help but she didn't appear so Lilleth sliced and buttered the fruit loaf herself, half hoping her sister would choke on a raisin.

Eva was sitting close to Jed on the settee when Lilleth carried the tea tray through, placing it on the coffee table in front of them, catching her sister's eye and glaring at her. She sat to the side of them in the leather winged armchair, slightly cut off from the conversation by Eva's back turned towards her.

'This is a delicious spread Lilleth. Your fruit loaf is second to none,' said Jed, diplomatically moving forward a little to peer around Eva.

With great satisfaction Lilleth noted the begrudging look on her sister's face. 'Thank you Jed. Help yourself to another slice, please do.'

'Yes, thank you, I will.' Jed helped himself to a couple more slices of cake.

'So, how was your holiday? Did you enjoy France?' Lilleth asked politely.

'Yes, I did,' said Jed, staring at the cake on his plate. 'It was good to get away. Paris is beautiful,' he said whimsically.

'What on earth did you find to do in Paris for five weeks?' Eva asked, laughing nervously. She was desperate to know why Jed had, all of a sudden, taken himself off on a long holiday, right out of the blue - just before Anna's funeral, it was.

Jed smiled, more to himself, a smile of secrets and memories but in the next instant he looked up and smiled at Eva and Lilleth in turn, saying cheerfully, 'Paris is a splendid city. There's plenty to do. I wandered around the galleries and went to some exhibitions. And I took thousands of photos – all of which I shall bore you with at a later date.'

They all laughed. Lilleth could sense Jed wasn't ready to be drawn on why he had taken off so suddenly. Anyway, it was his business.

'We will look forward to seeing your photos Jed dear,' she said. 'I'm sure they're all wonderful.' Jed smiled gratefully, taking a moment to bring himself back to the present.

'So, what have you two ladies been up to in my absence?'

'Brewing!' said Lilleth, a wicked twinkle in her eye, knowing how much Jed liked their home-made wines.

'Splendid! But will the dandelion be up to last year's standard, I wonder?'

'We'll find out soon enough,' said Lilleth, sipping her tea and looking forward to their lunch-time wine-tasting get-togethers which often carried on way past dinner time.

Jed bit into a slice of cake, a few crumbs settling on his full grey beard as both ladies watched, entranced.

Eva fidgeted in her seat, trying to think of something to say, and then she remembered their interesting bit of news that she could be the first to tell him. She put her plate of unfinished cake back on the table.

'The cottage,' she blurted out quickly, suddenly worried Lilleth would get there first.

'Jed,' Eva continued, making sure she had Jed's full attention. 'We were at Anna's will-reading a few weeks ago.'

Lilleth shot her sister a warning look. For some reason she wasn't entirely sure of, Lilleth had already decided not to mention Anna's will to Jed. But it was too late now, she knew there would be no stopping Eva if she thought she had some hot-off-the-press gossip. Although she continued to glare at her.

Eva fidgeted, trying to ignore Lilleth but uncomfortable enough to tone down her sensational news. 'Well, it turns out she owned a little cottage, top of Rowan Road. Apparently, she bought it years ago but then she married and moved away and the cottage, as far as we know, has been empty ever since.'

Jed had been a close friend of all three of the Delaney sisters since they were children and Eva expected Jed to be more interested in this news about their slightly aloof elder sister who had suddenly married at the age of nineteen and moved to the other side of the valley, barely keeping in touch with any of them.

Jed was staring at the cake on his plate. All he could do was nod in agreement. Lilleth had been watching Jed's reaction with a much greater understanding than Eva and was not in the least surprised by his reticence.

'Anyway,' continued Eva, somewhat frustrated by Jed's lack of reaction. 'Anna made a will and in it,' she paused in a final attempt for effect but both Jed and Lilleth were transfixed by the tea things on the coffee table. 'In it, she left the cottage to her grand-daughter, the youngest one, what's her name?' she asked, looking to Lilleth for confirmation but barely waiting a second for an answer. 'Oh, we can't remember. And we hear that she's on her way here to claim her stake, as it were.'

'Eva!' reprimanded Lilleth, feeling she had finally over-stepped the mark.

Eva did not like to be chastised and sniffed sharply in response and then slightly modified her words. 'She's expected here any time soon, but no-one seems to know her intentions.'

'She had two grandchildren, didn't she?' asked Jed.

'Yes, two girls,' answered Lilleth gently, hoping to stop Eva from speculating any further. Jed finally looked up and smiled at Lilleth.

Eva poured herself more tea, banging the teapot down on the table, hoping to break the spell between Jed and Lilleth and wondering what it would take for her to have that effect on him.

Chapter Five

Abbie drove back from the hospital having been given the all clear to go back to work. In fact, she'd already notified the college she would be leaving and fortunately they let her go without having to work any notice.

Abbie had been at Luisa's for over a week and could happily have stayed in the security of her cosy flat indefinitely but really there was nothing to stop her from going to her new life in the Lake District. She was as ready as she could be. And aside from the understandable trepidation she felt, she was keen to get to her new home. Hopefully this was going to turn out to be the best thing she'd ever done.

The car was fully loaded, and Abbie drove off with Luisa beside her already hidden behind an open map.

'Lou, I don't need a map just yet! I do know my way out of town.'

'OK, OK, I'm just getting prepared,' said Luisa folding the map away. She would be staying the night with Abbie to help her get settled and then return by train the following day on Sunday.

Having been on the motorway for a couple of hours Abbie pulled into a service station for a break. Luisa volunteered to get the teas - it was cold outside but good to get some fresh air. Abbie had the same idea and got out of the car to stretch her legs for a few minutes. Trying not to spill the hot teas, Luisa ran from the service station just as it started to rain. They got back in the car banging the doors shut as it poured; bullets of raindrops hammered on the roof and streamed down the windscreen. They sat there in the damp steaminess drinking their tea.

'Lou, I just want to say how much I appreciate all this.'

'Don't be daft. I'm just making sure you go so I get my settee back.'

'Seriously, not for just putting me up, but all this; travelling down with me and staying over – you're a great friend.'

'Oh shh, you'll have me weeping in a moment.'

'Well, I just want you to know how grateful I am. I couldn't have managed it all without you. You're always there for me. And it means a lot. I just wanted you to know.'

Luisa was uncharacteristically quiet, shuffling to get comfortable in her seat. 'You could manage on your own if you had to,' she mumbled but Abbie didn't seem to hear. Luisa wondered idly if Abbie would ever get back together with Jack – she hoped so, she liked Jack. He had phoned a few times over the last week, but Abbie was either out or wouldn't speak to him at that moment, saying she would phone him back.

'Did you speak with Jack in the end?'

'Yes, he caught me last night. Your home phone rang while you were in the bath.'

'How is he?'

'I don't know. He was OK, I suppose, I didn't ask.' Abbie was put out that Luisa was concerned for Jack, after everything that had happened.

'Oh Abbie, it's a shame to leave things like this. Did you talk about things much, resolve anything?'

'I didn't really feel like talking last night. I've got too much going on – I can't think straight. I said I would contact him in a while when we know what's happening with the house.'

Luisa nodded, understanding. They finished their drinks, aimed their cups out the window into a nearby rubbish bin, and Abbie drove off but the rain was getting heavier by the second and she reduced her speed, staying in the crawler lane.

'God, this weather is awful. I can just about see where I'm going - I might have to pull over.'

'You can't just pull over on the motorway. Just take it easy, keep your distance and we'll be OK.'

'Why does it have to rain, today of all days?'

Luisa laughed. 'You'd better get used to it. The Lake District is in one of the wettest parts of England.'

'Is it?'

'Yes, I'm sure it is.'

'Mm,' Abbie wasn't sure what to make of that.

They drove in silence for a long time. Abbie was concentrating hard, relieved that the rain was easing off and Luisa was doing her best not to fall asleep.

'Wake up sleepy head, I need your navigation skills.'

Luisa opened the map and traced her finger to the location they'd both studied many times over the last week. 'OK, you need to turn off at junction thirty-six.'

'Yep, that's just coming up. What then?'

Luisa reached down into her handbag for the piece of paper with the hand-written directions. 'We're heading for Kendal, so look out for any signs. Here we go, thirty miles. The village of Kirkby Bridge should be sign-posted before we actually get to town.' Luisa peered again at the map. 'Mm, should take us off left – I hope!'

The road seemed to go on for ages.

'Where's the sign? For goodness sake! I'm so excited - I can't wait to get there,' screeched Abbie, like a child impatient to see the sea.

'There it is, Kirkby Bridge,' said Luisa, looking back at the piece of paper. She read the directions; 'Winnifred Cottage, 25 Rowan Road, passed The Green Man pub. Top of steep hill. Set back, long front garden.'

Abbie drove slowly through the charming village of Kirkby Bridge. Dainty cottages with pretty country gardens were dotted along the roadside. Even Luisa was inspired and found herself smiling, hopeful that everything was going to turn out for the best.

'It's strange – I don't remember it being called Winnifred Cottage. And I don't remember it having a long front garden either. I was sure it was right on the roadside.'

'Does any of this look familiar?' asked Luisa.

'Not really but it's been a long time since I was last here.'

'When was that?'

'When I was fifteen or sixteen.'

'Why did you stop coming?'

'I don't know really. I suppose because I'd started my A levels and there was always so much work to do – couldn't just take off for the summer anymore. And then I was at university – same thing, I never seemed to have the time.'

'So, you haven't been back since then?'

'I came back a couple of years later, only for a few days, when my grandfather died.'

'What was he like?'

'A grouchy old whinger. Nothing like my gran – who knows what drew them together.'

'Your gran used to come down south didn't she?'

'Yes, once a year, she'd come down and stay with Mum and Dad for a week and I'd try to get over when I could. But I never came back up here to see her, not until last year when she went into the nursing home and I finally realised, too late of course, that she wouldn't be around for ever. I feel bad about that now.'

Abbie realised she didn't know where she was. 'I'm afraid I don't even know where Rowan Road is.'

Luisa spotted a very tall and thin elderly lady coming out of an off-licence. Presumably her booty was stashed in her very large handbag.

'Quick pull over here.' Luisa swished down the window. 'Excuse me, hello?'

The old lady eyed her cautiously before approaching the car.

'Do you know where Rowan Road is?' The old lady bent over a little, peering into the car, looking from one to the other as if they weren't to be trusted. She straightened up, remaining silent, as if debating whether or not to tell them. Reluctantly, she did. 'You're almost there. Turn right here, straight on and over the little bridge across the river, the road after that all the way up the hill is Rowan Road.' She straightened up even taller, hoiking her handbag decisively in the crook of her arm and watched as the car drove off.

'Thank-you,' called out Luisa. 'Wow, friendly lot aren't they? You probably have to live here for fifty years before you're accepted into the village inner circle.'

'Don't say that. I'll be about her age by then.' They drove on in silence, each very aware that in the next few minutes all would be revealed, and Abbie would discover whether all the recent events in her life had culminated in something that made absolute sense or she would end up feeling, yet again, that fate was against her. 'Look, there's The Green Man Pub,' she yelped, unable to contain her excitement. 'What did you say? Straight passed is it?'

'Yes, and on up to the top of the hill. Is any of this looking familiar yet?'

'No, nothing,' said Abbie feeling horribly uncertain of everything as she drove over the quaint little stone bridge and on passed the pub and up the steep hill glancing around, desperate for something to jolt her memory. They passed pretty lime washed and sandstone cottages with distinctive slate roofs, but all too soon they were heading out of Rowan Road and back onto a country lane which looked like it was about to take them out of the village. Abbie and Luisa looked at each other, confused.

'I'll turn around, we must have missed it.' Abbie reversed the car in a lay-by and headed back in the direction they had just come. Looking to their left now, Luisa was relying on Abbie to identify Winnifred Cottage, but she was still drawing a complete blank. Nothing along this road looked like the place she used to visit all those years ago. They were back at the bottom of the hill outside The Green Man again where there was a small parking area.

'Quick, in that space there. We'll walk up,' said Luisa.

Abbie's heart was pounding with anticipation as they walked up the steep hill. They slowed down, taking in every building, determined the cottage wouldn't escape them this time. They came level with two small cottages that had been converted into shops. One was a florist's and the one next door was a shop selling camping gear. They were at the top of the hill now and there didn't appear to be anything else around.

'OK, the camping shop is number 24 so we must be close.' Luisa looked beyond the shops, further back from the road, remembering the directions stating that Winnifred Cottage had a long front garden. 'There! That must be it.'

Abbie looked in the direction Luisa was pointing and then followed as her friend took off to investigate. They walked through the space where the garden gate should have been, but Abbie couldn't make sense of anything. This was most definitely not her gran's old home. She followed Luisa along the long narrow path, her heart sinking with every step.

'Here we are,' said Luisa stepping aside as they reached the door. A tatty wooden plaque confirmed that it was indeed Winnifred Cottage.

It was a tiny place and tumbling down from the look of it. Judging from the small windows, it would be dark and pokey inside. And almost worst of all, Abbie noted with a sense of foreboding, it was painted pink.

Chapter Six

Luisa looked at Abbie, the look of disappointment on her face was heart-breaking.

'Come on Abbie, never judge a book by its cover - it might be gorgeous inside.' Luisa was aware she sounded much more optimistic than she felt.

Abbie rummaged in her bag for the keys. It gave her a much needed few seconds to adjust her mind to the contradiction between what had been in her imagination over the last few weeks and what she was looking at now. She turned the key in the lock and pushed the rickety door open. It was worse than she thought inside; dark and dusty and smelling of damp. Luisa let Abbie go in first; glad her friend was unable to see the look of horror on her own face that she was unable to conceal.

The door opened onto a square room with a fireplace in the middle of the wall to the left. A door to the side of it led through to a second slightly smaller room with a corresponding fireplace. A few empty packing cases were pushed into the corners of each room. The sound of Abbie's heels echoed on the wooden floor as she walked despondently about the place, any interest fading fast. All the woodwork had been painted black. The walls may have been white at one time but now they were discoloured and dull and what with the tiny windows, the whole place was dark and gloomy.

Abbie was choked with emotion. She couldn't speak for fear of crying and she was grateful that Luisa had gone to explore a little room at the back.

'I don't understand,' she mumbled to herself. 'Gran never lived here.' She looked about her, desperately trying to feel some inspiration. But she hated it. And worst of all, she was stuck with it. She had no-where else to go.

'Abbie, come and look out here.'

Abbie slunk in.

'Isn't it sweet? The kitchen, and it's got everything you need. OK, it's a bit old but it all looks functional, just needs a bit of a clean. Look over there, it's even got a little pantry. They're all the fashion now and yours is original.'

'Mm, along with the original damp, original dust and original no hope. This is much too small and dark to ever be a gallery or photographic studio. It's useless.'

'Oh, come on Abbie. This isn't like you. There's bags of opportunity here, starting with the fact that this whole place belongs to you. No rent, no mortgage. What a fantastic thing.'

'Yeah, I know what you're saying, I'm just a bit disappointed that's all.'

'Listen, you've had a lot to deal with over the last few weeks. You need to give yourself some time to adjust to everything. Moving all the way up here is a huge thing. Give yourself some time to think what you want to do next.'

'Yes, you're right.' Abbie attempted a feeble smile and then grimaced. 'I thought I knew what I wanted to do next but now I'm not sure if I'll ever be able to.'

Luisa smiled patiently. She'd already peeked in the bathroom which led off from a tiny hallway across from the kitchen next to the back door. It was filthy and needed to be completely gutted but she didn't linger and thought it best to keep Abbie away for the time being. She was determined to focus on the positive – she just needed to find it first.

Luisa lifted the latch on a narrow wooden door. 'What's in here? Oh look Abbie, the staircase is in a cupboard. Come on, let's have a look.' Luisa's long legs scaled the steep windy stairs easily and Abbie followed much less enthusiastically.

They came up onto a narrow landing. A door to the right led to a small bedroom, and fortunately it didn't need any major work doing, just decorating. As part of a rather odd formation, another similar sized bedroom led off the first one. Neither Abbie nor Luisa had seen anything like that before and didn't know quite what to make of it. More boxes were stacked along the inner wall. Back on the landing, another door straight ahead led into a larger bedroom that spanned the cottage front to back. Luisa was over by the furthest window, peering out through the dirty glass.

'Abbie, come and look. This is amazing.'

Abbie joined Luisa and looked out onto the most amazing view she had ever seen. The sight of the fells and valleys gave a sense of magical tranquillity. Abbie breathed out a gentle sigh that might have been relief. This was truly beautiful. She scanned the landscape picking out farms and homes dotted randomly about, giving a sense of remoteness to their inhabitants yet with the comfort of knowing their neighbours weren't too far away.

'It's beautiful,' whispered Abbie. Luisa could see that her friend was completely transfixed; the surrounding landscape obviously appealing to her artistic sensibilities. And she was finally smiling, too.

'I tell you what,' said Luisa, 'let's leave this cleaning thing for a while. I've just realised I'm starving and I bet you are too. Shall we get over to that pub for some lunch?' Luisa was keen to get out while on a high note.

They stepped outside and Abbie dutifully locked up, thinking that it was hardly necessary as no-one in their right mind would think of breaking in. It was raining steadily as they walked back in the direction of the car and across the road to The Green Man.

Inside, the comforting smell of a log fire and food lifted Luisa's spirits although Abbie still looked incredibly glum. They stood at the bar, Luisa trying to catch the attention of the barman while Abbie stood there looking lost.

'Quick Abbie, grab that table over there by the fire.'

Luisa came to sit opposite her with a large glass of red wine for each of them. She had a couple of menus tucked under her arm.

'Are you hungry?' said Luisa opening her menu.
'Starving,' said Abbie.

They looked at each other and smiled, laughing a little, thinking the same; how nothing ever seemed to make them lose their appetites. They placed their order and very soon their food arrived; two dishes of lasagne, piping hot and wafting steam in their faces.

'Mm, this is delicious,' said Luisa. 'At least you know you've got a good pub just over the road and one that does gorgeous food too.'

'Yes, that's true,' agreed Abbie, feeling a little better for eating some hot food, although she couldn't stop a horrible image forming of her spending half her life in this pub, rather than staying in that dreary place that was supposed to be her new home.

'It's a beautiful village,' said Luisa.

'Mm, it is,' said Abbie, staring into the flames of the open fire.

'What are you thinking?'

Abbie looked at her friend and smiled feebly. 'How quickly can I sell?'

Luisa gave her a stern look.

'Where to start? My thoughts are all over the place,' said Abbie shaking her head, bewildered. 'The cottage – I don't understand anything about it. I've no idea why Gran owned it or why she left it to me. And what about the other cottage, the one she lived in, what's happened to that?'

'Quite a mystery then. Perhaps all the answers are in those boxes,' said Luisa trying to keep the conversation upbeat and not really understanding why Abbie was so unhappy; the place had definite potential.

'Try not to be too disappointed. It's amazing how buildings can be transformed. You must have seen the programmes on TV. You know, where they turn a mouldy old warehouse into luxury apartments or something.'

'Yes, I know what you mean. But that's usually for people with a million-pound budget and a team of family and friends who have the complete range of building skills to build a castle. And then when they, ooops, go over budget, Mummy and Daddy bail them out with another half a million.' Abbie banged her elbows on the table and buried her face in her hands. 'Oh God Luisa, what have I done? I don't even know anyone up here. Have I been really stupid, doing this?'

'You have me on the end of a phone. Anytime, day or night. You know that. And Jilly. And before you give me a look, you know she'd be there for you, if you needed someone to talk to. If I wasn't around, say.'

Abbie didn't comment on this. She was suddenly thinking about Jack. He'd always been her main source of inspirational advice and consolation when needed. 'You didn't answer my question.'

'Which was what?'

'Have I been stupid, coming here?'

'Well, that's entirely up to you Abbie. You've made your decision and now it's up to you what you do with it.' Luisa took her glass of wine and looked away, into the fire.

Abbie did the same, happy not to meet her friend's look, wondering what she'd done to cause

Luisa to be so unusually abrupt. After just a few moments of silence Luisa spoke.

'Anyway, it'll probably look a million times more promising once we've had a tidy up and a clean. So, shall we dump our stuff over at the B & B and get stuck in? Did you see it – Kirkby Bridge Bed and Breakfast as we drove in?'

'Yes, I did but I was tempted to stay here and have another wine,' said Abbie, relieved that Luisa had resumed her usual cheerfulness.

'Nope, come on, work to do. We'll come back here later.'

They collected their bags from the car and headed further down the hill to the B & B. They had taken the precaution of booking a couple of rooms, just in case Winnifred Cottage wasn't ready for them to stay in overnight. They hadn't even thought that it might be in need of work. As it was, it would take some considerable time and a lot of work before it was ready.

They were welcomed by Mrs Gilbert; a very short, fragile-looking old lady who was surprisingly full of energy as well as questions for Abbie and Luisa, but they were in too much of a hurry to give more than the briefest of answers.

Abbie and Luisa were given rooms either side of the landing. They dumped their things inside, changed quickly into old jeans and sweatshirts and went out again. On their way they stopped at a general hardware shop and bought buckets and mops and an assortment of cleaning solutions and then made their way back to the cottage. Abbie was lagging behind, unable to summon any enthusiasm.

She hoped, as she turned the key in the lock, that it wouldn't look so shockingly awful as it did earlier but as she stepped inside, the dismal feeling overwhelmed her again.

'OK, let's start upstairs shall we?' said Luisa. 'Or do you want to have a sort through down here?'

'No, leave it, I'm not sure I'm ready to tackle this lot. Let's concentrate on making upstairs liveable.'

But first Abbie bravely aimed for the bathroom. 'Hot water? Dare we hope?'

Luisa waited as she heard Abbie struggle to turn on ancient taps that had obviously seized up long ago. Abbie re-emerged. 'We're going to have to boil kettles I'm afraid. Crikey, that room is disgusting.'

'Do we have a kettle?'

Abbie visibly sank deeper into despair. She had brought a kettle with her, but it was packed away in a box somewhere in her car. The thought of having to unpack everything in order to find it was almost too much.

Luisa was already back in the kitchen. 'It's OK, there're pans here we can use.' Luisa looked warily at the electric cooker. And then she had a thought and twiddled some knobs – it didn't seem to have any life. She flicked on the light switch but of course – nothing. 'But we don't have electricity,' she mumbled, feeling finally defeated herself.

Abbie joined her in the kitchen. 'What did you say?' She saw that Luisa had filled a large saucepan with water and placed it on the cooker and worked the rest out for herself. She smiled feebly at Luisa suddenly feeling guilty; her good friend had come all this way, giving up her weekend to help and all she could do was moan and be miserable.

'OK, that means we've only got a few hours of daylight left. Let's just do what we can and then we'll get back over to The Green Man for dinner. How does that sound?'

Luisa smiled back; relieved to see Abbie had finally found some sense of positivity.

Chapter Seven

Having swept the old floorboards, dusted and washed as much as they could in cold water, Abbie and Luisa weren't convinced the place looked much better. They descended the stairs in near darkness and dumped their buckets and mops in the kitchen to be dealt with the next day.

Abbie took some comfort from the dark; while everything was hidden from view she could avoid thinking about it and that maybe she'd made a terrible mistake in coming here. She sighed deeply, knowing that tomorrow was another day and with the daylight would come the harsh reality of decisions that she would have to face.

Abbie and Luisa walked back to the B & B in weary silence. They were tired and cold and even Mrs Gilbert took pity on them as they entered the hallway and held off with her questions. She just smiled and assured them that there was plenty of hot water and that dinner could be ordered from six-thirty.

'Something smells very good actually,' said Luisa as they climbed the stairs to the first floor.

Abbie nodded in agreement. 'Shall we eat here tonight? I don't fancy going out in the cold again.'

'That's fine by me. Let's meet back down here, in that little bar area over there at about seven?'

'Yep, sounds good. See you in a while.'

They went into their respective rooms, each looking forward to a long hot bath and a quick nap. Abbie sat on the bed in her pretty little room. It was decorated entirely in white with dashes of sparkle here and there – a shiny bronze lamp was on the bedside table and a couple of gold-framed pictures above the bed. A tiny dormer window looked out onto the glorious surrounding countryside. It was idyllic but instead of cheering Abbie, it only made the contrast between it and number 25 Rowan Road seem even greater. Abbie had booked to stay at the B & B for just a few days, but she wondered now if Mrs Gilbert would give her a favourable rate if she were to extend her booking to several months!

Abbie soaked in the bath, running the water as hot as she dared. The bubble bath had produced more bubbles than she'd anticipated from the basic looking complimentary bottle. Her bones and muscles slowly thawed, feeling heavy now with tiredness. She lie there thinking back to the early start they'd had that morning and the incredible excitement and anticipation she'd felt then. Wow, that morning seemed like weeks ago already. And how different she felt now.

After she'd dried and dressed, she lay down on the bed for a rest and set the alarm on her mobile phone for a twenty-minute snooze. She placed the phone on the bed beside her and noticed how pretty the white bedspread was, fingering the dainty lace and idly wondering if it was hand-made and if it was, how many hours had it taken to make, just for her, a stranger, to lie upon it. And for some reason, all this made her feel like crying.

Abbie arrived at the bar first. Luisa smiled over when she saw her and perched next to her on a high stool. She picked up the waiting glass of red wine and raised it to chink with Abbie's.

'Here's to you, your new home which *is* going to be fantastic and all your forthcoming adventures up here in The Lake District. Cheers.'

'Cheers,' said Abbie. 'You make me sound like Peter Rabbit.'

'Well, he had a fair bit of fun, didn't he?'

Abbie gave her a look and took a long swig of wine.

'I feel so much better for a bath,' said Luisa. 'Don't you?'

Abbie agreed. Luisa look refreshed and, as always, naturally beautiful but Abbie knew that her own bubble bath hadn't had that effect on her.

'Aaron just phoned me. He'll be home a week earlier than he thought,' said Luisa.

Ah, that's why she looked so radiant, thought Abbie, sipping her wine. Thoughts of Jack suddenly came to mind, but she pushed them away, diverting her attention by picking up a menu and studying it intently.

Mrs Gilbert was keeping her expert eye on them and when she felt they were ready to order, she showed them through to the cosy dining room at the back of the house. Half a dozen tables were set for dinner but only a couple were occupied. Abbie was grateful for the quiet. She and Luisa took a table in the bay window with a mystical and beautiful moonlit view of the fells in the distance, their sharp edges rising up against the dark sky. They chatted and watched as Mrs Gilbert took orders from the other tables before disappearing into the kitchen to reappear only minutes later laden with plates of hot food, smiling and chatting with her guests all the time. In the next moment she was at their table taking their order.

'How many Mrs Gilbert's are there?' said Luisa watching as the old lady vanished through the swing doors into the kitchen once again.

Abbie smiled and nodded, acknowledging that Mrs Gilbert did indeed appear to have incredible energy for one little old lady. She wondered what her secret was. At the moment Abbie felt she barely had enough energy to eat although when their food arrived, it smelled, looked and tasted so delicious, she had no problem finishing her plate of home-made chicken and mushroom pie with fresh spring vegetables.

'Is it me or does she keep giving us funny looks?' said Abbie.

'Oh, I don't think so. She's probably just making sure we're OK,' said Luisa who had also noticed that the proprietor of the B & B had seemed particularly vigilant in ensuring her two new guests were comfortable. And here she was back at their table yet again.

She began clearing their plates. 'So, you're moving in to Winnifred Cottage, are you now?'

Luisa and Abbie looked at each other across the table, pretty sure they were thinking the same thing;

news travels very fast in this little village. Abbie smiled and nodded, reluctant to offer any further information, curious to know who was providing Mrs Gilbert with hers. But the old lady simply returned her smile and disappeared with the dirty plates.

'Did you mention -?' began Abbie.

'No, I never said anything,' said Luisa, knowing exactly what Abbie was going to ask. Neither of them had mentioned Winnifred Cottage to Mrs Gilbert when they'd checked in, so they were obviously already a talking point in the neighbourhood. Abbie fidgeted, uncomfortable with the thought of being gossiped about and wondering what else was being said.

Mrs Gilbert was back and handed over a dessert menu to each of them. 'So, what are your plans for the place? It'll be grand to see someone living there again. It's been empty for so long now. The previous owner bought it, with such dreams and the like, but it wasn't to be. Such a shame.'

Before Abbie could answer, a couple at the next table caught Mrs Gilbert's attention and off she sped to take their coffee order. Abbie was, all of a sudden, very keen to have a conversation with Mrs Gilbert.

Frustratingly, she left them alone for some time, delivering coffees and clearing tables. When she finally returned to take their order, it was Abbie's turn with the questions.

'Did you know the previous owner – of the cottage?'

'Ah, yes, I did,' said Mrs Gilbert, smiling a pensive smile of happy memories. 'Anna Baker.'

'Yes, she was my grandmother.'

Mrs Gilbert looked Abbie directly in the eye, her broad smile filling her face. 'I suspected as much. The same eyes. How wonderful.'

'Did you know her well?'

'Yes, dear, I knew her very well. We went to school together when we were little. We were good friends – she was Anna Delaney then, of course. And we remained good friends for a good while later. Until she moved, really, to the other side. And then we lost touch.'

'Moved? To the other side? How do you mean?'

'After she married, of course. She moved to the other side of The Lakes. Such a shame, leaving her lovely Winnifred Cottage behind. I don't think she ever came back to the area again. But understandable of course, in the circumstances. I had no idea that she'd held on to the little place – through all these years. But it is such a sad thing – to lose touch with your friends.'

Mrs Gilbert shook herself back to the present and looked between Abbie and Luisa, surprisingly familiar with the ways of the world and not at all backward in coming forward.

'Are you two? Just friends, or?'

Abbie and Luisa looked at each other, highly amused and answered in unison.

'Just friends!'

'Well, you make sure you don't lose touch. Good friends are hard to find so be sure to look after each other. And now what are you having for dessert? The red berry crumble is going down like hot cakes at the moment.'

Tucking into berry crumble, Abbie's mind was working overtime.

'She's known Gran nearly all her life; she'll be able to explain all about the cottage,' she said, looking anxiously about for Mrs Gilbert to return to the dining room. 'I wonder why they didn't keep in touch.' Abbie paused and then laughed. 'That was funny – she thought we were a couple!'

'Yes, very funny. I know we're close friends but really!' They sipped their coffees in silence. Abbie was thinking how lucky she was to have a friend like Luisa and vowing to herself never to lose touch when suddenly Mrs Gilbert reappeared at their table. Abbie was ready with a deluge of questions. But not tonight.

'Well my dears, I'd love to hear your plans for the cottage. And I'm so delighted that you're here, but I must get myself off to my bed. I've an early start in the morning. Tom is in the kitchen. If you need anything, just pop your head around and he'll look after you. Breakfast is available from seven in the morning until nine-thirty but for now I'll bid you both good-night.'

Chapter Eight

Despite feeling exhausted, Abbie spent a restless
night going over the day's activities. How her
excitement in the morning and on the journey up to
The Lake District had turned to disappointment on
arriving at the awful, dilapidated place that was now
her home. And now having met Mrs Gilbert, a
childhood friend of her gran's, hopefully she would
be able to throw some light on the mystery of
Winnifred Cottage. Abbie was impatient for the
morning to come so that she could capture Mrs
Gilbert for a long chat.

Looking forward to a full English breakfast to set
them up for the day, Luisa and Abbie were
disappointed to learn in the busy dining room that
the chef, Tom, was at home with Flu, leaving Mrs
Gilbert to cope single-handed. A young couple who
were visiting The Lakes for a walking holiday
informed them that a cooked breakfast was still on
the menu, but Mrs G had warned them that it could
take a while to get around to everyone. It appeared
that all the guests had collectively decided to go easy
on their hostess and had opted for simple choices of
tea and toast or cereal.

Abbie and Luisa did the same and it was soon
evident that there wouldn't be an opportunity to

speak to Mrs Gilbert any time that morning – the poor woman was run off her feet.

Abbie led the way up the weed-strewn garden path, looking up at Winnifred Cottage with a slightly different take from yesterday. It was still a mess of a place and she was still heavy-hearted with disappointment but there was a mystery to be solved here; this little dwelling obviously held a real significance for her gran and she'd very much like to find out what it was.

Back inside and ready to tackle more cleaning, it was clear that their efforts so far hadn't really improved the appearance of the cottage. It was still dark and dingy inside, not helped by heavy grey clouds outside and the constant drizzle of fine rain laying on the dirty windows.

In the kitchen with a sudden sense of determination, Abbie spread out the few papers she had from the solicitor and set about making a number of phone calls. Eventually - and miraculously - she thought, the electricity supply was back on which meant they could heat water to do some proper cleaning. She dreaded to think when the heating and hot water system would ever be up and working.

Luisa flicked the light switch. 'I don't believe it – it still works,' she said, looking up at the bare light bulb.

'Ah, they don't make them like they used to,' smiled Abbie. The weak light cast a soft glow around the room and it could have been quite cosy, with the dark skies and steady rain trickling down the windows, but the kitchen was freezing cold and smelled of damp and the light only showed up, in even more detail, how much work needed to be done.

The wind was getting up and they glanced towards the ceiling as something loose rattled ominously on the roof. Luisa tried to smile encouragingly.

In silence they filled saucepans and put them on the ancient stove to heat. The hot, soapy water was comforting on their cold hands and they spent the entire morning scrubbing cupboards and floors, skirting boards and paintwork. The black gloss would have to go, decided Abbie, it was so depressing and overwhelming in such a small space.

It wasn't a pleasant job or an easy one; clearing away years of grime and decay and there were some unidentifiable deposits inside the kitchen cabinets that Abbie didn't want to even think about.

They worked almost non-stop until past lunchtime, and all they'd really tackled was the kitchen and the small back hallway, neither of them brave enough to venture into the bathroom.

Abbie looked about her at the clean worktops and stove. It was still a tatty room with its hotchpotch of fixtures and finishes but even so, she felt a glimmer of satisfaction that at least it was now scrupulously clean.

Luisa was peeling off her rubber gloves, sighing deeply.

'We've hardly scraped the surface,' she said. Abbie noticed how weary she looked, aware that her friend still had a long journey home that evening.

'I reckon we need to call it a day,' said Abbie.

'No, there's still so much to do. I came up here to help and I'm not going to leave you with the place looking like this.'

Abbie smiled. 'It's fine, really, you've done more than enough for me already. And anyway, we've made a start, that's the important thing and I've got plenty of time to get on with it – it's not as if I've got to be at work tomorrow morning. Let's get cleaned up, drive out somewhere for a late lunch and just enjoy the rest of the day.'

Luisa smiled but didn't answer for a while. She looked about contemplating how long it was going to take Abbie to get straight. 'It's going to take quite a lot of money to get everything the way you want, isn't it?'

'A lot of it can be done gradually, over time.' Abbie was surprised at her own optimism.

'What about furniture? Have you decided whether you're going to bring some things from the house? And what about money? It's going to take longer than you thought before you're up and running and earning money from here.'

'I don't think that's ever going to happen,' said Abbie, accepting total defeat on that score. 'I'm OK for a while, I've got some savings. I was hoping to use them to set up the business but no, not from here. I'm thinking of contacting the local college, see if I can get back into teaching again or set up my own classes at a village hall or somewhere.'

Luisa was pleased and relieved to hear Abbie had options in mind. 'If you ever need some help, you know, financially, you know where I am.'

Abbie thanked her, for what felt like the thousandth time that weekend.

In the end they didn't drive out anywhere for lunch. After they had pottered around for a bit and returned to the B & B to clean and change, it was getting closer to the time for Luisa to leave for the station and her train back home. Besides, the rain was hammering down and they agreed that the easiest thing would be to hot-foot it back up to The Green Man for a simple bar meal.

They drove to the train station in silence; Luisa absorbed in her worries about Abbie and Abbie pretty much worrying about herself too. In the station car park, she took Luisa's weekend bag from the boot, the proverbial lump in her throat preventing her from speaking.

Abbie walked with her friend towards the platform and they hugged at the barriers.

'When are you coming back for a visit?' asked Abbie, hoping she didn't sound as desperate out loud as she felt inside.

'Soon,' confirmed Luisa. 'I can come back in a few weeks, if I'm invited?'

Abbie was surprised and delighted. She didn't dare hope Luisa would want to make the long journey again so soon. 'Of course you are! I'd love to see you back whenever you can.'

'And I look forward to seeing the place transformed,' she teased, albeit with a slightly serious note in her voice. 'I know you can do it, and you'll see; it'll be worth all the hard work – in the end.' Luisa gave Abbie one last kiss on the cheek and a quick hug before getting on the train.

Abbie walked away, turning every few seconds to wave as the train pulled away, until finally they were out of sight of each other. Her happiness at the thought of Luisa coming back in a few weeks quickly faded as Abbie drove back to the B & B. She parked and sat there for a few moments feeling very alone.

Back inside, Abbie stood in the hallway like a lost child. She loitered for a few moments, pretending to look at a selection of leaflets on local attractions and hoping that Mrs Gilbert would appear from one of the many doorways. Perhaps she could persuade her to sit for a few minutes and they could talk about her gran and their old times and where exactly Winnifred Cottage fitted into the story. The walking holiday couple came down the stairs into the hallway and waited at reception to check out. They turned and smiled at Abbie who was feeling conspicuous now, still not sure what to do with herself. She glanced through to the dining room, wondering if perhaps Mrs Gilbert was in there setting the tables ready for dinner. She'd already decided to stay in for something to eat.

The woman of the walking couple noticed the direction of her gaze.

'We were told earlier that the restaurant is closed tonight,' she said, almost apologetically.
'Apparently Mrs Gilbert has now gone down with the Flu. The chef has come back in, just to help out with the basics. But anyway they've decided not to serve food tonight, sorry.'

'It's OK, it's fine,' said Abbie, smiling bravely but feeling dispirited at having all her plans for the evening scuppered in one go.

Abbie couldn't face sitting in the bar on her own and reluctantly climbed the stairs to her room. Books and magazines held no appeal and she was in bed before nine o'clock, feeling weary rather than tired. On the bedside table her mobile phone rang and looking across Abbie was irritated to see it was Jilly calling. Having already answered Jilly's text yesterday, letting her know she'd arrived safely, Abbie let the call go to voicemail.

At eight o'clock the following morning, the phone rang again. Thinking it was the alarm, Abbie fiddled with the buttons until eventually the noise stopped. But then she remembered she hadn't set the alarm – it had been a phone call. Before Abbie could work out who'd phoned, the caller began ringing again. It was Jilly.

'Hi Jilly.'

'Hi, are you OK? Did you just cut me off?'

'No. Well, yes, but by accident. I didn't mean to.'

'I phoned you last night – you didn't answer.'

'I was tired.'

'At nine o'clock?'

'I've been busy. For God's sake Jilly!'

'I'm sorry to be fussing,' said Jilly calmly. 'I was just worried about you; I wanted to know that everything's OK, you know, and that you're settling in.'

'I'm OK,' said Abbie, really wishing she could leave it at that, but instead she tried to engage in conversation with her sister without letting on how bad it really was. 'It's early days yet. And there's a lot to do.'

'Yes, of course. It takes a long time to make a place a home.'

Abbie wasn't sure how to take that remark. Her sister didn't agree with her decision to move up here – was she still trying to make her point?

'Luisa came back yesterday, didn't she? Was it alright, the first night on your own?'

'Yeah, fine,' said Abbie, not willing to admit that she'd be staying at the B & B for a few more nights yet.

Jilly could sense her sister was in one of her 'not talking' moods. 'OK, I'll let you go and I'll call you again in a few days. Shall I? Is that OK with you?'

'Yeah, of course.' Abbie had a bad feeling Jilly was on the verge of announcing she was planning a visit. Thank goodness she hadn't. She dressed quickly and went downstairs for breakfast but once again the dining room was closed due to staff sickness. A note of apology had been placed on the reception desk.

Chapter Nine

Abbie had no real plans for the day. She hadn't thought past breakfast and now even that idea had been ruined. She'd hoped to have a full English fry-up and sit quietly in the bay window drinking tea for most of the morning -putting off any decision-making.

She went back up to her bedroom, grabbed her jacket and five minutes later was driving up the hill on the road that would take her out of the village. As she reached the top, she glanced over towards Winnifred Cottage; tatty, falling down and pink. She sighed, confused with an overwhelming mix of emotions. It had obviously been of importance to her gran at some time but what didn't make sense is why she had allowed it to fall into such disrepair.

Abbie drove on. She didn't know where she was going but she knew she didn't want to spend the day all alone in the cottage. After a few minutes she saw a sign for the Harper Shopping Centre. It was only ten miles away and in that instant she decided to head there. She'd find a café and have breakfast and perhaps afterwards do some shopping. After all there were plenty of things she needed.

As Abbie drove into the shopping centre multi-storey car park she felt a rush of relief as she read the information board. Inside she would find these stores and their lovely familiar names - John Lewis, Debenhams and Marks and Spencer almost made her feel like she was home again. She smiled at the idea of being able to lose herself for a few hours. It would be as if she were back in Hampshire or maybe in London on a shopping trip with Luisa – almost anywhere in the country, in fact. And she could forget, for a while, that she was stuck up here in miserable, damp, drizzly Cumbria.

Abbie parked and took the lift to the ground floor. She would start at the bottom, she decided, and make her way, floor by floor, back up to the top. The bright lights and warmth inside the centre were comforting, so too were the crowds of shoppers that Abbie could lose herself amongst. A small café to her right caught her attention; it was busy enough, but a selection of tables was still available. Abbie tucked herself at a small one in the corner and studied the menu, feeling a little conspicuous to be sat eating on her own but when she looked around, it was obvious that it was of no concern to anyone else. Abbie relaxed, shook off her jacket and got herself comfortable. There was a friendly level of chatter, the clatter of cutlery and music in the background - and the delicious smell of good coffee. Abbie glanced around surreptitiously; the fried breakfast looked good. She ordered the whole works for herself and a Colombian coffee.

After three coffees, Abbie was literally energised to begin shopping. She spent ages wandering around almost every department in John Lewis from shoes to tights and socks to the make-up counters where she resisted the urge to reinvent herself with a completely new look. Just in time she managed to remind herself that one hundred pounds worth of cosmetics might change her look but not much else.

Abbie wandered around the linen department, unable to get her head around colour schemes and room designs. She bought a bed-set in plain white cotton and then inexplicably, she bought a selection of bath towels in lime green, ruby red and cerise. A few hours later and after several trips back to the car to deposit her bags, she decided she'd bought enough for one day. After one last trip back down to the Marks and Spencer's food department, Abbie came away with two more carrier bags of provisions; if the B & B dining room was still closed tonight, then she'd have a private feast in her room. She had also bought a few things to keep up at the cottage.

Weary after her long shop, Abbie put the last bags in the car and hesitated after she'd slammed the boot shut. Not sure what to do with herself now, she decided to have a cup of tea before heading back. But it was well into lunchtime now and the cafés and tearooms were busy and so Abbie queued at a baker's and came away with a large tea and an apple Danish pastry which she took back and ate in the car.

Reluctantly she started the car, unable to think of any other means of avoiding returning to Kirkby Bridge. As Abbie drove out of the car park and away from the shopping centre, she acknowledged a feeling of calm; she felt much more relaxed than she had for the last couple of days. So, it was true, evidently, what they said about retail therapy. She looked across to the passenger seat which was full of her shopping as was the back seat and the boot. She was pleased with her purchases and made a snap decision to drop her bags off at the cottage, just quickly, and then she'd head back to the B & B for a rest. Maybe Mrs Gilbert would have recovered sufficiently to be persuaded to sit for a while and enjoy a little chat.

Abbie drove the windy roads back to the village. It was no longer drizzly, and the clouds had thinned enough for a light haze of sunshine to appear. She was lifted by the stunning views, unable to believe that she hadn't even noticed them as she was driving in the opposite direction earlier in the day. This was her neighbourhood she reminded herself; all of this was right on her doorstep, here to be enjoyed whenever she wanted to, just minutes away. Abbie smiled. Maybe, just maybe, everything was going to turn out all right.

Just a little way ahead, a white Vauxhall van with dents in the side pulled out in front of her. Her stomach flipped; it was Jack. What on earth was he doing up here? But then as she drove closer, coming to her senses and seeing the number plate, she realised it wasn't him. He was hardly the only person in the country to own a Vauxhall van and anyway, she thought sardonically, his had more dents in it.

Abbie drove on, stuck behind the van and wishing it would turn off. She smiled as she thought of Jack. He could easily afford a new van, but he insisted on keeping 'Suki' as he called it – just on the basis that there was an S and a K in the number plate. He'd had it over ten years and used it for carting about his photographic equipment and exhibition material and was stupidly affectionate towards it, saying he loved every single dent of her.

It was all a daft ruse really; a chance for Jack to laugh at himself, she knew that. He also owned an old Jaguar convertible that he'd spent a fortune on having restored. It was a beautiful, elegant car that he loved driving – Abbie loved being driven around in it too. But Jack would insist on teasing his friends; boring them with statistics on how economical the van was and how many miles to the gallon he got. Abbie smiled wryly; she missed Jack and the Jaguar, and she missed Suki the white van too.

As Abbie came into the village at the top of Rowan Hill and Winnifred Cottage appeared to her left, she prepared to feel the usual dread that seemed to overwhelm her each time she came here. But, so far, nothing. She parked up the little dirt track of a lane that ran alongside the long front garden and which didn't seem to go anywhere or be used by anyone. Once out of the car, she was suddenly inspired to walk around the garden, taking in its proportions and potential, as if seeing it for the first time. It surrounded the cottage on all sides and had to be at least a hundred feet to the back and the front. Having made a complete circuit of her land, Abbie came back to the car, wondering if it would be feasible to extend the cottage in some way that would provide her with the space to create a studio or gallery. There was plenty of room, but it depended on the local building regulations and, of course, the cost. Feeling a tinge of the old excitement she'd had when she first arrived, Abbie made a decision to look into it.

Grabbing as many bags as she could in one go, she unloaded the car, making several trips to and from the cottage. She placed the teabags and packets of biscuits on the kitchen worktop which immediately made the little ramshackle room look more homely. Abbie smiled at the absurdity of it.

As she walked back through the living room to the door, she looked across at the mass of bags she'd piled up on the floor, tempted to peek inside at all her purchases; to pull out the bright bath towels and the copper kettle. Again Abbie smiled; she'd bought bed linen but had no bed to put it on; she'd bought cushions but had no settee or armchairs and the stylish clear glass table lamp would have to sit on the floor for a while until she bought a little table for it!

But Abbie left all the bags where they were, untouched. She felt a twinge of excitement and wanted to retain the feeling, albeit very mild. She pulled the door to and locked it, pausing and looking up at the cottage. Abbie would do her best to transform the place, bring it back to its former self, and she allowed herself to wonder, for a few seconds, what the place would bring to her, in return.

Back at the B & B, a young friendly face at reception introduced herself as Mrs Gilbert's grand-daughter and informed Abbie that her gran was still unwell and probably wouldn't return for a couple more days. However, Tom the chef, had made a full recovery and would be opening the dining room that evening – business as usual.

Abbie took a nap, sleeping much longer than she intended and when she awoke, didn't feel like getting dressed for dinner and so stayed in her room. The bags of Marks and Spencer treats she'd bought helped make the decision, the only mistake being the now slightly warm bottle of white wine – she should have bought red.

With her one-man feast carefully spread out on carrier bags on the bed, Abbie picked up a couple of local newspapers she'd bought yesterday at the train station after dropping Luisa off. At the time, she thought they'd be useful if she needed to look up a local estate agent but for the moment Abbie threw the papers aside. Maybe ultimately, she would sell Winnifred Cottage but to do that before she'd even given life up here a chance would be silly and defeatist – she could hear Jilly's disapproving tone already, reproaching her for giving up too easily. She did not intend to give her that satisfaction.

Anyway, somewhere between the John Lewis linen department and arriving back at the cottage this afternoon, Abbie had already decided to put everything she'd got into making her new life a success. She'd loved this part of the world since a child and now she'd been given an opportunity to make it her home – she owed it to her grandmother at least to put a decent amount of effort into making it work.

The following day Abbie returned to Harper Shopping Centre but instead of a two-hour breakfast, she searched the larger furniture shops and bought a bed, a small settee and an armchair, a couple of rugs and a set of tables. She'd selected carefully making sure everything was in stock and could be delivered within the next few days.

The rest of the week Abbie woke early and after a quick coffee in her room, set off to the cottage to begin a full day's cleaning. She swept up piles of dust, washed all the paintwork, reached into the ceiling corners to remove cobwebs and even washed the inside and outside of the ground floor windows. The bathroom she left until last, literally dowsing everything in boiling water, several times, before going in with the bleach and limescale remover.

Abbie paced impatiently on the morning the furniture was due to arrive. Everything felt serious now and permanent too, and it also meant that she had no reason to stay at the B & B any longer.

Chapter Ten

It was a wrench to finally leave the B & B. Mrs Gilbert had reappeared a couple of days previously, but she looked frail and tired and so once again Abbie had to wait for another opportunity to be able to talk with her.

Mrs Gilbert gave a generous discount on Abbie's bill. With her bags loaded in the car, she stood on the doorstep and kissed the old lady's cold, smooth cheek, feeling that she'd known her a lot longer than just the last few days. But they had a connection, and despite the fact that they'd had only the briefest of conversations, Abbie had a feeling Mrs Gilbert was to become a good friend to her.

'Now, I'm only down the road, always here if you need anything.' Abbie was comforted by the reassurance that they were practically neighbours. She smiled and waved as she reluctantly made her way to the car and drove away, up the hill to Winnifred Cottage.

Inside, and alone, this was the moment Abbie had been dreading since she'd arrived.

Despite all the new furniture in the lounge, it still felt empty in there. Abbie sank down wearily on the squashy over-sized sofa, which looked almost too big for the room. A brand-new TV was positioned in the corner, it's spaghetti of leads and wires lay strewn on the floor. She leant her feet on the edge of the new coffee table, bare except for the new clock sitting in the middle. She shivered even though it wasn't cold.

Abbie looked about the room; she'd enjoyed her shopping sprees but now she'd lost her enthusiasm. Lamps were still in their boxes, cushions and curtains were stuffed in carrier bags. She had no idea when she would get around to assembling the flat-packed bookcase. Abbie rested her head on the back of the sofa, raising her eyes to the dingy ceiling and then down the walls that desperately needed painting. She was so tired, the ticking of the clock seeming to get louder, hypnotising her as she closed her eyes against it all and fell asleep.

She awoke much later when the room was in darkness - unfolded her stiff limbs and went over to the window, staring out to almost complete darkness apart from the twinkling lights of cottages dotted here and there. It wasn't late, but she didn't want to stay in the dark curtainless room, alone with her thoughts.

In the kitchen, she made a mental note to put a brighter bulb in as she flicked on the kettle. She'd placed some of her own kitchen things around and some new items but hadn't organised anything properly yet. Teabags were in their box and the sugar was spooned straight from the bag. It reminded her of the staff room at the college where she used to work; a good and happy life that had disappeared a long time ago.

Abbie sipped her tea, leaning against the sink, looking despairingly at the disorganised kitchen but reluctant to move. There was time enough of the evening left to do something constructive, but Abbie couldn't summon an iota of inspiration. She was stuck in place – immobilised, suddenly over-taken by a weary and draining tiredness.

With her mug of tea, Abbie climbed the stairs having decided to give up the day and go to bed. It felt strange to go to bed so early and Abbie smiled grimly to herself as she realised the last time she'd gone to bed at seven o'clock, it had probably been as a punishment.

The smile disappeared from her face immediately as she entered the bedroom. Carrier bags containing pillows and sheets and a new duvet were piled against the wall, all unopened. She wished she'd made the bed up earlier – she'd have to do it now. And that definitely felt like a punishment, along with being alone in this dreary place.

Chapter Eleven

A couple of weeks on and Abbie had at last
unpacked all the bags and boxes of her purchases. It
was nearly into May but still cold at night and she'd
had to buy an electric blanket just to make it bearable
to get into bed. She pulled the duvet right up tight to
her chin and her feet were so cold, she nipped out of
bed to pull on a pair of socks, getting back under the
covers as quick as possible.

Outside the strength of the wind could be heard
forcing its way through the creaking trees.
Somewhere nearby, a dustbin had blown over and
the windows were rattling in Abbie's bedroom. She
didn't expect to be able to sleep tonight, even
without this terrible weather. The unfamiliarity of the
place was still honing her awareness to all sorts of
noises that in other circumstances would just be
normal. The creaking of the old woodwork, the
sound of the fridge clicking on and off, a rustle of
something outside. Her imagination could create all
sorts of horrors if she let it. Accepting her fate of a
sleepless night, she lay there trying to occupy her
mind with a mental plan of what she should do
tomorrow.

Just as Abbie was finally relaxing, having made
great headway on her to-do list, she heard the most

horrendous gut-wrenching noise. It came from the attic or maybe the roof – she wasn't sure but she was out of bed in a second, out on the little landing, listening hard. Above the howling wind, she could hear the rain lashing against the roof and the sound of something sliding, something heavy. And there it was again, and then the same noise but now higher up. The awful sliding noise continued and then after a second of silence, several crashes, one after the other, as something smashed to the ground outside.

Immediately Abbie realised that in the middle of this wild storm, she had just lost several tiles off her roof. There was no way she was going outside tonight, and she just hoped they hadn't caused any further damage to anything else on their way down. She climbed back into bed, tired and weary and resigned to totally scrapping tomorrow's to-do list in favour of finding someone to mend her roof.

Abbie finally fell asleep just as it was getting light and as soon as she awoke, washed and dressed and went outside to discover that at least half a dozen roof tiles had smashed onto the hard-standing to the side of the cottage.

The rain had stopped but the sky was still a block of grey cloud. She needed a builder and quick. Abbie was sure she'd seen a builder's van parked nearby and as she looked down the road she could see quite clearly that it was still there.

Not knowing whether the builder lived there or was just working there, Abbie made an instant decision to go and introduce herself. After a quick cup of tea and a slice of toast, she checked herself over in the bathroom mirror to make sure she didn't

look as bad as she felt after such a terror-stricken and
sleepless night.

Chapter Twelve

Miriam Walker was driving home to The White House; a large roomy Victorian house halfway up the hill. She'd just been to the Cash and Carry shopping for supplies for The Honey-Blossom Tearoom, her business that adjoined the side of their home. As she drove past the little cottage at the top of the hill, she saw her husband standing in its doorway, chatting and laughing with the young woman who had recently moved in. She wondered, begrudgingly, what the joke was about. Typical, she thought, of Alistair to waste no time in making himself known to the new female in the street. Miriam wished she had time to stand around chatting all morning.

She reversed onto the drive making it easy to unload all the boxes from the back of the car through the back door straight into the kitchen. Alistair appeared just as she lifted out the last box, balancing it on one arm so she could slam the boot shut.

'You decided to come home then. Good timing – I've done all the donkey work.'

'Don't start Mim, I've only been gone five minutes. I've been talking to our new neighbour, Abigail. She's got a problem with her roof.'

'Has she? Really?'

'Lost some tiles in the night. I said I'd take a look. From what I can see at the moment, she's lucky she didn't lose the lot.'

Miriam appeared not to be listening, but she heard every word. The thought of a substantial building job for Alistair with its boost of income was very welcome. Pity he would be employed by the young, slim and attractive woman who became Miriam's enemy the moment she moved in. What were her intentions regarding the cottage? What if she wanted to turn it into a tearoom or café? It could put Miriam out of business, especially as she had the added advantage of that long front garden that could be turned into a huge parking area. Oh well, she concluded, if Alistair got the roof job, perhaps he could find out what was going on.

Miriam looked up at the clock as Alistair was checking the receipt from the Cash and Carry which he always did, and which always irritated her.

'I'm off to pick the girls up. Take these boxes through to the tearoom while I'm gone.'

Miriam snatched her keys from the worktop and went back out to the car. Alistair grabbed a stack of boxes and took them through to the extended part of the house at the side which they had converted into The Honey-Blossom Tearoom, thinking that an occasional 'please' from his wife would be a nice thing. He banged the boxes down hard on the counter and heard the tinkle of crockery inside, groaning instantly at the thought of Miriam's displeasure if he'd broken anything. He brought the remainder of the boxes through much more carefully.

One side of the tearoom was a wall of glass with three sets of French doors opening onto a pretty garden at the front of the house. They had removed a large part of the hedge to expose the sign advertising cream teas and freshly baked cakes which worked well in attracting passers-by – both walkers and drivers. The tables and chairs were neatly stacked along the back wall. They always closed for winter but in a few weeks time after some serious cleaning and polishing, they would be open for business. It would be a bumper year hopefully, thought Alistair. A good long hot summer is what they needed - the last couple of years had been complete washouts.

It was difficult enough being a self-employed builder and when Miriam had suggested they build an extension, almost doubling the size of the house so that they could open a tea room, it had seemed a great way of earning some extra income. And he thought it would be a nice hobby for his wife, something for her to do now that the twins were at school age. Neither of them had reckoned how much work was involved outside the 10:00-4:00 opening times. And with two ever-increasingly energetic four-year olds, it was becoming more and more difficult to keep up with it all. Their work/life balance was definitely out of whack.

Miriam pulled up outside the school and got out of her car, strolling along the pathway with a couple of minutes to spare. She was conscious, at forty-four, of being one of the eldest mothers waiting at Whistles Nursery School. She could easily have felt intimidated by all the young faces, barely past their teenage years some of them, and their trendy, skimpy clothes, but Miriam valued being able to wear expensive quality, sophisticated clothes and being able to drive a brand-new car.

Having discovered on the return journey that Daddy was at home, both girls went squealing in search of him as soon as they were released from their car seats. They quickly found him in the lounge, squatting on the floor surrounded by multi-coloured wires and cables, trying to set up the new DVD player.

One of his daughters clung to his neck like a monkey while the other leapt onto his back.

'Hello, you two. Did you have a good time at school?'

'Yeah,' they screeched in unison. Alistair instantly gave up with the DVD, succumbing totally to his adored daughters, rolling gently onto his back on the carpet and letting them clamber all over him. He never would have imagined that little girls could be so fun-loving. Despite the pretty frilly clothes their mother dressed them in, they were brave and boisterous, loving their rough and tumble games with Dad. Honey was definitely the braver of the two, witnessed one time by a hysterical Miriam who caught her jumping backwards off the coffee table, landing squarely onto a huge leather bean bag. Blossom, although the gentler one, was always close behind her sister.

Miriam took advantage of the few minutes she knew the girls would be safely entertained with Alistair. She disappeared into the tearoom to unpack the boxes. When she'd finished she returned to prepare lunch.

'Come on you two, go and wash your hands ready for lunch. Quick now.'

Blossom and Honey raced each other out of the room. Miriam looked over at Alistair as he picked up the DVD instruction manual.

'I've just unpacked the stuff from the Cash and Carry. Half of it is smashed – I'll have to phone them to complain.'

Chapter Thirteen

Eva and Lilleth had been arguing all morning. Eva wanted to go to Winnifred Cottage and meet their great-niece but Lilleth said it was too soon and they should wait until she had had more time to settle in. Eva craftily suggested they just go for a walk and pass by and maybe just knock to say 'hello'.

They took the bus into Kirkby Bridge and got off at the stop just down from The White House. Both women strolled along, preparing themselves for the long, steep climb up Rowan Road. Lilleth thought it funny that her sister wasn't complaining about her achy knees or her creaky hip as she normally did if she had to walk anywhere. But she was keen to go for this jaunt – to satisfy her itching curiosity.

'Are you OK there, Eva?'

'Oh yes, I'm fine. She better not be out after all this.'

Lilleth smiled, knowing that if their great-niece wasn't at home, the moans and groans about achy knees and creaky hips would surely begin.

As they got to the top of the hill, they could see that the light was on in the cottage although nothing else about it looked any different. Eva was keen to find out whatever she could but Lilleth didn't want to appear nosey or interfering.

'Let's just walk by. She's bound to be busy.'

'Mm, we'll see,' said Eva bounding on with amazing energy. She reached number twenty-five first, Lilleth drew level with her sister and tried to link arms.

'Come on, let's not make a nuisance of ourselves.' Eva shook her off, wishing she'd come on her own.

'Come away Eva. She'll not even be settled in yet.'

'I want to find out what she knows – about this place.'

'For goodness sake, what will she think of us just turning up like this? Come on, we're going.'

But it was too late – Eva was heading up the garden path and rapping on the knocker, smiling her fake smile as Abbie opened the door.

'Hello, can I help you?'

'Hello. You must be Abigail. I'm Eva and this is my sister Lilleth. We're your Great Aunts.' Abbie smiled bemused by the pushy woman. She stood back from the door and looked at Lilleth who gave her an apologetic smile.

'Would you like to come in?' she asked, rather surprised at their sudden appearance.

Eva and Lilleth walked inside; Eva marching off, assuming authority to look around as she pleased. Lilleth smiled again, taken aback for a moment at the family likeness in Abbie.

'Your grandmother was our sister,' she said, as if that explained everything. 'We just wanted to come along and say hello.'

'Oh, I see. Yes, I knew Gran had relatives up here, but I didn't realise you were so close by. That's lovely.'

'We live quite nearby but we often come into the village – it's so pretty, you know.' Poor Lilleth was feeling quite awkward now at having just turned up, uninvited.

'We were surprised Anna left it all to you.' Eva's voice sounded out loud and crisp as she returned to the front room. No-one seemed to know how to respond, so Eva continued.

'Lilleth and me are actually her closest relatives, you see.'

'I was close to Gran too,' muttered Abbie, not quite getting Eva's point but feeling the need to defend her gran's decision. After all, the cottage belonged to her, she could have left it to a cat's home if she'd wanted to.

'Yes, you made sure you kept in touch with her – I understand.'

Eva's tone was beginning to grate on Abbie and the implication, if she was reading it right, was deplorable.

'And you didn't – I understand,' she replied, with equal force.

Lilleth wanted to crawl away and hide. Her great-niece was absolutely right, they had hardly had any dealings with their elder sister apart from Christmas and birthday cards for years. They had no business being here and making assumptions. Abbie seemed to be a lovely young woman, Lilleth thought, she would like to get to know her better. And here was

Eva throwing accusations at her and ruining everything.

Lilleth took satisfaction in that Abbie's retort had actually managed to silence her sister who appeared to be lost for words. A feat not even attempted by many and succeeded by far fewer.

Abbie looked across to Lilleth who was still standing by the door. They exchanged sympathetic smiles, their thoughts connecting in that instant, both convinced that each knew what the other was thinking, as their expressions relaxed into knowing smiles. They moved towards each other, and Lilleth patted Abbie on the arm.

'It's lovely to have met you. Come by and see us when you're settled and have more time. We're at Gordon Cottage, over at Flanders Way.'

'Yes, OK, I will, thank-you,' said Abbie, meaning it and knowing for certain that she would visit and probably soon – attracted by the calm presence of this lady – the sister of her lovely Grannaliese.

'Come along Eva, we've interrupted Abbie long enough.'

Eva, silently and amazingly, simply did as she was told.

As they started down the hill, it started to drizzle. Fine, misty rain that soaked in seconds. 'Typical,' moaned Eva. 'This damp is going to set my knees off again.'

Lilleth felt the cold too but wasn't about to admit as much to Eva.

'Shall we pop in to Miriam's - see if she's open for business?'

'Good idea.'

They turned off the footpath into the garden of The Honey-Blossom Tearoom, but it didn't look promising. The signs weren't up yet and even though they could see Miriam pottering about inside, they could also see the tables weren't set up ready for customers.

'They really should stay open for the winter months,' grumbled Eva, repeating a favourite mantra of hers, and continuing through the garden. Lilleth hung back a little. While she agreed with her sister that it would make sense for the tearoom not to close during the winter – rumour had it that Miriam and Alistair were struggling financially – it was obvious that they weren't open today. But Eva had already caught Miriam's attention through the French doors.

'Any chance of a cup of tea?' Lilleth thought she would never be surprised at the cheek of her sister. She hurried across the garden to join her just in case her cheekiness descended into rudeness and Lilleth's much practiced damage limitation skills were called into play. She smiled through the glass at Miriam who didn't look pleased to see them. Tight-lipped, and concentrating on sorting out some cutlery, she looked stressed, tired and worn out. Lilleth wondered, as she often had before, what inspired Miriam to want to run a tearoom. Her outward demeanour, her sophisticated clothes and distant manner made her appear more like a lawyer than someone who made pots of tea, sandwiches and cake. hen again Miriam could take care of herself and would take no unwelcome nonsense from Eva.

Miriam tried unsuccessfully to smile at the ladies peering in expectantly through the window. This was the last thing she needed today. She was already behind with what needed to be done to open the tearoom in time for Easter. Honey and Blossom both had a tummy bug and Miriam felt as though she had spent the entire night tending one or other of them. And on top of that she and Alistair had argued that morning. She had raised the idea again of using some of the garden to make a dedicated car parking area. Alistair was against the idea, saying it would cost too much. The tearoom was losing money and Alistair seemed to be losing interest in it altogether. Miriam's certainty that by spending on the car park, they would be able to attract more customers was not convincing him.

Miriam wondered if she could get away with politely but firmly telling the Delaney sisters that she wasn't open yet. But it was obvious they were expecting preferential treatment. She sensibly reminded herself that Eva and Lilleth, retired and wealthy, with plenty of time to sit around drinking tea and eating cake, were among her best customers - she really ought to look after them. She unlocked the doors.

'Hello. Nice to see you, are you coming in? We're not actually open for a week or so but it's fine, come in. I'm sure I can rustle up something.' She lifted down a table and pulled out a couple of chairs. Eva was first inside.

'My goodness, it's dreadful out there. Mind you, it's not much warmer in here.'

Lilleth followed her sister, smiling her well practiced and perfected smile of apology at Miriam.

'Two teas ladies?'

'Yes, just tea, that would be lovely,' said Lilleth quickly, not wanting to put Miriam to any more trouble than they obviously were already.

'Unless you have some cake?' said Eva. 'A couple of slices of cake. Yes, that'll do. Anything you've got but nothing with chocolate, or that awful plastic cream and no nuts – I'll be digesting them all day.'

Miriam went through to the main house still with her pretend smile fixed on her face, which dropped as soon as she was out of sight. The tearoom wasn't set up yet for serving so she would have to make their tea in her own kitchen. It was a good job she had a fresh cream Victoria Sandwich in the fridge. And with Blossom and Honey both on very simple food diets, at least it wouldn't go to waste now.

Miriam carried the tray back across the hallway and as she passed the stairs, she heard two little voices calling out to her.

'OK, I'll come up to you in just a minute.'

Miriam unloaded the tray onto the bare wooden table. She felt a little better when Lilleth said a quiet thank-you and wondered how it was that two sisters could be so different; one calm, gentle and polite while the other seemed to be in a constant state of irritation about something or other. What had happened in their respective past lives to give them such different perspectives on simple daily life? Her thoughts turned to her own two girls, lying upstairs unwell while their mother was too busy to sit with them. How would their upbringing and childhood affect their developing characters and personalities?

'So, Miriam, what are your plans for this season? I hope you're not planning to serve any take-away burgers or anything like that. I notice that The Silver Spoon Café have started doing that, and they're selling all day breakfasts too. What a nonsense – an all-day breakfast. Well, that's one place we shan't be frequenting anymore. Shame, too, they do a gorgeous home-made Victoria Sandwich.' She dropped a piece of Miriam's shop bought cake onto her plate in obvious displeasure. Miriam didn't know where to begin with her defence; all her cakes for the tearoom were home made, she wanted to say, the one on Eva's plate was kindly donated from her own food store.

'I need to see to the girls – they're not very well today. I'll be back in a minute.' Miriam made her escape not trusting herself to keep quiet if she stayed any longer. She ran up the stairs, two at a time, and checked on the twins. They were a little flushed and had just a slight temperature but otherwise they were chirpy enough, snuggled together in the same bed watching television. It was nice being able to watch over them while they were unwell. She reminded herself of how different things would be if they were still living in London. She would have had to continue working, paying a chunk of her salary to childcare, and wondering what the point of having children was if she had to be stuck in an office all day, as a solicitor, specialising in family law of all things.

'I don't think that's very professional just wafting off and leaving us on our own,' said Eva, miffed. She fancied some conversation with Miriam who pretty much knew most of what was going on in the community.

'She hasn't wafted off. She just told you – her children are unwell. For goodness sake Eva, you are quite unreasonable at times.'

Eva looked up in shock, she opened her mouth to respond but closed it again. It wasn't often that Lilleth ever lost her temper and this was the second time today someone had managed to shut her up. She drank some tea, wondering idly if there was a full moon that night.

Lilleth took a deep breath and lifted her cup in a slightly shaky hand. She disliked confrontation of any sort, although she had had to get used to it since letting her sister move in with her. Sometimes Eva's grumbles and grievances were just too much for Lilleth's easy going, live and let live disposition. Sometimes she just went too far.

No-one could accuse Miriam of being unprofessional for looking after her sick children but even so Lilleth often felt slightly prickly in her company. Miriam always appeared to be anxious and uncomfortable around people – not the ideal persona for someone running a tearoom. Lilleth was quite relieved that she and Eva had been left alone.

They heard a vehicle pull up outside and wondered, somewhat ominously, if another customer had arrived hoping the tearoom was open. Their eyes fixed on the French doors, they were both relieved and delighted to see Alistair come in.

'Good morning ladies. Wow, it's wicked weather out there. Raining quite hard now. You two have got the right idea, I see.'

Eva and Lilleth liked Alistair. He was always in good humour, never a mood or a down moment with him.

Alistair grabbed a stray mug from the counter. 'Mind if I join you?' he asked, pulling up a chair before they had a chance to answer, knowing full well they would love a few minutes of his attention. Lilleth poured him some tea from the pot. It must have looked a cosy scene to Miriam when she hurried back to check on the old ladies and saw her husband chatting and joking with them. Instead of joining them, she turned immediately and went back into the house to continue with her chores. She was relieved that she could now leave Alistair to look after Eva and Lilleth but felt irritated to see him so relaxed and easy. Wasn't he supposed to be building a shed for Jim Peters – how come he always seemed to have time for sitting around and chatting?

Chapter Fourteen

Abbie laughed at the sound of Alistair singing, badly, on her roof. This was his second day here; he'd found a lot of work needed doing and was likely to be around for a while yet. She liked having him about - he was good company; totally over the top jolly and he kept calling her 'gorgeous' which made her laugh.

She was off now to go and get something special for their lunch. Yesterday she was only able to offer him a cheese sandwich with not too fresh bread but today she wanted to make a bit more effort – he deserved that just for his entertainment value alone.

As Abbie got to the end of the garden path, a white van caught her eye as it whizzed past. She sighed, annoyed with herself; every time she saw a white Vauxhall van, it didn't mean it was Jack's. There were hundreds of white vans around, she told herself. There, for instance, was Alistair's parked outside her cottage. And she could see another one further on, stopping outside the fish and chip shop. She needed to stop this paranoia.

As Abbie walked down the hill, she could see Alistair's wife in her garden potting up some hanging baskets. Abbie tried to catch her attention as she came alongside The White House; she was sure

Miriam had noticed her on the opposite side of the road but kept her head down now, concentrating on her gardening. Abbie resolved to make more effort on her way back. It was a good thing to get to know your neighbours, she thought, especially if they were all as friendly as Alistair.

She bought a fresh, crusty baguette in the bakers and a couple of apple turnovers – a speciality of Mrs Kelly's. She then bought some honey roast ham and fresh salad. On her way back up the hill, Abbie stayed on the left-hand side of the road, she could see Miriam still in her garden, lifting the hanging basket up onto its bracket.

'Hello,' called out Abbie. 'I've just bought something nice for your husband's lunch,' she said, showing her the baker's paper bags. Miriam glanced up briefly, just long enough to cast Abbie a derogatory look before turning away and going back inside her house, banging the door shut.

Abbie wasn't exactly dumbstruck – she could think of plenty of things to say but there was no-one around to say them to!

Alistair was at the kitchen sink washing his hands when she returned.

'Are you alright?' he asked.

'No. I just got a very strange look from your wife. Have I done something wrong?'

'Ah, don't worry about Mim. She can be an awkward cow sometimes. Not exactly the easiest person to get along with.'

Abbie was taken aback. Hearing him talk like that about his wife surprised her. He must have picked up on her uneasiness; he looked as though he regretted saying it. And then Abbie felt sorry for him. What a shame, she thought, for such a nice guy to have such a grouchy wife. Good job he was so jovial – it would have to do for the both of them.

'Here, I've got some things for our lunch.'

Alistair perched on a stool watching Abbie make up two ham salad baguettes, and what seemed like the twentieth cup of tea for him. She was self-conscious and a little uneasy of him watching her every move.

'So how are you getting on, up on the roof?' she asked as she handed him his plate.

'It's getting there, although I might drag it out a bit so I get more of your delicious lunches.'

'Ah, thank-you. We even have one of Mrs Kelly's turnovers for dessert.'

'Just the one? Do we have to share?'

'No, of course not,' said Abbie laughing. 'One each I meant.'

'OK, although I wouldn't mind sharing my apple turnover with you.'

He was funny, thought Abbie, feeling a little uncomfortable as she sensed her cheeks reddening. She did enjoy his company but then thoughts of Jack came to mind. She was reminded of the silly banter they used to enjoy together; their playful teasing and silly discussions. It almost felt disloyal to him to be sitting here laughing and joking with Alistair. And then Abbie pulled herself up; it was Jack who had been disloyal and anyway there was nothing going on here – Alistair was married. And to the scariest woman in the neighbourhood.

They ate in silence for a while and then Abbie made a conscious effort to steer the conversation to safer territory. She asked how long he'd lived in The Lake District and he proceeded to tell his story of how he'd moved here from London after he married Miriam. He missed the buzz of the city and was obviously disappointed that Miriam didn't want to go back. He didn't have much good to say about his wife, but he spoke lovingly about his two young daughters.

Abbie was content to let him ramble on – perhaps he just needed someone to talk to but when he turned the tables and started asking her questions, she clammed up, not feeling at all comfortable talking to him about Jack or the history of events that had led her there. For some reason which she couldn't define, she avoided confirming or denying that she had a boyfriend somewhere.

Abbie swiftly concluded the conversation by excusing herself, saying she needed to go out for a while – it was beginning to feel a little claustrophobic in the little kitchen. Alistair noted the rather abrupt ending to their cosy lunch and was annoyed with himself for maybe going too far. He'd specifically noticed how vague Abbie had been about whether she had a partner or not. That was OK, he quite liked women who had some decorum and didn't spew out their life history in the first few seconds. It usually meant they were single. He put his plate and mug over by the sink.

'Will you be back before I leave? It's no problem, I'll just close up when I go.'

'Yes, I'll be back. I won't be that long.'

Abbie began to walk up and out of Rowan Road which took her to the quieter outskirts of the village. She took some deep breaths; feeling more relaxed by the minute and gently but firmly reprimanded herself for verging on paranoia - all over a friendly builder fixing her roof. She would have to get it into her head that things were different up here. This was a small village, a long-established community. People here were generally very friendly – apart from builders' wives of course.

Abbie continued walking, and a little further on she saw a sign pointing in the direction of a narrow lane which was not much more than a farm track. Abbie's heart sank as she read the sign – Art Gallery. She couldn't believe it, an art gallery right here on her doorstep. Yet another blow to her dreams. Although Abbie had accepted that Winnifred Cottage would never be suitable for what she needed – she still harboured a hint of her dream deep down and hoped that some day she would have her own studio and gallery. Was there room for two in this neighbourhood? Probably not, she conceded. Abbie walked down the secluded lane, and if it weren't for the signpost, she'd feel as though she were trespassing on very private property – but she had to find out what this gallery had to offer.

On the left was an old cottage facing directly onto the lane. With its interesting collection of pottery and sculptures on the wide window cills, it looked intriguing - Abbie would have loved to be able to push the front door open and peek inside. Just a little further on, Abbie noticed a small barn which was obviously the home of the gallery. There was a display in the window of various paintings and sculptures but the sign on the door had been turned to 'Closed'. Abbie tried to see around the window display, desperate but frustrated not to be able to get a glimpse of what it was like inside. She walked around the place, reluctant for some reason to leave but it didn't seem that anyone was about. A collection of out-buildings was scattered randomly, one with its door left propped open, was a storeroom for all sorts of art paraphernalia. Abbie couldn't resist sticking her head inside. It took a few seconds for her eyes to adjust to the lack of light, but she found it totally inspiring and exciting as little by little the odd shapes in the darkness became clearer and she could make out old easels leaning against each other, and stacks of canvasses propped against the wall.

A plump and fluffy tabby cat brushed the back of Abbie's legs making her jump. It's meowing sounded loud amidst the tranquillity. As much as she would have loved to be able to meet the owner, Abbie didn't want to be caught snooping around. She made her way back onto the lane, heading toward the main road again, knowing it wouldn't be long before she would return to this wonderful place.

Back to reality, and as Abbie descended the hill she was surprised not to see Alistair back working on her roof. Perhaps he had finished for the day but as she let herself in, she saw his tool bag just inside the door. She was surprised to find Alistair settled in her kitchen, as if he were waiting for her. He certainly looked pleased to see her.

'Hi, I see you've finished for the day. Have you got time for a cup of tea before you go?'

'I was hoping you'd say that,' said Alistair with enthusiasm.

Abbie turned away to fill the kettle and as she switched it on, she suddenly felt him behind her, his arms enveloping her. She turned automatically to face him but was trapped between him and the worktop.

He was standing close to her, much too close and as she held up her arms in defence, her hands were forced onto his chest.

'What the hell do you think you're doing?' She thought she was speaking calmly but was surprised to hear a definite tremble of fear in her voice.

'Come on Abigail, you're a friendly girl.'

'What?'

'Let's not play games. It's OK to feel lonely and find yourself needing someone.' Alistair leaned in and tried to kiss her.

'I don't need anything!' Abbie felt as though she was shouting but in fact her voice came out just a whisper. 'For Christ's sake, I only made you a sandwich.'

Alistair finally took a step back. 'And the rest. You've been lapping up the attention. You just like to play, do you?'

Abbie had escaped to the other side of the kitchen, putting as much distance as she could between them. She wanted him out of her home, but the thought of angering him was frightening her. His jovial, happy-go-lucky personality had all been a total front. That wasn't the real Alistair Walker.

What if all that energy and passion were turned to anger? The thought made her feel sick.

'You're talking nonsense. I think it's better if you leave.'

'I'm going. I'm not into games with silly girls.'

Abbie was relieved to see him move to the doorway. He didn't appear to be angry, thank goodness. On the contrary, he was actually laughing. He was mocking her; a snide smile creeping across his face which perversely seemed scarier to her than perhaps his anger would have been.

Chapter Fifteen

Abbie woke earlier than usual, washed and dressed in record time, making sure she put on her most unflattering scruffy jeans and shapeless jumper, lest she be accused of trying to seduce anyone.

She'd spent the previous evening going over and over the last few days, wondering suspiciously whether there really was anything wrong with her roof apart from the few tiles that needed replacing. Had Alistair plotted this right from the start, from the moment she'd knocked on his door and introduced herself? Did he imagine that she had a thing for builders? She opened a bottle of wine and then started on herself; had she perhaps led him on, just as he'd accused her? True, she liked him being around; he was good company, he was funny and made her laugh. But no, she wasn't attracted to him. And she hadn't led him on. That was the truth. Unless buying someone an apple turnover from Mrs Kelly was code for something else, in these parts.

The shock of it all and the self-recriminations were easing now but anger was beginning to set in. Abbie dashed over to the window yet again, peering down the hill towards The White House looking for the dreaded sight of Alistair Walker making his way up to her home. Fortunately, there was no sight of him. He was usually here by now so hopefully he'd made the sensible decision of staying away, but even so Abbie felt agitated and restless and didn't want to spend the entire morning twitching at every little sound. She didn't really want to be indoors at all and decided that the best thing would be to go out for the morning. She considered going for a walk up in the hills, she hadn't really looked around the area much yet but then she decided against it - it wasn't very sensible to go exploring in these parts alone.

Her mobile phone started to ring on the bedside cupboard, and she answered without looking at the caller display.

'Hello?'

'Hi Abbie, it's me Jack.'

'Oh Jack, hello, how are you?' This was a lovely surprise; one she wasn't prepared for and it was impossible to hide the delight she felt at hearing his familiar voice.

'I'm fine. And you?' Jack was also pleasantly surprised – he hadn't expected Abbie to be so affable.

'I'm OK.' She said, unconvincingly. She would have liked to tell him about Alistair; spill out all the awful details so that Jack would agree what a total bastard he was. She sighed and sank down onto the edge of the bed, thinking it was probably best not to say anything. Jack might put his own spin on things and think that she was encouraging Alistair in some way. She probably shouldn't care what Jack thought, but actually she did. 'It is beautiful down here.'

'Yeah, I know. It's a shame we never got to go there together.'

Abbie forgot that Jack used to go to the Lake District for a holiday every summer with his parents when he was a boy. She always thought it funny that they were possibly in the area at the same time, maybe year after year, long before they'd even met.

'And how's the cottage? Luisa mentioned that you're planning on setting up a studio or gallery.'

At first she was surprised that he'd spoken to Luisa but then again, knowing her good friend, she'd probably phoned Jack to check he was OK.

'Well, no actually, it's no good for that at all. It's much smaller than I thought it would be, and dark and pokey.' Abbie laughed lightly; it felt good to have a proper moan. With Luisa, she felt obliged to try to remain upbeat and positive – Luisa had been so supportive of her. And when she spoke to Jilly on the phone, she didn't dare admit what a disaster it was turning out to be. But now it was so easy talking with Jack, she could be herself and he would understand exactly what she meant.

'That's a shame. You'd never be short of inspiration, living and working up there. It could've been perfect.'

'Yes, you're right; the place is definitely perfect.'

There were a few moments of an awkward pause; Abbie wondering what the reason was for Jack phoning but not wanting to push him to finish the conversation. And then it was as though he'd read her mind.

'Anyway, the reason for me ringing is that the repairs to the house are nearly finished and I wasn't sure if you were thinking of selling or renting and maybe, I don't know, if you want me to do anything

103

to help – put it on the market or whatever? I just
wanted you to know, that I'm happy to help.'

'OK, thanks Jack. I haven't really thought about it
that much to be honest. But I will give it some
thought, and then I'll get back to you, at some point,
if that's OK?'

After speaking with Jack, Abbie wandered back
over to the window, looking out on the spectacular
landscape; showing a hundred different shades of
vibrant green after all the recent rain. She smiled at
Jack's excuse for phoning. She was in regular touch
with the builders who were working on her house
and she knew that it wouldn't be finished for quite
some time. It was his way of keeping in contact with
her. She still didn't know exactly what had happened
on the evening that the house caught fire, but she
decided that, for now, keeping in touch with Jack
was OK.

Abbie often thought of her great-aunts; the two
sisters who appeared to be so different – well, she
knew that feeling. Normally, she didn't like to call
on people without prior arrangement, but they had
invited her to visit anytime and without their
telephone number there wasn't much else she could
do.

Abbie changed out of her sexless baggies into a
more suitable pair of smart black jeans and a thick
woolly jumper. Gordon Cottage, Flanders Way - she
looked it up on the map and headed out of the
village. Setting off on her journey she had been
worrying how to find her aunts' home when all she
had of their address was Gordon Cottage. But as it

was, it wouldn't be difficult to spot a dwelling out here in the middle of nowhere. And at last, in the distance she saw a cottage and felt instinctively that this was the one. It was a gorgeous day and Abbie half expected to see the ladies in their garden but as she pulled up outside, there was no-one about although the front door was wide open.

Abbie let herself in the gate and walked into the most perfect country cottage garden. It was packed with plants; shrubs and borders just ready to burst into bloom. There was just about a sense of order to the crammed full garden and Abbie knew that in a few weeks time all would become clear when the contrasting colours and textures would all be perfectly displayed.

There was still no sign of either Eva or Lilleth but suddenly, she heard voices from the open doorway and started towards it but stopped again. They were arguing.

'What are you saying? That because this is your house, I'm not allowed to touch anything?'

'No, don't be silly. You know I'm not saying anything of the sort.'

It was easy to tell which sister was doing the shouting and which was doing her best to stay calm.

'I do contribute to the upkeep of the place. I would've thought I have the right to move a piece of furniture if I care to.'

'Of course you can. I just wished you'd checked with me first because as you see that chair was hiding a bare patch of carpet which is rather ugly.'

Abbie stood still on the spot, debating whether or not to go back to her car. She didn't want to be discovered listening to their ranting, but she didn't want to interrupt them either.

Eva finished the argument with one final retort before storming out to the garden.

'Buy a new carpet then. You have enough money.' Eva appeared in the doorway with a look of spite on her face that matched the tone of her voice, neither of which relaxed at the sight of Abbie.

'Oh, it's you.'

Abbie couldn't prevent herself from thinking what an unpleasant woman her Great Aunt Eva was.

Lilleth appeared behind her sister, wondering who she was talking to. On seeing Abbie, she came straight out into the garden to greet her.

'Hello Abigail. This is a nice surprise. It's lovely to see you.'

'Hello. I hope you don't mind me just dropping in like this.'

'No, of course not. It's lovely that you've come.' Lilleth linked her arm through Abbie's, in a wonderfully affectionate way that Abbie found very comforting. They walked towards the cottage.

'We don't get many visitors these days,' she said curtly, and Abbie wasn't sure whether or not she imagined it, but she thought she saw Lilleth raise accusatory eyebrows in the direction of her bad-tempered sister.

Lilleth led her to a bench set against the wall of the cottage and they sat down, looking over the garden.

'How are you settling in?'

'Not too bad, I'm getting there slowly. I had a bit of a nightmare with the roof.'

'Oh dear, what's happened?'

'Some tiles fell off in the storm the other night.' Abbie paused, choosing her words carefully, wondering if Alistair had a reputation around here. 'Alistair Walker has been working on it all week.'

'Ah, yes, Alistair. Lovely man. Mind you, that wife of his, Miriam, have you met her? She's a bit of a sour puss.'

'Yeah, I tried smiling at her the other day. It didn't go down too well.'

Lilleth smiled knowingly. Abbie decided to push a little harder. 'It makes you wonder how someone as friendly as Alistair could end up with someone like Miriam.'

Lilleth sighed, long and deep, as if her lifetime of experience of human relationships suddenly weighed heavy on her. 'It takes all sorts. And no-one knows what goes on behind closed doors, as they say. Perhaps it's a case of opposites attracting. Shall we go inside for a cup of tea?'

Abbie agreed. Her great aunt Lilleth was easy company and Abbie was reluctant to leave this safe sanctuary. Lilleth put the kettle on the cooker and lit the gas with a match. She set the table with three cups and saucers and the sugar bowl and went to the fridge for milk.

'Ah, we're out of milk. Abbie dear, pop into the store there and fetch me a pint from the big fridge, would you?' Lilleth indicated a small room to the side of the kitchen. Abbie went inside the windowless room which had been purposely built as a food store, sort of an old-fashioned utility room. It was cold and dark, and Abbie pulled the light cord just to the side of her. There was a chest freezer over in the far corner and next to it a fridge. Abbie took out a pint of milk and smiled, highly bemused at the paraphernalia spread all over the floor. It was almost completely covered with demi-johns filled with an amazing kaleidoscope of coloured liquids, all bubbling away soon to become wine of various descriptions.

Long shelves lined the walls, straining under the weight of bottles which appeared to be grouped in some sort of filing system relating to wine type and vintage. A small pine dresser next to the doorway held a collection of even more bottles and jars in different shapes and sizes, some with odd looking berries bobbing about inside.

And tucked in a particularly dark corner, there were at least half a dozen Rumtopf jars which Abbie knew all about. Jilly had made a Rumtopf concoction many years ago when they were teenagers; filling the pot throughout the year, adding fruit every few weeks and then topping it up with rum. On Christmas Day, after a year's worth of anticipation, Jilly served bowls of the sweet syrupy fruit to the whole family – it took the rest of the day for them to sleep it off, vowing never again!

Abbie wondered in what context her two aunts opened a few bottles. There was far too much in that room for an occasional tipple. She made a mental note to be sure to accept any invitation to a party here. Abbie handed the milk to Lilleth conscious of her own amused smile. She could bet that that little dark room and its contents had put smiles on many faces in the past – and probably headaches too!

Eva had come in from the garden and was silently and expertly knocking back some bread dough before dividing it equally into two bread tins. She put them in the oven, wiped the worktop and was just washing her hands as the telephone rang. Taking the hand towel with her, she went into the lounge to answer it, returning barely a minute later at which point Abbie almost did a double take. Where had Eva the grouchy old lady gone? And who was this smiling, twinkley-eyed woman who had taken her place?

'You need to set another cup, Jed's on his way over,' said Eva. Abbie was entranced. Whoever this Jed was, he certainly did it for Great Aunt Eva. Abbie sat down at the table in the middle of the kitchen and waited. She was intrigued to meet the man who could put a smile on Eva's face.

Eva had disappeared from the room and when she returned a few minutes later, Abbie noticed that she'd removed her apron and had changed her plain black sweater for a dark purple one. She'd combed her hair and applied a hint of red lipstick. Abbie looked across the table at Lilleth who was warming the pot with water from the kettle before filling it and stirring the tea and then covering the pot with a brightly coloured knitted tea-cosy.

Abbie heard the click of the garden gate and almost held her breath in anticipation. He knocked on the open door before coming into the kitchen.

'Morning ladies.'

'Good morning Jed,' welcomed Eva. 'Take a seat, tea's brewing.'

Jed sat down opposite Eva, while Lilleth poured tea for everyone.

'Jed, this is our great-niece Abigail.'

'Pleased to meet you,' he said politely, shaking her hand gently across the table. She liked the look of Jed with his wild grey hair and matching but much less wild beard.

'She's Anna's grandchild,' said Lilleth to clarify, although it really wasn't necessary; Eva had never married and Lilleth didn't have children.

'Yes, I can see that. Your eyes, violet grey, exactly the same as hers.' Jed stared for just a moment; shocked at the likeness. Abbie was shocked too because no-one in her life except Jack had ever commented on the odd colour of her grey-ish eyes or referred to them as being violet. Eva and Lilleth were both equally shocked that Jed Tobin had such a specific memory for the colour of their elder sister's eyes.

Several seconds of silence followed while each of them was lost in their own respective thoughts.

'This is a nice surprise and as I said it's a great pleasure to meet you my dear.'

Abbie couldn't help but be charmed by the very likeable Jed.

Eva fidgeted in her seat, agitated by the competition for Jed's attention and irritated that the other person seemed to be winning and worst of all that Lilleth seemed to be enjoying the whole of it.

'Abbie has inherited Winnifred Cottage and has come up here to live,' continued Lilleth.

'Ah, have you?' Jed's face clouded over with a whimsical look that took him back in time.

110

'What are your plans? What work do you do?'

'Well, I'd hoped to create some kind of art gallery or photographic studio in the cottage, something along those lines but it's not quite right for that really.' Abbie could have continued talking about her dream, but she was stopped in her tracks by the look of surprise on Jed's face, the second time in a few minutes. His shaggy eyebrows were raised so high, they almost met his hairline. Abbie would like to have known what was so surprising about her wanting to open a gallery, but she didn't have the chance to ask. Eva had reached the point where she had had enough of listening to this meaningless chit-chat and dived in to change the subject.

'We have a new batch of turnip wine on the go Jed – should be ready in a few days. Are you feeling brave enough to come over for a few glasses at the weekend? Do you remember the last time we made turnip wine?'

'Remember it? That stuff was lethal – it wiped my entire memory for the whole of the month.'

Eva flashed Jed the widest of smiles which unfortunately seemed to be wasted on him. He was still completely preoccupied with other thoughts and the whole turnip wine conversation quickly fizzled out.

Abbie finally arrived back home about mid-afternoon. She'd had a lovely time at Gordon Cottage but felt restless now and wandered slowly around the cottage running her hand along the walls and gazing into the empty fireplaces – how many years since they'd held a welcoming warmth?

111

Something told her that this cottage was a theatre of secrets. And she now believed that Lilleth, Eva and Jed had been key players in the performance.

Abbie felt something as she stood there, convinced that something magical had happened within these walls. She wondered what she could do with this space that Grannaliese had left for her. And whether she could re-capture and continue something of that magic.

Chapter Sixteen

It had rained almost continuously over the last few days and Abbie kept looking at her upstairs ceilings, worried that an ominous damp patch might appear at any moment.

Alistair hadn't returned to Abbie's home since the day he had made a pass at her. Fortunately, she hadn't seen him around the village either, although she'd definitely gone to great lengths to give The White House a wide berth – not wanting to run into either Mr or Mrs Walker.

The problem was that the repair work to her roof needed to be finished. And there was also the matter of the bill. She owed Alistair for his work and this was making her feel quite uneasy.

Also nagging at her conscious was Miriam Walker. Abbie remembered Miriam's reaction to her when she'd tried to be friendly and she cringed at her stupid comment about buying something special for Alistair's lunch. No wonder Miriam had given her such a look. She felt a need to make contact somehow, to find a way of letting her know that she was in no way encouraging her husband into anything improper. She didn't have a clue how she was supposed to do that but knew she had to at least try.

It took a couple of days for Abbie to pluck up the courage to go into The Honey-Blossom Tearoom. She struggled to find an excuse to stop by and then came to the realisation that she didn't need one - she would simply pop in to pay her bill.

Charged with bravado first thing on Monday morning, Abbie set off for the tearoom ready to face whoever might be there. Miriam didn't see her as she entered the garden. The tearoom still wasn't officially open for business, but all the tables and chairs were set out in readiness. Eva and Lilleth had popped by a couple of times when luckily Miriam wasn't quite so stressed. She had been quite relieved to see that she hadn't managed to scare away two of her best customers and made a particular effort to welcome them.

But right now, she didn't look too welcoming to Abbie as she went inside. Miriam was shaking out a pink linen tablecloth before laying it neatly onto a small square table. As the cloth lowered, she saw Abbie standing by the door and simply looked at her – her face completely expressionless.

'Hello. I'm sorry to interrupt you.' Abbie began.

Miriam grabbed another tablecloth flapping it out of its creases so violently, Abbie flinched. But then the notion that she was being intimidated, when in fact she had done nothing wrong, strengthened her.

'Your husband did some work on my roof, but I haven't received the bill yet.'

A few seconds of silence followed while Miriam smoothed the cloth down.

'I'd like to settle up,' said Abbie, getting irritated by this petulance.

114

'I don't have any dealings with my husband's business,' said Miriam, a sarcastic emphasis on the word business suggested she wasn't talking about roof trusses and broken tiles. 'I'll get him to call you about it. I take it he has your number.'

'No, don't ask him to call. I'd just like the bill. He can post it through the door, please. Thank-you.'

Abbie left the tearoom not waiting for a response and resisting the urge to slam the door behind her. She marched up the hill back home, hoping to stomp off her anger.

Eventually after several worrying nights of rain, Abbie decided to contact another builder to finish the work. She took out the local business directory and picked out a builder. He agreed to call the following day to check over her roof to see if there was anything else that needed doing.

He arrived bang on time and Abbie invited him in to explain the situation, editing out the bits where the previous builder had made an unwelcome pass at her. He was a friendly man, introduced himself as Tom but Abbie was on her guard and resolved, at first, not to even offer him a cup of tea. He took a good look in the loft, then examined the roof from his ladder before confirming that a good job had been done with nothing left outstanding.

As Tom was folding his ladders away, Abbie, on the spur of the moment, asked if he could prepare a rough estimate on the cost of an extension to the cottage. She wasn't committing to anything, she reasoned, it would just be interesting to know what sort of figure was involved.

She explained what she had in mind; a single story, self-contained building, at least one large room, bright, lots of windows and a smaller workroom/darkroom. They walked about on the lawn, measuring in strides the approximate size although Abbie found it incredibly difficult to visualise the finished structure and was worrying that what they'd mapped out wouldn't be big enough. Tom scribbled some notes and figures on a scrap of paper and Abbie told herself to stop fretting. She'd just wait until the quote came through and then she would have something to work with – she'd have plenty of time to confirm measurements if she decided to go ahead with it.

Tom left with a cheery smile and promised to get the quote in the post to her within the next few days. He seemed like a genuine guy, Abbie thought, feeling a little mean that she hadn't offered him a cup of tea.

Chapter Seventeen

Miriam Walker was in a good mood. Her parents had taken Honey and Blossom to stay with them for a few days. The girls would love it; trips to the beach every day and though it was still too cold to be able to stay there long, they would be well wrapped up and allowed to paddle, just in the shallow water in their wellies. Miriam smiled as she imagined her highly excitable daughters screeching as they ran back up the beach away from the waves as they surged towards them. Someone was bound to fall over and get soaking wet - Miriam smiled wryly. She had no cause to worry; they were in good hands. Her parents would whisk them home for a hot bath afterwards, make them little cups of hot chocolate and read them stories.

Miriam's attention was brought swiftly back to the task in hand – the batch of cherry and almond muffins baking in the oven. She opened the door and was immediately swathed in heat together with the buttery, sweet smell of home baking. The muffins were cooked perfectly, and she placed the tray on the worktop which was becoming rather crowded with fruit cake, banana bread and mini, individual sized versions of old classics that were seemingly the next hottest thing in tearooms - according to the mass of food and catering magazines she'd been reading all winter.

Miriam surveyed her wares, pleased with herself for having made everything on her list – and there had been no disasters either. Everything had turned out to her exacting professional standards. She flicked the kettle switch, popped a teabag in a cup and went through to the tearoom for a quick final check, knowing as she went that there would be at least half a dozen more quick final checks before tomorrow morning.

Last year she'd packed in too many tables, too close together and it had looked cluttered and cramped. Now she'd removed half a dozen of them and stacked them up in the corner which wasn't ideal but as she stood in the centre of the room, turning slowly, running her eyes over the random arrangement, she knew it looked much better. Miriam didn't like the clean, straight lines of the extension – it had been Alistair's design but was just a cold square box to her, devoid of any welcoming character whatsoever. She did her best to make up for it with soft furnishings and pretty colours. She'd bought new table linen in different shades of pink and green, from the palest cherry blossom and pistachio to fuchsia cerise and evergreen pine. Miriam smiled; pleased with the result. Small clear glass vases were in place ready for a single pink gerbera to be placed in each in the morning when they were delivered. And that was it – everything was ready. Tomorrow they would be open for business.

Miriam turned to leave and looked admirably at the shining French doors - that had been a hard job, cleaning all three sets of them yesterday. But it was worth it - they were positively sparkling. She must remember to put the warning stickers back on to stop people walking into them. Miriam picked up a small notebook from the counter and scribbled a reminder to herself.

She stood and gazed out to the garden which she'd tidied over the last couple of weeks, but it still needed a lot of time spent on it – she'd asked Alistair a couple of times, but he'd been too busy. She couldn't complain about that – it could only be a good thing if he had plenty of work. Of course, the best solution for the huge time-consuming garden would be to turn it into a parking area for her customers. Miriam was convinced it would make a huge different to the success of her business. She made another note in her book to speak to Alistair about it.

Back in the kitchen in the main house, Miriam drank her cup of tea. It had started to rain, and she hoped it wasn't raining wherever Honey and Blossom were today, and she really hoped it wouldn't be raining tomorrow for her opening day.

Chapter Eighteen

Miriam unlocked the French doors and pulled one open. She looked out onto the sodden garden and inhaled a deep breath bracing herself for the season's first day of business. It had rained solidly throughout the night - she had woken many times, anxious about today and although it had stopped raining, it was drizzling now, a fine mist of hazy rain. It was cold too, colder than it should be for the time of year and Miriam pushed the door shut, resigned to the fact that it was very unlikely anyone would bother to turn up for her opening day. It wasn't the weather for early tourists to be out walking, stopping off for tea and cake on their way back. They would stay in their hotels making use of the in-house facilities; the swimming pool and sauna, the gym and beauty treatments. Even those in the B & Bs would probably stay cosied up, after a full English breakfast of course, in the guests' lounge, reading their books and newspapers in front of a roaring log fire. They would have no need to venture out for refreshment.

Miriam was rather hoping one or two locals would turn up though. She'd put the opening details on a board outside on the pavement for the last few days and advertised in the local and parish magazines but again why would they want to leave their warm, cosy homes to come out in this weather?

Miriam shivered. It wasn't that warm inside, she thought, turning up the thermostat on the wall a good few degrees. She wandered from table to table tweaking things in place and fussing with the fresh flowers, thinking sadly how they might not even be seen at their best.

A sharp tap on the glass made her jump and she turned around to see Mrs Gilbert smiling in expectantly. Miriam signalled from the other side of the room that the door was open and went over to greet Mrs Gilbert as she stepped inside.

'Hello Mrs Gilbert. I'd heard you'd been unwell, are you better now?'

'Hello dear. Yes, much better thank-you. I thought for a moment I'd got the day wrong. I was sure you were opening up today.'

'Yes, that's right. Today's the day – it's just a bit quiet at the moment, probably because of this rotten weather.'

'Ah, that won't stop folk around here. Lord, we wouldn't do anything at all if all we did was wait for it to stop raining.'

It amused Miriam to still hear some people talk to her as if she'd only just arrived. She'd lived in the area for five years now.

'I just wanted to call in,' continued the old lady, 'and wish you luck for the season.'

Miriam had guided Mrs Gilbert to a table close to a radiator and laid with a pale green tablecloth and a pretty pale pink gerbera. This was her third year of opening the tearoom but when she thought about it,

Mrs Gilbert had always been there on each of her opening days.

'What can I get you?' she asked kindly, slightly overwhelmed by Mrs Gilbert's loyal support.

'A pot of tea and some cake I think.'

'What sort of cake?' Miriam had her notebook and pen in hand. 'Shall I bring the board over?'

'No, don't worry about that. Choose me something. Surprise me! Let's live dangerously,' she laughed.

Miriam smiled as she went behind the counter thinking how nice it would be if everyone was so easily pleased. First, she took the tea things to Mrs Gilbert's table and then she sliced a generous portion of double chocolate fudge cake, filled a tiny china jug with cream and placed them on the table.

'There you go – double chocolate fudge cake, filled with chocolate cream and cherry conserve, topped with chocolate fudge sauce and fresh cream if you like. It doesn't get much more dangerous than that!'

Mrs Gilbert laughed again and then Miriam was about to make a comment about it being dangerously fattening but considering how tiny and frail Mrs Gilbert was, she wasn't sure if it was appropriate. She stood there for a second watching her pour a generous amount of cream carefully over the cake and wondered how on earth she managed to run the B & B on her own at her age.

Miriam heard the door open behind her and turned to see Jed Tobin's smiling face as he quickly closed the door, wiping his feet courteously on a non-existent mat and rubbing his cold red hands together. 'Ah, it's lovely and warm in here,' he said appreciatively. Miriam was immediately pleased with herself for turning the heating up. Without waiting to be asked, he called out his order to Miriam who appreciated his decisiveness as she returned to the counter.

'A mug of coffee please, Mrs Walker, and a toasted tea cake. Make that two – I need some insulation in this weather. Morning Mrs Gilbert.'

Mrs Gilbert smiled and nodded in acknowledgement as she placed another forkful of rich, moist chocolate cake in her mouth.

Jed took a newspaper from the rack on the wall, holding all the main dailies, and sat at a table in the far corner. Miriam brought him a large mug of coffee. She knew he didn't like to be bothered with jugs and bowls of sugar, so she made it as she always did with two large spoons of sugar and plenty of cream.

'Lovely. Just how I like it. Thank you Mrs Walker. Hope this is going to be a busy and successful year for you – for all of us actually. We could do with a good year for a change.'

'Thank-you, yes, let's hope so.'

Miriam set his teacakes down on the table and looked up as the door opened again. The two Delaney sisters walked in chattering away at each other. Jed looked up and smiled at them as he folded his newspaper - placing it on the table, knowing full well that his quiet reading time was over already.

Miriam got out of the way while they settled themselves at Jed's table, knowing it would be a few minutes before they would be ready to order.

To her amazement the door opened again, and another elderly couple came in. Bill and Renee were red faced and watery eyed from the cold, despite being wrapped up sensibly against the weather.

They looked at Miriam and nodded questioningly at their little dog, Mick, a soulful looking Scottish Terrier, ensuring, as they always did, that it was OK to bring him inside. Miriam automatically glanced around the tearoom checking there was no-one obvious who might object. Mrs Gilbert wouldn't mind, of course. And neither would Jed Tobin – he loved animals of all sorts. Lilleth would be OK, it was only Eva who might have something to say. But then, she always had something to say.

Miriam nodded at them. They looked half frozen. She took her notebook and pen ready for their order as they took the table nearest the door ready for a quick exit if need be.

'It's so lovely to see you open again,' said Renee, a little out of breath and getting redder in the face as she thawed out. She was short and slightly plump with her matching husband sitting opposite.

They look like bookends thought Miriam affectionately as she smiled at them, glad to have another happy couple in her tearoom. She waited patiently with pen poised while Renee continued as she tried to settle Mick at her side.

'We went for an extra long walk this morning, right over to West Heights. My goodness, it was cold, wasn't it Bill? Anyway, we didn't mind because we'd already planned to stop off here on our way back – I've been looking forward to hot buttered crumpets since breakfast.' Renee laughed at herself and then added, 'It's a real shame you're not open throughout the winter. We do miss this as part of our routine you know.'

Miriam was touched but didn't know how to respond so she just smiled and wiggled her pen self-consciously before writing 'crumpets' on her notebook. She looked over at Bill.

'And what can I get for you?'

Bill was studying the newly styled menu; first, to see if there was anything new this year to tempt him and secondly to confirm that his old favourite was still there, which it was. 'Two hot fruit scones please,' he said looking up with a happy, contented smile.

'And to drink?'

'Tea please,' they said in unison. Miriam brought the tea things to their table then ran through to the main house. She wasn't planning to offer crumpets this year and had taken them off the menu, but Bill and Renee had been so kind with their comments she didn't have the heart to tell them. There were some crumpets in her freezer that she could quickly defrost in the microwave before toasting. When she returned to the tearoom, she was pleasantly surprised to see another three tables occupied.

There was a pleasant babble of lively chatter but above it all, coming from the far corner of the room, she could hear Eva Delaney moaning about the lack of service.

Acknowledging the other visitors on her way, Miriam went back to the counter to collect her pad and heard Eva exclaim loudly. 'Service. Over here,

125

please,' closely followed by embarrassed shushing from Lilleth.

Miriam was in too good spirits to let Eva's rudeness spoil her mood. She arrived at their table with a genuine smile, feeling as though she had all the patience in the world. While she waited, Jed asked for another mug of coffee. Lilleth quickly ordered one of the new additions to the menu; a mini banana bread loaf and finally Eva noticing that crumpets were no longer on the menu, asked for those. She was thrown when Miriam reassured her that the omission was, in fact, a mistake and that they were still available. Eva mumbled something inaudible before announcing that she would have the sweet and sticky treacle tart instead.

Miriam left the table thinking what an appropriate choice she'd made. Perhaps the sticky tart would sweeten her up – she definitely needed it.

Miriam got around to the other tables as quickly as she could. Everyone seemed happy when she finally got a few moments break; looking across, with great satisfaction, at her full tearoom. It was very warm, and coats were hanging on the backs of chairs as people settled in their seats. She poured herself a glass of water, leaning against the sink as she drank. She thought she heard Alistair's car pull up on the drive and turned her head to listen. The slamming of the front door confirmed that he was home although Miriam wasn't expecting him back during the day. She cast a careful eye over her customers and gauged that it would be alright to leave them for a minute or two.

As she dashed through to the house, she heard Alistair slam his keys onto the kitchen worktop.

'Is everything alright?'

'Yes,' was his simple reply although obviously it wasn't. He was flicking through his work diary, yanking the pages so violently, Miriam thought he might tear them out if he wasn't more careful.

Miriam wasn't in the mood for an argument. Literally, she was in the best of moods because of her busy morning but also her head was buzzing with thoughts about the car park. And after such a successful start today, Alistair could hardly refuse. She would have liked him to go through and see the tearoom full of customers, but she could tell this wasn't a good time and really needed not to fall out with him right now.

'I thought you were at that woman's house, what's her name? The new porch woman. I didn't think you'd be back until tonight.'

'Yeah, it's not quite – going to plan,' he snapped.

Miriam gave him a questioning look, and he snapped back again.

'A few setbacks, that's all. I'm off somewhere else now.' Alistair left his book on the side and slammed out of the house with not even a peck on the cheek for his wife.

Out into the drizzle Jed, Eva and Lilleth finally left the tearoom together. Jed was walking them to their bus-stop but Lilleth soon found herself walking behind the other two on the narrow pathway. Eva had linked arms possessively with Jed and Lilleth was left to plod along behind. Soon the drizzle turned to rain and within moments it was coming down quite hard. Jed was OK in his tweed fisherman's hat and Lilleth was more than OK as she pulled out her compact umbrella and flicked it open, sheltering smug and content underneath, feeling a little wicked but smiling to herself all the same. She would lay a fairly high stakes bet that her sister wouldn't let go of Jed to come and shelter with her. And she was right.

Lilleth's smile soon disappeared as the number nine bus passed them up the hill. She and Eva automatically looked at their watches ready to incriminate the bus driver for setting off before his time and daring to go without them. It should have left at a quarter past and both their watches confirmed that it was two minutes after that and there wouldn't be another one out to their part of the country for another hour. They didn't fancy waiting in a cold, damp bus shelter for an hour and luckily Jed came to the rescue.

'Come back to mine. And I'll drive you home from there.'

'Are you sure Jed?' asked Lilleth, grateful for the offer but not wanting to put him out. Eva just wanted her sister to shut up – and to get inside the warm somewhere, out of this horrible weather.

'Of course I am. Come on, let's go.' Jed turned around decisively, forcing Eva to take her arm from his. He passed the two ladies to begin walking in the opposite direction briskly up the hill, leaving Eva and Lilleth doing their best to keep up with him. Eva was walking quite apart from Lilleth at first but by the time they reached the top of the hill, she'd edged closer and closer until she was finally sharing the shelter of Lilleth's umbrella. Finally, they reached Jed's cottage, thankful to be able to get out of the rain at last.

'Come on in. I'll make us a hot drink, warm us all up.'

They liked the sound of that. They were cold through and the idea of thawing out with a hot cup of tea or two in Jed's warm and cosy cottage was very welcoming.

Several cups of tea later, Jed provided some lunch in the form of tomato soup and crusty bread and then as they were all comfortable and warm, settled snugly around the little log fire, it seemed the only appropriate thing to do was bring out a bottle of his favourite Cabernet Sauvignon. It was getting dark by the time they had finished the bottle and Eva and Lilleth reluctantly stretched themselves out of their armchairs, rosy cheeked from the fire and the wine. Jed phoned for a taxi for them while they wrapped up ready for the cold. It was still raining.

Miriam was on the phone to her mum who was telling her where she and her grand-daughters had been that day and what they'd all been doing. Miriam had already had two almost identical versions of the day's events from Honey and Blossom when she spoke to them each in turn. Their conversation lasted barely a minute as they were tempted away by some fun distraction probably from their grand-dad. Miriam phoned every evening at about this time to make sure everything was OK with her parents and to speak to the girls and say good-night.

She missed them terribly, but it had been a busy non-stop day, so it was a good thing they were out of the way. While she was on the phone Alistair had come in and had gone straight upstairs to shower. Miriam was a little surprised that he hadn't stopped for a quick word with his daughters but then again, she had barely got a nod from him before he disappeared.

Miriam said her good-byes and went into the kitchen to open a bottle of wine. Alistair reappeared, washed and freshly shaved. She was pleased that his grumpy mood had passed, although he was quiet now, and thoughtful.

'Lasagne's in the oven, just needs a few more minutes,' she said. But still no reaction. His mind was definitely elsewhere. Miriam's hopes for a chat about the future of the tearoom were fast slipping away, as Alistair sat at the kitchen table and engrossed himself in the newspaper. Miriam dished up in silence, only just managing to resist the temptation of banging the plates down in front of him to get his attention. She sat down, took a deep breath and calmly poured a generous measure of wine in their glasses – if she had to get him drunk to talk to her, so be it.

Miriam tip-toed through the meal, making light conversation and topping up Alistair's glass a couple of times. They finished up and Miriam loaded the dishwasher as quick as she could, suggesting to Alistair he open another bottle – anything to stop him disappearing into the living room to switch the television on.

'I had a great day in the tearoom.'

'Yeah, you said already.'

Miriam sighed inwardly, her spirits deflating by the second.

'I know. I'm just saying – it was a good start. Very encouraging for day one. And if it carries on like this….' At last, she'd caught Alistair's attention; he jerked his head round to face her.

'What?'

'Well, if it carries on this good, we can really go ahead with the parking area.'

That was as far as she got.

'For God's sake,' he shouted. 'One day selling a few bits of cake isn't going to pay thousands of pounds for a bloody car park.'

Miriam was visibly shocked at his temper. She jumped, annoyed with him and herself for allowing him to have this effect on her. She didn't really think a small parking area would cost thousands of pounds, would it?

The problem was Alistair took care of all their finances and Miriam had always been happy to leave that side of things to him. But right now, she was wishing she'd involved herself more and then she could argue her case with more conviction. As it was, Alistair had just made her feel silly. She wanted to bring up the fact that he was busy too, with plenty of work coming in but she felt out of her depth already, not knowing what expenses had to be paid or when. She let the matter drop and Alistair took his chance to disappear out of the room. Within seconds Miriam could hear the television blaring out.

She stayed in the kitchen sipping her wine, unable to shake the feeling that this argument, this stalemate, wasn't really much to do with the tearoom or a few car parking spaces either.

Chapter Nineteen

As Abbie was scrambling eggs, free-range from a farm just outside the village, she could hear whistling and it was getting closer. She recognised it as the postman and heard a light plop on the doormat as she finished spreading creamy eggs onto her toast before going through to the front room to collect her delivery. Just one envelope. Abbie smiled at the quality stationery, knowing before she even turned it over to see the hand-written address, that it was from Luisa. She took it back to the kitchen, perched herself on the new stool she'd bought and placed the envelope on the worktop, enjoying the anticipation while she ate her breakfast and sipped her tea. The postmark stood out clearly and Abbie's stomach flip-flopped as she realised that it was Jack's birthday today.

Abbie and Luisa regularly spoke on the phone. At the beginning Luisa phoned almost every other day and Abbie had only just managed to convince her that it wasn't necessary for her to keep checking up. She finally opened the envelope and inside was a notelet, a whimsical picture of a stream over-hanging with weeping willow trees, the sun shining and wildflowers in abundance.

Hi Abbie,

Just a quick note – glad to hear things are coming together and you're settling in up there. That's really fantastic. I hope you like the picture on this notelet, it reminded me of your gran's little painting – I think. It's very pretty anyway!

If it's OK with you I'm coming up to visit in a couple of weeks – I have some news. Aaron is off to Finland so I can come for a long weekend if that's OK? I'm looking forward to seeing the place transformed and to meeting your two aunties – and Jed, of course!

See you soon,
Luv Luisa x x

Abbie placed the card back on the worktop. She sipped her tea thinking through the mixed feelings crowding her mind. She was more than pleased that Luisa was visiting soon – that was definitely something to look forward to. And what was her news, she wondered. But Luisa was expecting to see a transformation and now Abbie wished she hadn't exaggerated her progress quite as much as she obviously had. Without doubt, the cottage looked different; with its new furniture and curtains and after all the initial manic cleaning, Abbie had done a good job of keeping up with it all. She'd even bought a few pots and hanging baskets to brighten up the outside – but she wasn't sure that this would pass as a transformation in Luisa's book.

And something more pressing was bothering her – the whereabouts of her gran's painting. Abbie picked up the notelet, Luisa was right; the picture was very similar in style to the little watercolour although she was sure her gran's painting was finer in detail and fresher in the way that it portrayed the light to reflect a beautiful early summer's morning. But where was it? She remembered having it with her at Luisa's, having rescued it from her near burnt-out home. And she remembered carefully wrapping it separately from the box of trinkets that her gran had given her, ready to be packed for the move. But she couldn't honestly remember having seen it since arriving here.

Abbie pulled open the stairway door and ran upstairs. There was only one place it could be. In the smaller bedroom she'd left some boxes, yet to be unpacked. They were full of books mostly and also her art and photographic equipment that she hadn't had the heart to deal with yet. She emptied a box of books onto the floor, stacking them carefully but the painting wasn't there. She started on the next one and finally, in the third box, she found what she was looking for. The little painting was neatly wrapped and lying near the top, cushioned between two fluffy bath towels. Abbie sat on the floor and unwrapped it, relieved and comforted by its familiarity. She'd studied it many times, wondering who had painted it and under what circumstances it had been given to her gran – with that interesting inscription on the back. She noticed now that it really needed a new frame; its thin rather basic looking one did it no justice at all.

Abbie took the painting back downstairs, hanging it on a stray nail in the middle of a wall in the main front room. It looked lost there and she resolved to have it reframed in something more suitable and hang it, pride of place, above the fireplace. And she'd make sure this was done before Luisa arrived. She sat down on the sofa; there was something else she wanted to do straightaway and that was to send a text to Jack wishing him a Happy Birthday.

Later in the week, pleased to have a legitimate reason to visit the gallery again, Abbie could see from halfway down the lane that there were lights on and it appeared that the gallery was open. First, she walked by the cottage, taking a long lingering look to see if anyone was inside. It seemed not.

She walked up to the gallery and pushed open the door, a little brass bell tinkled announcing her arrival as she stepped inside. There was no-one around and she looked about for a few moments, content to have the place to herself for a while. It had a nice feeling; light and bright, yet warm and cosy, a homely place. A young woman, in her early twenties, appeared from a back room.

'Hi. Can I help you?'

'Hi, do you offer a framing service here?'

'We certainly do.' The young woman breezed confidence in her gently voice, her smile was friendly and welcoming.

'That's brilliant. I have this picture here.' Abbie placed the wrapped painting on the counter. 'It's twenty by twenty centimetres, could you give me a price?'

'Well, it depends what type of frame you choose, of course.' The woman flicked through the pages of a folder and turned it around on the counter for

Abbie to see. There were rows of prices for different sized pictures, under different headings for different frame styles.

The woman pointed to the appropriate row. 'Prices for that size start here and as you can see, it goes up if you want something more ornate. Just depends what you want to pay really.'

'I want something nice, to really set it off.' Abbie unwrapped the painting and couldn't help notice the young woman's momentary look of surprise, a flicker of recognition maybe. But the moment was soon gone as the assistant pointed out some examples on the wall close by.

'The cream frame with the fine antique gold edging, just over there, would look good I think.'

Abbie followed her gaze. 'Yes, I think you're right. Or even the one next to it, just slightly heavier but I think it would be perfect.'

'Definitely, although I will warn you, the one you've chosen is quite expensive,' the gallery assistant flicked over the page in the folder. 'Yes, one of our very most expensive actually.'

Abbie turned around to look at the painting on the wall, she moved in for a closer look. 'It's OK, I really like it. I'd like to go with that one, please.'

'Of course. Just let me input all the details.' The young woman took the order and printed off a copy for Abbie.

'You have a beautiful place here,' said Abbie, trying to take it all in, always collecting ideas for her own gallery that she was determined she would have one day.

'Yes it is, but it's not mine,' the girl laughed. 'I only work here, just four afternoons a week.'

Well that explained why it was so often shut thought Abbie.

'Nice job,' said Abbie. 'Let me know if there are any more going. I've not long moved here, and I need to find something. Something part-time at least.'

'It is a good job, I know I'm very lucky. The owner is an old friend of my parents so that's how I came by it. But I'm off to university in September – all being well,' she laughed. 'There'll definitely be a vacancy then.'

'I'd truly love to work here but I think I ought to try to get something before then.'

'Well, if you're not too fussy, I do know that there is a job going over at The Green Man pub. They're looking for lunch-time staff.'

'OK, thanks. I'll give it some thought.' Abbie decided there and then to pop into the pub that afternoon to make enquiries.

'Good luck. I'll give you a call when your painting's ready.'

Back home and the postman had been. Abbie picked up two envelopes, neither of them bills or junk mail; they were both addressed to her in actual handwriting. She tore open the first one, quickly realising from the business heading that it was the quotation from Tom the builder. Abbie pulled a grim face; it was a hefty figure although she hadn't had a clue what to expect in the first place. She folded the quote up and put it back in its envelope, resignedly - it didn't change anything; it still wasn't feasible to set up a gallery of her own from Winnifred Cottage, not in the immediate future anyway.

The second envelope was much smaller, felt like it had a card inside but interestingly no stamp on it which meant it must have been hand posted. Intrigued, Abbie carefully tore it open. It was from Lilleth inviting her to an evening 'do' at the weekend to celebrate the opening of the first bottle of Turnip wine. Lilleth had written that she would be delighted to see her there. How could she possibly refuse?

On Saturday evening, Abbie pulled up outside Gordon Cottage at seven-thirty. The front door was hooked open on the pleasant but slightly chilling evening and Abbie could hear jovial voices from inside. She knocked and called out 'hello', stepping into the warm, homely kitchen. Great Aunt Lilleth appeared in an instant, her cheeks glowing and beaming a smile at Abbie who gathered the party was already in full swing.

'Hello Abbie, my dear, come on in. We're just getting started on the Blackberry – last year's vintage and a little more potent than we expected. We're waiting for everyone to arrive before we open the Turnip.'

Abbie was a little overawed at the seriousness of what she thought was just an excuse to open a few bottles of home-made wine. As Lilleth ushered her through to the lounge, she didn't really know what to expect.

The heat from the blazing log fire hit her as she entered the room. A collection of people with roasted rosy red faces sat around chatting – some she recognised but most she didn't. One familiar face she was very happy to see was that of Jed Tobin. He looked pleased to see her too and was out of his chair immediately, pouring her a drink.

'Are you going to be brave Abbie and go straight in with a Blackberry or are you going to play safe with the Raspberry?'

Abbie was at his side, marvelling at the assortment of bottles with their intriguing coloured liquids. She had no idea how brave it was to try the Blackberry and decided to stick with caution - for the time being anyway.

'I'm afraid I'm going to be a lightweight and go for the Raspberry.'

'Coward!' teased Jed. 'You won't escape the Turnip, you know. That's Lilleth's pride and joy; she'll be positively insulted if you refuse a tipple.'

'I wouldn't dare,' giggled Abbie, enjoying herself already.

After barely a couple of minutes, Eva appeared, possessively, at Jed's side but Abbie was reluctant to relinquish her party partner. A quick glance around the room showed that apart from Mrs Kelly from the bakers, she didn't know anyone else there. Unfortunately, Eva was determined and quickly linked arms with Jed before leading him away, leaving Abbie alone clutching her Raspberry wine. She smiled as Jed winked conspiratorially at her, before raising his eyes to the ceiling. She knew then that she would get to talk to him again later that evening.

In the next instant, Lilleth, the perfect hostess, swept her off to introduce her to some of her far-flung neighbours.

Some considerable time later, her head buzzing trying to remember faces and names and locations, Abbie loitered in the empty kitchen for a few moments. She placed her empty glass on the draining board, conscious of the sticky fruity taste in her mouth. She poured herself a glass of water.

'What are you doing out here on your own? Come on through, we've started on the Turnip wine. It's a pretty potent brew this year – better get in quick before it's all gone.' Lilleth put a gentle arm around Abbie's waist and steered her towards the door, whispering in her ear as she opened it. 'Mrs Whippit has already tripped on the rug - half landed in Fred's lap. Poor sod, he didn't know whether to be pleased or frightened!'

Lilleth beamed at her and Abbie was suddenly taken aback by her Great Aunt's beauty; her smooth pale skin, highlighted with rosy cheeks. Her soft, kind blue eyes were positively twinkling, matching the outrageously dangly earrings that sparkled from frail, stretched earlobes that looked as if they couldn't really take the weight.

The room was lively with noisy laughter and chatter. Lilleth led Abbie across the room and took possession of a bottle of Turnip wine.

'We'll just hang on to this one,' she said, handing it to Abbie. 'Stash it somewhere safe. It's your own secret supply!' And then she flitted over to the other side of the room, checking on friends and food and empty glasses. Abbie was left on her own, feeling incredibly conspicuous with a bottle of treasured Turnip wine in her hand. She poured a glassful, liked the look of it, took a sip and liked the taste too. She sidled to the edge of the room, sinking back into a large leather armchair, surreptitiously sliding the wine bottle to the side of the chair, out of general sight but still nicely within reach.

She smiled to herself; feeling like an eccentric old lady. It obviously ran in the family.

Abbie lost track of exactly how long she'd sat there but guessed it must have been some time judging by the giddiness she felt when Jed pulled her to her feet for a quick shimmy to some big band number. The music was loud but the laughter and chatter even louder as Jed whirled her around the room amidst a kaleidoscope of faces.

Momentarily she saw Mrs Gilbert swaying gently in her own little world, a small glass held precariously to her chest.

After a few more spins she caught sight of Eva topping up her own glass and then Lilleth and Mrs Kelly trying to dance something between a waltz and a foxtrot and, very worryingly, nearly tripping over each other's feet. Everyone was having a ball. When the music finally stopped, and the room stopped spinning, Abbie and Jed came to a gradual halt. Abbie was giggling, out of breath, but reluctant to let go of Jed as she was giddy with spinning as well as from the Turnip wine. Abbie caught a glimpse of Eva giving her an unfriendly stare from across the room.

Some time later and after even more Turnip wine, Abbie grinned at her reflection in the bathroom mirror – her flushed face was beetroot red, matching exactly all those other faces at the party. She placed her hands on her cheeks; they radiated intense heat. As she went back through the tiny hallway into the kitchen, she could feel cool air from the open door and headed for the welcome coolness, stepping outside into the starlit garden. Jed was sitting on the garden bench, apparently deep in thought. She didn't want to interrupt him, but he'd already sensed her presence, turning towards her and beckoning her to join him.

'Come and sit down, Abbie. It's OK, I'm on my own.'

Abbie smiled, sitting down next to Jed. 'Yes, I see you've escaped.'

He was cradling a whisky glass, filled with a generous measure.

'And I see you've given up on the fruit wines?'

Jed smiled silently, leaning forwards, resting his elbows on his knees. Abbie felt an odd suspense, just for a moment, of words unspoken.

'How are you finding it, living at Winnifred Cottage?' he asked, a little whimsically thought Abbie. She wasn't sure how to answer, sensing that Jed wanted her to say something much more positive than she felt. She aimed for the middle ground.

'Well, you know, I'm getting there. It's just going to take a while, to get everything the way I want it. It's been empty for such a long time.'

'Fifty years,' cut in Jed, gazing deep into his whisky glass.

'Oh. You know the place? When my gran lived there?'

'Ah, she never actually lived there. It was the plan, but it never happened,' said Jed quietly, shaking his head.

Abbie leaned in a little closer, curious and eager for Jed to continue. But just at that moment, a couple of noisy women appeared in the garden, immediately spoiling the opportunity of a quiet chat with Jed. As she turned back to him, he was already getting up from the bench, although before he left, he leant close to her and whispered, 'I knew your gran very well.'

Jed went back into the cottage, stopping on the way for a quick word with the noisy women. Abbie couldn't hear what he said but both women beamed flirtatiously at him before laughing congenially, lapping up the attention. Jed certainly knew how to charm the ladies, observed Abbie, wondering if he'd ever worked his charms on her lovely Grannaliese.

Abbie sat; deep in thought in the welcome silence now that the noisy women had followed Jed back inside.

Chapter Twenty

Abbie awoke, opening her eyes cautiously against the early morning light. After the previous evening's cocktail of potent fruit and vegetable concoctions, she expected a whopper of a hangover. But as her eyes tentatively tip-toed around the bedroom, focusing on solid objects without a hint of spinning, she was amazed that she felt no nausea, not even a headache.

With a contented smile Abbie closed her eyes and snuggled further down under the duvet and just as she was working out how to get back to her aunt's place to collect her car, she fell back to sleep.

Eva had been phoning Jed on and off since she'd got up over two hours ago but wasn't getting an answer.

Jed had heard the phone ringing but chose to ignore it. He was busy, delving into old boxes in the smallest bedroom that he used as a storeroom, engrossed in looking through old photographs, lost in a past world. He sat at the old desk wallowing in his happy memories, smiling, musing and remembering.

It was getting near to lunchtime and Jed decided to wander over to the gallery. Rhona would be going for her break soon and he felt like pottering about in there for a while. He pushed open the door, the bell above rattled and he saw Rhona over the far side of the gallery, placing a new collection of watercolours on the wall, standing back and studying the display. She looked up and smiled.

'Julian came by this morning, took the last of his other paintings away – there were only a couple left and he asked me to put these up. It was OK to do that, wasn't it?'

'Of course, my dear. Julian's a regular.'

'That's what I thought. And these are exquisite, aren't they?' Rhona looked at the paintings, admiring the artist's talent. They were of the local landscape; the fells and valleys and lakes.

'They certainly are. Wish I could paint like that,' said Jed with a twinkle in his eye. Rhona laughed and pulled a face as she went back to the counter. 'Are you going off to lunch dear?'

'Yes, I was just going to go.'

'No need to hurry back if you've got things to do, I'll keep shop in here for a while. Anything particular need doing?'

'Not really, I'm pretty much on top of things. Oh, there's some post there for you, just come in. Don't worry about that little package back from the framer's, I know what that is – I've got to give the woman a ring to let her know her painting's back.' Rhona grabbed her jacket and handbag and opened the door, calling over her shoulder to Jed. 'OK, see you later. Have fun!'

Jed smiled as she banged the door shut. He sat behind the counter and looked around, drumming his fingers, not quite sure what to do with himself now

146

that he was there. He opened the post; a couple of bills and some junk, and three letters from artists – one local, the others further afield asking for their work to be considered for exhibiting in the gallery. Jed put them to one side to look at later. He sighed. He didn't have the energy to deal with this side of things anymore – not with the kind of vitality and enthusiasm these young budding creators deserved. And Rhona would be leaving him at the end of the summer, so he had to think about what he would do then. One particularly good idea had come to mind, but he needed to act on it - sooner rather than later.

Jed picked up the parcel that had come back from the picture framing company, and opened it, curious to see what it was. He opened the box and lifted out the picture, carefully unwrapping the tissue paper to reveal a watercolour painting of a summertime meadow. He could hardly believe what he was looking at; he almost gasped aloud and he was sure his heart stopped beating for a good few seconds. Jed placed the painting on the counter and took a deep calming breath, placing a hand on his chest to steady himself. Suddenly he remembered something; he picked up the painting and turned it over, and there it was – the inscription, 'To my dearest Anna, my inspiration for everything I do.' It was dated 1958, Jed smiled weakly, he turned twenty-one that year.

He wrapped the picture up again and placed it back in the box then ran his hands through his mass of wild grey hair and sighed deeply, contemplating what he should do. He knew instantly who'd brought the painting in and he was delighted to know that it obviously meant a lot to her judging by the very expensive frame she'd bought for it. He wondered how much she knew about it, probably nothing significant, he concluded. Jed nodded as if in confirmation to himself. The idea he'd been mulling over for a little while now, was definitely the right thing to do.

It was lunchtime and Jed knew he should eat soon. His digestive system had always been a weak point and he suffered terribly if he missed a meal or was ever tempted to eat something rich or exotic. But right now, for good or bad, he didn't want to eat. He wanted to paint. He hadn't worked on anything for years. But seeing this watercolour in front of him had stirred up all sorts of feelings and memories.

He left the gallery, taking the painting with him, and turned the sign to 'Closed' on the door. He went around the side of the gallery to his studio, up the wooden stairs, unlocking the door to his private space and once inside he started to sketch.

Abbie was dreaming – her mobile phone was ringing but when she ran into the room, it wasn't there. She proceeded to run from room to room looking for the elusive phone. She woke to realise that it really was her own mobile ringing downstairs in the kitchen in her handbag. Abbie knew she couldn't move quickly enough to reach it in time and so she lay there and let it go to voicemail. The clock on the bedside cabinet showed it was eleven thirty; she had to get up and get ready for work.

Abbie had gone along to The Green Man and asked after the bar job, she'd had a quick chat with Tony, the landlord, and started the following day.

She thought it would give her an opportunity to meet people and get to know the local community better. And the income would help prevent her from digging too much into her savings. But the summer season hadn't really started yet and the lunchtime shifts she did on Mondays, Wednesdays and Sundays were unbearably quiet and boring.

Abbie was on the landing as her mobile rang again and she took the stairs two at a time at break-neck speed down to the kitchen, grabbing her bag and rummaging frantically for her phone, just managing to see that it was Jilly before she answered, automatically but inexplicably irritated.

'Hello!'

'About time! Where were you? I was getting worried.'

Abbie didn't want to admit that she had only just got out of bed and she didn't feel like going into an explanation of how she'd had such a good time at a party given by two old ladies in their seventies.

'I was upstairs and didn't hear my phone down here.'

'You need to get a landline installed.'

'I know. I will.' Abbie's limited patience was disappearing fast. Had her sister phoned just to tell her what to do?

'Listen, I haven't got long. I'm on my way to pick Molly up from nursery but I wanted to let you know as soon as we'd decided.' There was a momentary pause; Jilly's for effect, and Abbie wondering what on earth was to come – it was obviously something she should be excited about.

'We're coming up. For a visit.' Another pause. This time Jilly was waiting for a reaction and Abbie was waiting, hoping for a suitable one to manifest itself. She managed to keep 'Oh God, no!' to herself.

Jilly felt obliged to fill the ominous silence. 'Soon. Well, quite soon. In the half-term holiday – end of May, just for the week.'

At last Abbie found her voice. 'Right. OK. That's good.' She knew she didn't sound at all convincing and was relieved when Jilly continued, like the trooper she was.

'We still need to sort out where we're staying and things, but perhaps you could recommend somewhere?'

'Yeah, of course, I will.'

Jilly had had enough of this going nowhere conversation and repeated her need to get going, saying she would phone again in a few days when perhaps Abbie would be able to suggest some hotels or B & Bs.

Abbie closed her phone, noticing that the low battery indicator was flashing. She sighed with relief; that would have gone down well if her phone had run out while talking to Jilly. Why was it she always felt so inadequate when comparing herself to her competent, organised elder sister? She perched on a stool, feeling tired and drained. And guilty too. Jilly was going to all the effort of bringing her large family all the way up the country to visit her and she'd hardly bothered to say two words of enthusiasm to her.

Abbie made a mental note to be more prepared for when Jilly phoned again in a few days. She would

150

ask around about local hotels and pop into the B & B to see Mrs Gilbert and see if she had any family suites or connecting rooms that would suit Jilly's needs.

She sat there for a long moment mulling over how different their lives were. Jilly and Glen had the girls Chloe and Freda who were sixteen and thirteen. Molly had been an unexpected addition to their family three years ago and Abbie remembered how Jilly had struggled with a new baby in her life at the age of thirty-nine. And as if that wasn't enough, just one year later Glen's ex-wife and mother of his two teenage twin sons upped and offed to Australia with her new partner. George and Joe, now eighteen and in the middle of their first year at university had strong objections to being uprooted and relocated to the other side of the world. Jilly and Glen had been happy to take them into their home. Abbie was still thoughtful, wondering what it was like having a home with five children aged from eighteen years to three. She sighed, shaking her head and conceding that she had no idea. She put the kettle on for a cup of tea.

Abbie took her filofax from her bag and flicked through while she waited for the kettle to boil. She counted how many weeks were between now and the end of May – only three. And then a thought occurred; hadn't Luisa's note said that she would be visiting in about three weeks? Abbie closed her eyes and sighed. How typical! To be on her own all this time and then for everyone to descend all at once.

Jed was reluctant to pull himself away from his painting, but he was beginning to feel light-headed and his noisy grumbling belly was really disturbing the peace and proving to be too much of a distraction.

He wandered back into his cottage and went straight through to the kitchen. He didn't need to ponder in front of an open fridge; his lunch would be the same staple as most days; a hunk of bread, some local cheese and whatever else he fancied with it – some pickles or chutney or salad. Halfway through cutting a thick slice, the phone rang. He guessed it would be Eva – only she would be so persistent. He considered ignoring it again but the thought that she might turn up looking for him changed his mind. He really didn't feel like chatting; he intended to be brief.

'Hello?' Fully expecting to hear Eva's forceful voice on the other end of the phone, Jed was totally unprepared for the soft, gentle tones that floated to him from a distance. Other than the person saying his name, he didn't hear the actual words, only the voice.

'Hello? Who's there? Anna? Is that you Annaliese?'

'Jed. Jed are you alright? Jed it's me – Lilleth. It's Lilleth here, can you hear me?'

Jed was brought abruptly back to his senses. What on earth had he been thinking?

'Hello Lilleth, it's you, of course. I'm sorry about that – I was miles away there for a moment.'

'Oh, don't worry. I have days like that. Anyway, I just thought I'd let you know poor Eva has been trying to get hold of you all morning, she must've phoned about ten times. She wanted to come over and track you down, but I stopped her and she's gone off in a bit of a huff.' Lilleth was aware she was rambling but her poor mind was working overtime and her reflex was to keep talking, as much as anything to prevent Jed from saying anything more that she might find worrying. 'But then I got to thinking Jed, it's not like you not to answer your phone or give us a callback. And I got a little bit worried myself. Silly of me, I know. And so, as long as you're alright, then that's fine.' Lilleth stopped, a little out of breath. She waited for what she hoped would be a sensible and coherent response.

Jed could hear the concern in his kind friend's voice and he felt ashamed for causing her to worry.

'There's no need to worry Lilleth, I'm fine, really I am. I've just been wallowing in old memories this morning. You know how it is.'

'Yes,' answered Lilleth gently.

'Actually, I think I've spent too much time here thinking on my own. I need to get out. How about making an old man very happy? And joining me for a spot of Sunday lunch?'

Lilleth laughed, with relief as much as amusement – thank goodness, Jed sounded like his old self again.

'And you'd be making an old lady very happy too. The Green Man in an hour?'

'Perfect. I'll be there.'

Lilleth replaced the phone smiling to herself, thinking what a very happy lady she was. Eva had stalked off and she would enjoy a very rare

153

opportunity of having the company of Jed Tobin all to herself for a couple of hours.

Abbie was bored. She'd been working at The Green Man for a couple of weeks and she was still trying to figure out its busy times. They didn't occur on her shifts, she knew that much. There were less than half a dozen customers dotted about in the pub and she couldn't be sure they hadn't all fallen asleep – she hadn't served a drink for at least half an hour. She'd wiped the bar top clean, polished the pumps and tidied the bottles and glasses but the lack of things to do just gave her too much time to think. She thought about Luisa visiting in a few weeks. And then Jilly and her lot visiting too. Please don't let it all happen at the same time, thought Abbie, already resigned to a knowing feeling that it would.

From her viewpoint behind the bar, she could see Jed and Lilleth walking down the hill together, arm in arm. She smiled to herself; they looked good together, she thought. She came out from behind the bar to collect a couple of glasses from a table over by the window with the hope of catching their attention and giving them a wave. As she reached the table, she was delighted to see them turn and enter the pub.

'Hello aunt,' she said, automatically giving Lilleth a peck on her powdered cheek. 'Hello Jed,' she said before doing a little woodpecker dance, unsure whether to kiss him or not. He obviously wasn't sure either and then the moment was gone.

'What can I get you both?'

Jed looked at Lilleth to make her choice.

'Just a coffee for me dear.'

'The same for me,' said Jed.

Abbie prepared their drinks.

'Are you off somewhere nice? And, how come, I mean, where's?'

Lilleth smiled before answering the first question and understanding perfectly the second even though it hadn't actually been asked.

'We're here for a bit of lunch. I'm not sure where Eva has got to – we had a few words this morning.' Lilleth smiled knowingly, her eyes twinkling at Abbie. 'No doubt she's enjoying some peace and quiet to herself, somewhere.' Lilleth raised her eyebrows cheekily and Abbie giggled in return. She pondered on how awful it must be to live with a sister you so obviously didn't get on with and then immediately felt a stab of something to her conscience – it might have been guilt, she wasn't sure. And if it was, she wasn't sure why either.

Lilleth was still smiling, Abbie observed, and she could see in that moment that Lilleth wasn't laughing at Eva, on the contrary, it was an easy, relaxed smile, revealing not just a patient tolerance but much more than that – a sincere understanding. Her kind eyes met Abbie's thoughtful ones and she smiled even wider and nodded as if to reassure her that everything was alright in her world.

Jed hadn't spoken during all this. He had been studying Abbie's expressions and mannerisms, bewitched by both and he was now moving away from the bar hoping Lilleth would follow. He had lots to talk about and it was all beginning to overwhelm him.

155

'Go and sit down and I'll bring some menus over,' said Abbie.

Jed and Lilleth took a table to the side of the open fire.

'I didn't know Abbie worked here,' Jed jerked his head towards Abbie behind the bar.

'Yes, I believe she started about a couple of weeks ago.'

'Does she need money then?' asked Jed, brusquely.

'Everyone needs money, Jed. Abbie's young and she may have inherited a property, but I suspect she still has to earn a living.'

Jed didn't answer and drank his coffee.

Gradually Jed warmed up and was chatting and smiling and laughing as usual. He was definitely out of sorts today, thought Lilleth; down one moment and up the next. Something was bothering him, and she had an idea what it could be although she wasn't brave enough to tackle it head on. And, as if reading her thoughts, Jed swiftly took the conversation in another direction completely.

'Did some painting this morning,' he said.

'Oh yes? Good idea, that porch of yours has needed a touch up since last winter.'

'Not that kind of painting,' barked Jed, looking across the table at Lilleth who was grinning, her twinkling eyes teasing – she knew exactly what he meant. 'Go on then, tell me what you're painting.'

'A picture! You silly woman.' There, he'd got his own back. 'Nothing special,' he continued gruffly. 'The chickens outside, the barn, some trees. It's good. To get back to it.'

Lilleth smiled although Jed wouldn't meet her eyes, looking down intently at his empty coffee cup. But the moment was significant; they both knew it. Jed was painting again, after all these years. His ghosts were being finally laid to rest.

Abbie suddenly appeared at their table, bringing them both immediately back to the present.

'Did you want to order food?' she asked. 'They have beef on the menu – it looks gorgeous.'

Jed looked over at Lilleth who nodded to his unspoken question.

'Go on then, two beef roasts and two more coffees and a drink for yourself, young lady.'

'Thank-you Jed,' said Abbie, clearing away their empty cups.

A good hour later Lilleth decided to make tracks. 'I couldn't eat or drink another thing. I'm going to make my way for the bus otherwise we'll be stuck here for another whole hour – how awful.' Lilleth laughed.

'I'll walk you,' Jed said, getting up and putting on his coat and hat.

As they left with a warm 'good-bye' to Abbie, they linked arms and walked to the bus stop a little further down. There was only one woman waiting there and she turned and looked at them as they approached.

'Oh dear,' said Lilleth.

'Yes, oh dear,' repeated Jed.

Eva, in the bus shelter, turned her gaze back away from them, and poor Lilleth knew the bus ride home was going to be a long and silent one.

Chapter Twenty-One

Miriam was frantic. Blossom had a temperature of over a hundred. After a restless night, she was whiney and listless, not even having the energy to resist being made to stay in bed all day. Miriam had made the decision not to take Honey to school either. After a sleepless night she wasn't up to the screaming protests of a four-year old being taken to school while her twin sister got to stay at home. It seemed a much easier option to let Honey stay home too, although a few hours later with the tearoom half full and Miriam constantly checking on Blossom and making sure Honey was OK, she wasn't sure her decision had been the right one after all.

But now, late in the afternoon, having taken Blossom's temperature yet again and read 100.2 degrees on the thermometer, she silently thanked herself for the foresight. She had to get to the hospital – fast. Alistair was needed home and she phoned him on his mobile. As it rang, she was trying to decide what was best; to leave Honey at home with him while she took Blossom to the hospital or close the tearoom early and all go together. As it was, Miriam didn't have the luxury of being able to make a decision; Alistair didn't answer his phone. As calmly as she could, she left him a message letting him know he was needed home urgently. She then went through to the tearoom and turned the sign on the door to 'Closed', looking around anxiously, feeling a sense of relief that everyone seemed to be finishing up and getting ready to leave.

Miriam tried Alistair's mobile again but still there was no answer. She ran up the stairs two at a time to check on Blossom, her temperature and general condition were unchanged and Miriam, feeling more desperate, couldn't decide whether that was a good thing or not.

She ran back downstairs and into the kitchen to locate Alistair's work diary. He had got out of the habit, over the last couple of weeks, of telling her about his work and where he would be each day. It made her feel uneasy not knowing where he was. She needed his diary and if he didn't call her back within the next few minutes, she would have to phone his customer's home number to get hold of him. She yanked open all the kitchen drawers until finally she found it.

Honey was calling for her, clinging to the baby-gate across the living room door, obviously picking up on the anxiety vibes coming from her mother. Miriam grabbed Honey's Wellington boots from next to the front door and placed them on the other side of the gate, crouching down and giving Honey a squeeze.

'Are you going to put your wellies on for Mummy, all by yourself, like a big girl, while I go and get Blossom ready?'

'Are we going out?' said Honey, confused but excited by the sudden activity after a day of not much happening – not even getting to play with her sister.

'Yes, but it's raining, so get your wellies on and I'll be back in a minute.'

Miriam knew that Honey would struggle putting her boots on by herself and that they would probably end up on the wrong feet, but the task would keep her occupied and quiet for a few precious minutes while Miriam organised herself.

She flung Alistair's work diary open, flicking through the pages to the current day. He had written 'Mr Roy Hancock' – the name wasn't familiar; she couldn't remember Alistair mentioning him. Next to the name he'd written his address and she didn't recognise that either as being anywhere local. Underneath he'd scribbled some brief notes about the work he was to do and right at the bottom of the diary section, he'd written his telephone number.

Miriam dashed back through to the tearoom, peering into the living room on her way. Honey was sitting in the middle of the floor with one Wellington boot securely in place, but she was struggling with the other one. In the tearoom, Miriam had mixed feelings; she was pleased that her last customers had finally left but she also felt guilty that she hadn't been there in her professional capacity to see them off and thank them for their custom. Well, it was too late now. She locked the doors and pulled the blinds across to confirm that she was closed and also to hide the dirty tables – they would have to wait until much later.

As Miriam dashed back across the hallway, she only just missed being hit by a low-flying

Wellington boot that had been thrown with surprising force - the window of the front door juddered as it hit it. And now a very cross Honey was attempting to escape over the baby-gate but had caught her welly on the top and was stuck. Miriam lifted her up and over and carried her into the kitchen, plonking her on the worktop and holding her there as she picked up her mobile and with some difficulty, with one hand, tapped in the number from Alistair's diary. Honey was wriggling and grabbing at the pages of the book making it difficult for Miriam to read. And she'd obviously messed it up as all she could hear was the annoying continuous tone that signified the number she had dialled was incorrect.

Miriam plonked Honey on the kitchen floor, a little too roughly and now she was close to tears.

'Go and bring your boot here,' said Miriam as gently as she could and with the biggest smile she could muster. But Honey's bottom lip was trembling, and it didn't look like she was going to move.

'Go on now, bring it here and Mummy will put it on for you. And then we'll see if there are any chocolate buttons in the cupboard.' Bribery was restricted to emergencies only, but Miriam considered this to be a definite emergency. And it worked; Honey ran out of the kitchen, her one welly boot thumping on the floor.

Holding the phone steady in both hands with her elbows resting on the counter, Miriam peered closely at the phone number in Alistair's handwriting. She tapped it in, carefully and deliberately, double-checking each number and could hardly believe it when she heard the same noise, confirming that this number did not exist. In desperation she looked at the diary page again, studying the numbers to see if she was reading any of them incorrectly. But no, it was quite clearly written. 'Damn Alistair,' she thought, he must have written it down wrong.

Honey arrived back in the kitchen and was swinging her retrieved welly against Miriam's backside rhythmically and annoyingly, as Miriam tried Alistair's mobile again.

'Stop that Honey. I'm trying to phone Daddy.'

But Honey had had enough and was whining about wanting chocolate buttons. Miriam heard the sound of a boot hitting the oven door.

'Wait, just a minute,' she snapped, whereby Honey threw herself face downwards into the cat basket and howled.

Miriam put her hand over her ear as Alistair's phone went to voicemail yet again. But this time she wasn't so calm – she shouted down the phone that she was taking the girls to the hospital and that she needed him to come back from Mr Hancock's - or wherever he was. She slammed the phone onto the worktop, wondering why she'd said that last bit, something deep inside her reluctantly acknowledging that she wasn't sure a Mr Hancock even existed.

Miriam was suddenly aware that everything had gone quiet. She looked over at the cat basket. Honey was still crouched over it but her red and blotchy, tear-stained face was staring up at Miriam. It must have been Miriam's crazed shouting that had shocked her into silence. Her little face looked bewildered, her mouth pouting mid-sob. Miriam scooped her up and sat her on the worktop and pulled on her Wellington boot. All the while Honey sat there, good as gold, without a fidget or a sound.

A few minutes later, Blossom, still in her pyjamas was bundled up in a couple of blankets in Miriam's arms. Honey had quietened down, seemingly aware of the seriousness of the situation. It was raining heavily and as Miriam pulled the front door shut, she shouted to Honey who had already disappeared out of sight, to come back to the car. She caught a glimpse of that young woman, Abbie, who'd moved into the old cottage, coming down the hill. Miriam dropped her keys and struggled to pick them up with Blossom, a heavy bundle, in her arms, conscious that Abbie was probably watching her.

Having locked the door, Miriam turned to the car on the drive and then let out a piercing scream as she saw Honey running at the end of the drive - towards the main road beyond. She ran as fast as she could but awkwardly with Blossom in her arms. Shaking all over with fear at what she would find, she almost collapsed with relief when she saw Abbie crouched down, her arm gently and protectively keeping Honey on the pavement.

'Oh my God! Thank-you, thank-you so much,' gasped Miriam breathlessly. Abbie looked up.

'Is everything OK?'

'I have to get my daughter to hospital. She has a temperature. And I can't get hold of my husband anywhere.'

The two women held each other's look for a second; a wealth of information and understanding passed between them.

'Can I do anything to help?' asked Abbie, holding Honey's hand and leading her up the drive following Miriam who was hurrying back to the car.

'Would you mind holding her?' she asked as she placed Blossom in Abbie's arms, opening the back door and lifting Honey into the car seat and fastening her in. Abbie followed Miriam to the other side of the car and handed the little girl back, watching as Miriam gently placed her daughter inside, making sure she was well wrapped up in the blankets.

'Would you like me to come with you?' Abbie asked, and for a second Miriam was tempted to accept her offer but then pride overtook.

'I'll be OK, thanks,' she said a little abruptly, feeling guilty for it as she climbed into the driver's seat.

Abbie didn't take it personally; she could feel Miriam's distress. She stood there on the drive, in the pouring rain, as Miriam turned the car and sped off, thinking compassionately what an awful lot Miriam Walker had to put up with.

Much later that evening Miriam poured herself a glass of red wine. Her two girls were tucked up in bed, fast asleep. They had spent a few hours at the hospital until Blossom's temperature came down. Miriam was told she had a virus and was given some antibiotics before taking her home. Honey had behaved like an angel throughout and Miriam decided she would plan an extra special treat for them as soon as Blossom was fully better.

As soon as they were in bed, Miriam went through to the tearoom and cleared up the day's mess and then prepared everything ready for the morning. She had a quick shower and started to sort the contents of the laundry basket. But then she stopped; surrounded by piles of washing grouped on the floor – she scooped it all up and threw it back into the basket. She knew what she was doing – keeping busy. To stop herself from thinking. She'd had an exhausting day, and with no help from her husband whatsoever. She deserved to stop now.

Miriam relaxed onto the sofa, sinking down and taking a sip of wine before resting her head back. It was nine o'clock and she still hadn't heard from Alistair. In another time and in another place, and definitely with another man, she might have been worried. Had he been in an accident? Or stuck somewhere and lost his phone? But a sickening feeling, call it gut instinct, told her she needn't worry. Not in that way, anyway.

It was while she was on her second glass of wine that her mobile rang on the settee next to her - she knew it would eventually. Alistair's name was flashing on the screen. She answered it calmly and let his frantic questions and concern free-fall for a while before interrupting him and simply telling him that Blossom would be fine, she was home and in bed asleep. She would explain everything when he got home. And then she virtually hung up on him.

Miriam heard Alistair speed onto the drive and seconds later he burst through the door, a look of anguish set on his face. Too little too late, she thought. She let him bluster on with his questions, answering calmly, briefly. He wanted to go up and kiss his daughter good-night.

'Careful not to wake her,' said Miriam, surprised at the deceptive gentleness of her voice.

Alistair disappeared upstairs and a few moments later Miriam heard the shower. She drained her glass and rested her head back, tired now, really tired with that exhaustive feeling of contentment after a trauma that finally turns out to be OK.

When Alistair came back into the room, he'd poured himself a glass of wine and sat in the armchair to her side. A few moments of awkward silence passed. Miriam didn't care enough to try to make it easier. She hadn't asked Alistair why he was so late home. She hadn't mentioned Mr Hancock or the dodgy phone number. There was plenty of time for all that.

After a while Alistair went up to bed, rather earlier than normal. Maybe he was tired too, thought Miriam, after his hard day's work. Or maybe he sensed the difficult questions to come and decided he needed all the rest he could get.

Chapter Twenty-Two

It was only just over a week until everyone; Luisa and Jilly and all her family would be arriving. And they would be full of expectations. Abbie sighed, heavy with dread. Luisa was expecting to see Winnifred Cottage completely transformed. Abbie wished now that she hadn't exaggerated so much, saying she'd been busy bringing the place back to life.

And Jilly would be even more demanding. Unless she saw Abbie living the ultimate dream life deep in the English countryside, Abbie would be a complete failure in her eyes. She wasn't sure how she was going to create this illusion but today, she was going to start with several tins of paint.

She'd put on her cleaning clothes; a scruffy old pair of jeans and what she realised now was an old shirt of Jack's that he used to paint in. It smelled of oils and turpentine. She touched the cuff; felt the roughness of dried brown paint, trying to remember the last piece she'd seen him working on. It had been a large painting of a horse's head; bold and dramatic in brown and black and red. He was much braver with his art than she ever was.

A knock on the front door shook her from her memories. She opened it to see Miriam on the doorstep.

'Oh hello. This is a nice surprise. Please, come in.' Abbie was genuinely pleasantly surprised on seeing Miriam at her door and with such a gentle smile, illuminating her face and transforming it into a friendly and pretty one. 'How's your daughter? Is she OK now?'

Miriam stepped inside, glancing around her immediate surroundings. She noted Abbie's work clothes and the tins of paint.

'I'm sorry to disturb you. I just wanted to come along and thank-you for yesterday; for helping me. My daughter's much better and home now. I'm sorry if I was a little abrupt, I was…'

'No really, it's fine,' interrupted Abbie. 'You had a lot on. I'm just glad everything's OK.' What she meant was she was glad her daughter was well again. Abbie got the feeling that everything in Miriam's life was most definitely not OK.

'This is such a gorgeous place,' said Miriam, turning on the spot and looking all around her. She was smiling, her face animated, as she took in the character of the place; the low ceilings, the tiled fireplace and the small square-paned windows. 'It's totally enchanting. You're so lucky to live here.'

Abbie followed her gaze silently, fascinated to see Winnifred Cottage through someone else's eyes. Feeling somewhat ashamed, she didn't like to admit what her initial reaction to the place had been.

'I've got family visiting shortly.' Abbie indicated the tins of paint. 'I thought I'd better get on with

168

sprucing the place up a bit otherwise they'll be wondering what I've been up to all this time.'

'I'm sorry, I can see you're busy, I should leave you to get on.'

'No, really, it's fine. I've been putting things off for the last two months, a few more minutes won't make any difference.' Abbie laughed, and Miriam smiled in return.

'Do you have plans to change it much?' asked Miriam diplomatically. She was seeing the cottage through tearoom owner's eyes and visualising how lovely it could be.

'Originally I came up here planning to convert it into an art gallery of sorts and a photographic studio. But it's just too dark and it's far too expensive to have it extended to how I'd want it.' Abbie cringed inwardly at the mention of building works; she still hadn't received a bill from Alistair for the repair work to the roof.

'That's a shame,' said Miriam, nodding absently and picturing small tables dotted about with crisp white linen cloths, a fire burning in the grate and the smell of baking in the air. She sighed, bringing herself back to the present moment. 'But it will look lovely when you've painted and brightened it up. Well, I really must let you get on with your work. Looks like you have a lot to do.'

Abbie was almost sorry to see Miriam leave. This was a different woman from the Miriam Walker she'd initially met, and she would have liked to chat for a while longer.

Miriam left, and Abbie turned to her tins of paint, keen to make a start.

Miriam took her time strolling back down the hill towards her home. She had taken Honey to school that morning despite her protests. Blossom would stay home for a few more days, and surprisingly Alistair had offered to help - in fact he was being overly helpful this morning. Miriam would rather he'd gone to work but didn't have the energy to ask why he could suddenly take time off. She couldn't face another argument. But while he was being so agreeable, she thought she'd take advantage of his rare good nature and have a leisurely walk around the local shops.

After just a few hours of hard work, Abbie was shattered. By the time she'd painted the ceiling of the main living room, her arms ached so much she didn't think she'd ever recover enough to be able to paint another stroke. She took a short break, made herself a sandwich and a large mug of tea and decided to bite the bullet and carry on. By late afternoon all the walls were painted, and the result of her hard work was amazing. The lightness and brightness of the room lifted her spirits and she resolved there and then to have the entire cottage painted before her visitors arrived.

Abbie stood back to admire her work. Tomorrow she would start on the awful black woodwork; rubbing it down and painting it in white gloss. It would be a long hard job, but she knew it would be worth it. She tried to picture the room through Luisa's eyes when she returned to the cottage soon and what would Jilly think, seeing it for the first time? She suddenly had a lovely idea; she would paint the smaller living room - maybe in a pastel colour; cream or pale yellow and turn it into a makeshift dining room. She would need to borrow a large table from somewhere - that could prove to be the difficult part - and then when they all arrived she could cook a special meal for everyone; invite Lilleth and Eva and Jed of course so that everyone could meet each other.

Abbie enjoyed a long, hot and soothing bath, musing over her idea and planning menu options, deliberating over how many choices she would need to offer to make sure everyone was happy. Sleepy and hungry after her bath, she didn't have the energy to cook anything too involved, and looking in the kitchen cupboards, she settled for a tin of chicken soup and the remains of some slightly stale bread, before finally falling into bed for an early night.

Miriam had an early night too - not so much because she was tired; she'd been tired for the last four years and had just about got used to it or resigned to it at least. She went to bed early simply because she'd had enough of the day and the sooner she got to sleep and it was over, the better.

Earlier on she had finally chosen her moment of courage to speak to Alistair about the wrong phone number in his work diary. She knew it would end in an argument with Alistair accusing her of accusing him. It did. And nothing was resolved.

Alistair had stormed out of the house presumably to the pub, thought Miriam. He wasn't back yet and she lay there in the darkness, irritated by her inability to get to sleep and blaming Alistair for it. With a mixture of sadness and anger she thought about their planned new life in the country. It had been evident almost immediately that Alistair couldn't settle but she wasn't convinced he'd really tried. He said he missed the buzz of London life but there was no way she was going to uproot the girls from this rural haven to go back there.

Miriam heard a key in the lock and the noise Alistair made trying to get in would have woken her anyway. Seething now, she heard him fall inside the under-stairs cupboard as he tried to hang his coat up. It took Alistair three attempts of tripping up the stairs to get to the top and Miriam was silently threatening all sorts of evils if he dared wake Honey or Blossom. She lay with her back to his side of the bed, eyes tight shut, she didn't even want to engage in a few seconds of conversation with him and pretended to be asleep.

Chapter Twenty-Three

Rhona could hear noises from above and knew that Jed was up in his workroom above the gallery again. He'd been in there a lot lately. She made two mugs of coffee and took one outside and up to Jed. As she entered, she could see him at the side of the room concentrating hard at a tabletop easel. Windows on all sides of the room let in an abundance of hazy sunshine creating a magical glow, lighting the paintings on the walls - all of them his.

'Here you go, your morning fix of caffeine to keep you going.'

'Mm, thank-you dear. You do look after me well. I'm going to miss you.'

Rhona smiled; she would miss the slightly eccentric, gentle old man too. She turned to go and then remembered the real reason for her going there. 'That painting that arrived the other day, you know the one, came back from the framer's? Well, it's disappeared. Have you got it?' Rhona wasn't worried, she knew that Jed had most likely taken it and she thought she knew the reason why.

'You mean this one?' Jed leaned forward and picked up the painting, holding it in front of him over the one he was currently working on. Rhona joined him at his side and studied both watercolours.

'I thought so,' she said. 'It's yours isn't it? I thought I recognised it when the woman brought it in. How weird is that? She brings your painting back to your gallery for re-framing, after all these years. I mean, she didn't actually mention that she knew this was your gallery. Is it a bit weird?'

'Well, yes and no.'

'Do you know her then?'

'Well, yes and no.'

Rhona tutted in frustration. 'Honestly Jed! I won't miss your teasing, you know!'

Jed smiled to himself, and placed the painting back carefully on his worktop, leaning it against the wall where he could see it.

'All will become clear, my dear, you'll see.'

'OK, if you say so. But what should I do – I said I'd phone her when the painting gets back from the framer's? Something tells me you're not going to give it back to me.'

'Quite right. Just leave it with me for a little longer. Actually, you could give her a call and tell her the gallery owner has taken an interest and is carrying out a little research on her behalf. Tell her I'll contact her myself. But don't mention any names - that's important. And I'll pay for the frame too.'

Rhona sighed, looking puzzled, but she knew there was no point in pushing for more information. Jed would reveal all when he was good and ready.

Lilleth had endured over two weeks of on and off sulking from Eva. And to make matters worse, Jed appeared to be lying low too. He hadn't called and invited himself for afternoon tea and although she'd

174

phoned him a couple of times with no answer, she didn't like to keep trying in case he thought she was pestering him too much. She understood his need to be alone occasionally. She felt that way herself sometimes.

Lilleth had finished dusting. She replaced the photo of her husband Harry on the mantelpiece. It was her favourite photo of him in his army uniform, just a few months before they married. She blew him a silent kiss and wondered fleetingly if it would be long before they were reunited and together again at last. As her eyes watered, she sniffed sharply, scolding herself for being so soppy. But she couldn't help herself; she was feeling a little melancholy and inexplicably lonely too. Eva's behaviour didn't help.

Today things seemed to have reached a peak. Lilleth was convinced that Eva was going out of her way to provoke her. She had used the last of the bread that morning and hadn't got a fresh loaf out of the freezer. Then she disappeared into the garden leaving Lilleth to do all the Monday morning chores they normally did together. And just now she'd walked muddy footprints all over the kitchen floor that Lilleth had just mopped.

'Eva, please, look at my clean floor.' Eva got to the back door and turned to look at the mess she'd made. She sighed dramatically and grumbled something that sounded like she would clean it up later.

'I'd rather you did it now,' mumbled Lilleth in return, feeling herself on the slippery slope of meeting like with like.

175

Eva swung round, grabbed the mop and began mopping the floor in a frenzy. 'You have to have everything your own way.'

'What's that supposed to mean?'

At first Eva ignored her, continuing with the mopping and as she finished, she gave Lilleth the strangest of looks and with the hint of a smile, she said, 'You nearly didn't have it all your way.' But then she made a quick exit before Lilleth could say any more. Although Lilleth already knew exactly what Eva was referring to. She had known for years – all along in fact. She'd often wondered how it would all come out; what particular situation or moment Eva was waiting for - to play what she thought was her trump card. Eva had made a choice, taken a gamble but ended up with no-one. She took no responsibility for her situation but was bitter, particularly towards Lilleth. And so, she'd hinted at it again today, but would she ever have the courage to say the words out loud? Lilleth hoped not but deep down knew her sister would want her moment of glory. But if and when it came to it, she would get a lot more than that.

Chapter Twenty-Four

Winnifred Cottage, having been tirelessly worked on from the bottom up, was bright and clean, if a little austere in its newly painted whiteness. And now Abbie was attempting to do something with the garden. There wasn't enough time to transform it completely, but she was so pleased with her efforts in the cottage, she was determined to do something to improve the outside area.

The hopelessly scraggy lawn had long since encroached on the narrow flowerbeds that had probably provided a pretty border at one time. If she could borrow a lawnmower from someone, a quick mow of the grass would instantly improve things as well as remove the nettles and dandelions that were threatening to take over. The worst part of the garden was the ugly concrete hard-standing that went all the way around the cottage. A collection of pots in different colours and sizes was the obvious answer, planted up with eye-catching colourful flowers like red geraniums and purple and pink fuschias. Abbie wondered where the nearest garden centre was. Miriam Walker would be the best person to recommend one. She had the most beautiful garden and she might be willing to offer some advice on what sort of plants did well in these parts.

Miriam was running late and now, here was the ultimate professional humiliation; she had customers knocking on the French doors wondering why she wasn't open.

It served her right; this was a direct result of last night's argument with Alistair and the consequent excess of energy that had sent her to the conservatory with a bottle of expensive Chablis. They had been saving it for a special occasion, but Miriam didn't reckon they would be sharing one of those any time soon and she took the bottle from the fridge, just her and it for company for the rest of the long evening.

Miriam had crawled into bed in the early hours, knowing for certain that she would suffer and be full of regret in the morning. Bright sunshine woke her much earlier than she felt was decent. The body next to her was completely silent. Not a snore not a snuffle. Miriam lay there anticipating some sort of movement any moment. But nothing. Now she was hardly breathing herself, straining to hear some sound, some evidence of life. Still nothing. Miriam was curious to know where this morbid train of thought was going. What if Alistair was dead? Lying there next to her. How would she feel?

Alistair coughed. A noisy congested choking sound shattered the silence in the room. Miriam sighed, throwing the covers back and getting out of bed, unable to deny the horrifying feeling of disappointment in discovering that her husband was still very much alive.

She looked at the clock – there was no time for breakfast. There was barely time to wash and dress.

And worst of all, she would have to admit failure and ask Alistair to take the girls to their Saturday morning ballet lesson.

Miriam went across the landing to the bathroom already going over in her mind the huge argument they'd had the evening before. It was about the garden again and converting part of it into a parking area. Miriam had started to keep notes on some basic financial matters; the in-comings and out-goings of the tearoom for a start, and already she had enough information to back up her case for the parking spaces. But it hadn't gone down well. Alistair was obviously uncomfortable with his wife's sudden interest in their financial affairs. He accused her of not trusting him to know what they could afford, and Miriam had counter-argued that as they were both so busy working hard, why were they always so short of cash? And then she really threw the red rag to the bull by intimating that perhaps he wasn't really out working at all.

The argument spiralled out of control after that with Alistair shouting that he'd never really wanted to leave London and Miriam shouting in return that maybe he should go back. Many things had been said in the heat of the moment but as Miriam brushed her teeth at breakneck speed, looking at her sad reflection in the bathroom mirror, she had to admit that the idea of Alistair going back to London was not one she regretted voicing.

Washed and dressed, she went into the girls' bedroom and gently encouraged them awake, tempting them downstairs with cartoon dvds and chocolate cereal. It was as she was securing the

179

safety gate across the living room door that she heard the tapping on the glass doors in the tearoom, realising that she had customers waiting outside for her to open.

It was busy inside The Honey-Blossom Tearoom by the time Abbie arrived and she wasn't even sure if there was a table free but then she spotted one right over in the far corner, sitting down to face the room and studying the menu. There were so many cakes to choose from and all home-made too, she couldn't help but be impressed. Miriam was something of a superwoman, she decided, putting so much effort into her business and while bringing up two young children. She withheld judgement on how helpful she thought Alistair would be with practical matters, but instinct told her he was something of a free spirit – and not in a good way.

Abbie watched as Miriam dealt with the busy tearoom single-handed. She wasn't in any hurry herself and sat there for a few minutes looking around and taking it all in. It was a lovely big spacious room and with the three sets of French doors it was amazingly bright inside, ideal for an art gallery thought Abbie whimsically, noticing the smooth white-washed walls - perfect for hanging paintings and photos. She noticed a stack of tables tucked away in the corner of the room, wondering if she could borrow a couple for her planned family feast. Suddenly Miriam appeared at her side.

'Hello Abbie. What can I get for you?' She looked tired, thought Abbie, but even so her wide friendly smile was genuine. 'It's lovely to see you.'

'Thank-you,' said Abbie, picking up on something. It was such a shame the tearoom was so busy, Miriam looked as if she'd like nothing better than to sit down for a chat. 'Just a cup of black coffee and a slice of fruitcake please,' she said, deciding that perhaps this wasn't the right time to ask Miriam about local garden centres and pot plants, or spare tables. The poor woman looked like she had a world of problems on her shoulders.

Miriam had just returned to the counter, smiling and welcoming a small group of tourists inside. They were noisy and excitable, chatting away as they pounced on an available table. Miriam appeared to collect the dirty crockery and to take their order. They were a happy lot, obviously on holiday and enjoying themselves, thought Miriam, feeling her spirits lift. This was one of the reasons she liked her job so much.

'Where are you staying?' asked Miriam, lowering her pad and pen. She was an expert on identifying different types of customer and this lot with all their chatter and laughter would take ages to decide what to order, and no doubt change their minds a dozen times before they did.

'We're at the B & B, at the bottom of the hill. Run by a Mrs Gilbert? Amazing woman.'

'Oh yes, I know,' smiled Miriam.

'She pointed us in your direction,' continued the woman. 'She recommended your scones; said they were the best she's ever had.'

Miriam was touched and slightly overwhelmed by the kindness of her neighbour.

'You're lucky with the weather,' said Miriam. 'It's been nice and sunny for a few days now. I hope it stays like it for you.'

'Yes, it's lovely,' said the other woman. 'We're planning to head over to the equestrian place but we're not sure if it's open every day. Mrs Gilbert had run out of leaflets, she was so apologetic, bless her. Do you have wifi here?'

'No, I'm afraid not. But I think I have some information on the equestrian centre in the house. I'll go and look, I won't be a minute.'

Miriam dashed back into the house, thinking as she went of the two things she had been planning to do for some time and was now determined to action soon. First, she wanted a display stand with information on local attractions and places of interest. And additionally, she was planning to get some leaflets of her own printed and distribute them to be displayed in return. Secondly, an ever-increasing number of people were asking if she had free internet access with many of them turning away and going elsewhere when she replied that she hadn't. She'd come to the obvious conclusion that this was definitely something to invest in.

Miriam rummaged through the kitchen drawers, making a mental note that they really needed sorting properly at some point – something else for her never-ending to-do list. She was sure there was a leaflet in here somewhere – they had been to the equestrian centre only last summer. That is, Miriam and the girls had gone with Miriam's parents. Alistair had cried off at the last minute due to a building emergency, whatever one of those was.

Miriam began grabbing handfuls of papers from the drawer and dumping them on the worktop, conscious that she didn't want to be out of the tearoom too long. At the bottom of the drawer, there were only a couple of Alistair's old work diaries. She lifted them up to see if there was anything underneath but there were only some old estate agent papers from the purchase of the house. Miriam threw the diaries back and was just about to pile all the paperwork on top but she stopped, thinking how odd, that those papers were lurking there. Surely, they were safely filed away years ago. And then she noticed something else; a less faded piece of paper with the name Fox & Co as the heading. Fox & Co were a major estate agent in the area, but not the one she and Alistair had dealt with five years ago. She picked up the piece of paper, it was a valuation on a house - for a lot of money. Miriam scanned the top of the paper, searching for a date. It was dated four weeks ago and then she scanned the details looking for confirmation of what she already knew in her heart. It was a valuation for her own home.

Chapter Twenty-Five

Abbie had bought four large blue earthenware pots to
start with and filled them with a variety of fuchsias
in a mixture of colours from the brightest hot red and
deep purple to the daintiest delicate pale pink.
Miriam had suggested Kirkby Growers, a small
nursery just outside the village and Abbie had gone
along and filled her car boot with pots and plants,
growing compost and plant food. She filled in with
white trailing Lobelia and variegated ivy and could
just imagine, with some sunshine and watering, how
they would grow and blossom and soon the pots
would overflow with an abundance of blooms. But
so far, that was not meant to be. Since Abbie had
planted up the pots it had rained continuously, and
she had to accept that there would probably be no
abundance of blooms by the time her visitors arrived.
Small buds of colour brave enough to peek through
were threatening to be bashed from their hold by
heavy raindrops. Dainty Lobelia plants hung weak
and limp, struggling to hold their own against the
harsh weather and if the weather reports were to be
believed, it wasn't likely to get better any time soon.

Abbie was putting the finishing touches to the
bedroom that Luisa would stay in. She had painted it
white, the same as everywhere else and had

continued with a simple rustic but cosy theme. She'd bought a white, heavily embroidered bedspread and then placed a red wool throw over the end of the bed. The rich red was picked up in the multi-coloured striped rag rug and a few pieces of warm antique pine furniture completed the room.

Obviously, she couldn't accommodate Jilly's large family, but she had emailed her sister with all sorts of information on places to stay in the area. She'd included as much variety as possible and had sent details on local B & Bs as well as self-catering properties full of character and charm. She didn't understand why, in the end, Jilly chose to stay at the large hotel, one of the Chandler chain, a few miles away in town. It could be anywhere in the country she thought scornfully. Although today she had to concede that it might turn out to be a wise choice. If the rain continued, it would be good for the family to have use of the hotel's indoor swimming pool and other sports facilities and activities for the children.

It had worked out perfect; Luisa was arriving on Sunday and they would get to spend some time together catching up before Jilly and her brood arrived some time on Monday morning.

Abbie was just finishing in Luisa's room by putting a box of tissues and a vase on the bedside table when her mobile rang. She looked around, very pleased with the overall effect and sat on the bed as she answered the phone.

It was just so typical of Jilly to mess everything up. She'd phoned to say there had been a change of plan and she was now arriving in Kirkby Bridge on Friday, a few days earlier than originally planned.

That meant Jilly would be here before Luisa arrived and so they wouldn't get a chance to catch up on their own after all. Abbie picked up a red love-heart cushion and hurled it across the room where it simply hit the wall opposite and landed with a flop on the floor.

Jilly would only be visiting for seven days but Abbie had an awful feeling it was going to seem like a whole lot longer.

Chapter Twenty-Six

Jilly had said she would phone Abbie when she and her family arrived at the hotel. It was now one o'clock and she had only just phoned. They'd checked in, after which the children had fought over bedrooms and had now unpacked most of their things.

Abbie was on her way over to meet them for lunch in the hotel restaurant. She took it easy in the torrential rain with visibility down to just a few yards, parking as near to the hotel entrance as she could. There was still a short distance to run to get inside and Abbie stood in the lobby, her wet hair flattened to her head, droplets of rain trickling down her cheeks.

She saw a sign for the restaurant and walked towards it through the bar area dabbing her wet face with a tissue. There was a small reception desk at the entrance to the restaurant where a woman asked for her room number.

'Ah no, I'm just meeting family here,' said Abbie, scanning the tables for her sister. She caught sight of Jilly and her family but unfortunately no-one appeared to be looking out for her. 'Oh, there they are. Is it alright if I go through?'

'Yes, of course Madam.'

Abbie went over to Jilly's table, willing someone to turn around and be pleased to see her. But they didn't; they all looked completely bored, even Molly, the three-year-old, didn't appear to have the energy to make a fuss. No-one was speaking, and they were all looking in different directions to avoid each other's gaze. Abbie wished she could just turn around and go back home but then Jilly saw her and got up to meet her, instantly giving her a hug.

'Where have you been?' she asked.

What lovely first words thought Abbie. 'It's quite a drive from where I live and it's pouring out there,' she said defensively.

'Yes, I know, I was getting worried about you,' said Jilly sitting back down. And now Abbie was annoyed with herself for getting annoyed with Jilly - so soon.

She took off her mac and draped it on the back of her chair, smiling at Chloe next to her. Chloe was sixteen, perfectly made up, with her fair hair beautifully styled, very straight and glossy. Abbie hoped her friendly smile conveyed the apology she felt she ought to offer for being such a bedraggled and disappointing looking aunty. Chloe sort of smiled back. Her younger sister, Freda, sat opposite. Her pale face was devoid of any make-up and Abbie wondered if that was in defiance to her sister's fine delicate features perfectly accentuated with eyeliner and lipgloss. Her dark hair hung limp and lifeless. They might look completely different, thought Abbie, but they both seem to have perfected the typical clichéd teenage look of stubborn boredom.

'Right, shall we order?' said Jilly, hoping to inspire her silent family into conversation even if it was only about food. She opened her over-sized menu which turned out to be the cue for the rest of her family to do the same. Abbie picked up her own menu even though she had no appetite - for any of this.

By the time the waitress arrived to take their order, Chloe and Freda had vaguely mumbled something about burgers. Jilly heard the two boys negotiating with each other over which pizzas they could share, and as the waitress took the orders, Jilly knew, with all the junk food on the table, she wouldn't be able to get Molly to eat anything half decent. Abbie noticed a very pained expression on her sister's face. This was a fine restaurant and she had probably hoped her family would at least use the opportunity to try something different. The waitress took away the huge menus and the table looked really bare now as everyone sipped their drinks in silence again. Abbie helped herself to some mineral water.

'The weather's awful isn't it?' said Jilly. Abbie smiled, nodding in agreement, trying to resist reacting as though it were a criticism.

'I hope we haven't come all this way for it to rain all week,' she continued, irritated and nudging her husband to do something about Molly in the highchair next to him who was blowing bubbles into her drink.

Abbie couldn't stop herself from commenting. 'I thought you'd come all this way to see me.'

Jilly looked at her younger sister as if she'd just spoken in a different language. She poured herself some more wine.

'What? Of course, we've come to see you. But it'd be nice if the weather was good too!'

Abbie knew she had her sulky face on and tried to snap herself out of it.

'So, come on, tell us everything. How's it all going? How far have you got with setting up the art gallery? You don't really say much about it when we speak on the phone.'

'I can't use the cottage as a gallery. It's no good for that,' Abbie snapped. All four teenage children were paying attention and listening intently now, mainly because Aunt Abbie was beginning to sound like they did when their mother asked them awkward questions.

'Oh, right. So, do you have any other plans for the place?'

'No. I'm not doing anything with it. At the moment. Just living there.'

'What about a job? Are you teaching again?'

'No, I've got a part-time job in the local pub.' Abbie cringed at what Jilly would think of that although she needn't have worried.

Jilly smiled. 'Oh well, there are worse jobs. It'll tide you over for a while and I suppose it's a good way to meet the local people.' Abbie was unable to speak; it seemed that she and her sister were in complete agreement on this matter. She wasn't sure whether this had ever happened before.

The food arrived, and everyone seemed to cheer up a little and even Abbie perked up as she tucked into her broccoli cheese bake which was delicious.

'Are you vegetarian?' asked Chloe, the first three words she'd spoken although she did sound genuinely interested.

'Oh no, I just liked the sound of this dish with all the different cheeses and vegetables. It's really nice.'

'Oh,' said a slightly disappointed Chloe although she saw an opening for expressing her cause. 'I want to be one, but Mum won't let me.'

'You only want to eat vegetarian because you think it will make you lose weight – which you do not need to do,' interjected Jilly.

'No I don't, that's not the reason why,' said Chloe, not very convincingly.

'Well, your mother's right in that way – you really don't need to lose weight.' Sensing that she was losing her niece's friendship before it had even begun, she tried to make amends. 'You have a lovely figure Chloe, all you need to concentrate on is eating healthy; fresh fruit and vegetables, things like that.' Abbie noticed she was losing interest in her cheeseburger and chips.

'Do you want to try some of this?' offered Abbie.

Chloe eyed the gooey yellow and green vegetable mess dubiously. 'No, it's OK thanks.' She plonked her knife and fork onto her half-finished meal and folded her arms with an attitude as if to say that she'd given up on food altogether.

Abbie felt it might be a good idea to change the subject.

'So, do you have a boyfriend then?' Judging from the surreptitious smile she was trying to hide, the answer was a 'yes' although judging from the look on Jilly's face, this was obviously another contentious issue between them. Abbie wasn't sure whether she should encourage this line of conversation but then Jilly swapped places with Glen so that she could clean Molly's face and hands of the fish fingers and beans she'd managed to smear all over them.

'What's he like then?' asked Abbie sensing that Chloe definitely wanted to continue.

'He's really nice.' Chloe smiled shyly.

'And what's his name?'

'Dex.'

'Does he go to your school?'

'No,' said Chloe vaguely.

This was like pulling teeth thought Abbie, desperately trying to extract some information that could lead to a proper conversation.

'I take it your Mum doesn't approve?' she asked, conspiratorially.

'No,' agreed Chloe, grimacing, although she still didn't offer any more information on the elusive Dex.

Jilly returned to her seat on the other side of Chloe who suddenly resumed her usual sulky silence, picking up her fork and poking around with her food.

Abbie was thinking ahead to Luisa arriving in a couple of days. She was looking forward to seeing her friend and if there were to be many more painful occasions like this, she couldn't get here soon enough.

At long last they had all finished. Jilly paid the bill, looking rather surprised at the amount – burgers and pizzas didn't come cheap in hotels. Abbie was about to offer to chip in but changed her mind, and then felt inexplicably uncomfortable and a little guilty too.

As the family walked towards the lifts, Jilly hung back walking alongside Abbie.

'They're all growing up so fast,' said Abbie, nodding at Molly who was running to catch up with her elder brothers and sisters and who were all having a go at pressing the button for the lift.

'Especially Chloe,' sighed Jilly, looking very weary. 'Teenage girls!' she said as she tried to smile.

Abbie smiled back, not really seeing what the problem was - Chloe seemed OK; a reasonably normal teenage girl if a little reticent and surely there were a lot worse things than that for a teenage girl to be.

'Why are you being so tough on her for wanting a boyfriend?'

'So tough, am I? I heard you both talking – trying to get her to tell you all about the wonderful Dex. Well, what she failed to tell you was that Dex is twenty-two years old and has a daughter by another teenage girl - that is, only the one as far as we know. However, he doesn't have a job or any means of supporting them. He sleeps on a sofa at a friend's house because his own parents threw him out due to a 'borrowed' credit card but of course that was all just a mix up. Chloe is of the opinion that we should take him under our wing, but I won't even begin on the arguments we've had about that.' Jilly paused for a fraction of a second, red in the face and out of breath. 'And I would appreciate it if you could not make out that I'm some sort of wicked witch of a non-understanding mother.'

'I didn't say that!' said Abbie, sounding horribly like a defensive teenager herself.

'You know what I mean. I'm not just trying to spoil her fun. Dex is not the sort of person you'd want your sixteen-year-old daughter to spend time with.'

'No, I see that. I didn't realise.'

The lift arrived, and Abbie looked at Jilly noticing that she looked a lot older than her forty-two years, in fact she looked completely exhausted. For a brief moment Abbie wanted to give her a hug but already it was too late; the lift arrived and the whole family bundled themselves inside, the children waving at her as the doors closed, leaving her standing there alone.

Abbie drove home through the torrential rain and got drenched again as she ran from the car to the cottage. In the kitchen she took off her mac and hung it on the back door, switching the light on even though it was only mid- afternoon. Heavy black clouds hanging low in the sky made it very dark inside. She flicked the kettle on although she could really have done with something much stronger after the awful start to her sister's family holiday.

Abbie cradled her mug of tea in both hands and stood looking out the window at the rain streaming down as far as the eye could see. There was something in the garden, close to the cottage, and she squinted through the haze of rain trying to make it out. Finally, she realised what it was - a stack of tables piled up right next to the wall. She'd asked Miriam if she could borrow a couple for her informal dinner party but there had to be at least six tables outside. She guessed that Alistair must have brought them over and just dumped them at the back of the cottage. He would have been glad she wasn't in. Now she would have to go out in the pouring rain and drag the tables inside.

The weather couldn't have been more appropriate; cold and miserable. Abbie felt awful. What had she been thinking? Was she trying to win Chloe over and score a point against Jilly by being understanding about her wanting a boyfriend – when she knew absolutely nothing about the situation? She must apologise. Now wasn't the time to phone, Jilly would be up to her eyes trying to manage her large family between a few hotel rooms. But she would apologise, and she would do it soon.

Chapter Twenty-Seven

Miriam had got yet another order wrong. She'd delivered the hot buttered scones to table three instead of table eight, but the occupants were so engrossed in conversation that by the time they noticed and called Miriam back, she didn't feel it appropriate to deliver lukewarm scones to the correct table. She reprimanded herself for not concentrating but her mind was all over the place at the moment. The troubles between her and Alistair had escalated, and she was fighting to keep her business, but the way she was going she'd have no customers and no business left to fight for. It was particularly busy in the tearoom today; the awful weather was bringing people in and while she was grateful for the business, she really needed to get her act together.

The door opened, and a rush of wind blasted a couple of young women who were sitting nearest to it. They cupped their hands around mugs of hot chocolate to warm them.

A large family bundled in, struggling to fit around the last available table and borrowing spare chairs from wherever they could. They didn't look particularly happy, thought Miriam. The parents looked stressed probably due to trying to occupy all their children in such awful weather and the children themselves all looked thoroughly bored although the younger girl seemed to be enjoying the tearoom surroundings. She was admiring the pink tablecloth and fiddling with the pink flowers in the vase which her mother promptly moved out of her reach.

Miriam left them to settle for a few minutes before going over to take their order. As she stood waiting for them all to make up their minds, she studied the woman's face; it looked familiar to her although she was positive they hadn't met before. It took a while to take the order as everyone seemed to change their minds at least two or three times. Miriam reckoned with some certainty that by the time she delivered their food and drinks, they would have forgotten who had ordered what.

Miriam had confronted Alistair about the valuation on their house that she'd found. The subsequent argument had been a defining moment in their lives.

There was no denying the flicker of shock on his face, but he recovered quickly and then dropped the bombshell that they were in terrible shape financially and the only way of resolving things was to sell the house, in his opinion. Miriam's instinct was to demand to know why he hadn't told her before, but then she knew why he preferred to keep her in the dark about things; like where he was and who he was allegedly working for. The less she knew the better for him. He'd been working all hours, supposedly, or had he? He'd been out of the house a lot – doing what? She found she didn't want to know. It had been the same in London; his little dalliances that he always insisted were nothing serious. It was one of the reasons they'd moved up here to The Lake District. How stupid could she be? There were plenty of women up here too.

Miriam assumed Alistair wanted to sell up and downsize. She also figured that he resented how successful the tearoom was and that it took up more of her time, meaning he was needed to pitch in more with domestic matters. But then he told her that he'd already been looking at properties in London and that if they got a good price for the house and tearoom business as was indicated on the valuation, they should be able to get a reasonably sized place back in London.

Miriam couldn't even contemplate the idea of leaving Kirkby Bridge and so they were at a stalemate. They hadn't spoken since about the situation or anything else, although both were totally consumed by their own thoughts.

Miriam prepared the order and lifted the loaded tray, taking it over to the family's table. Jilly was organising things; dishing out teacups and mugs of hot chocolate to the appropriate person.

'Whose is the carrot cake?' asked Jilly. No-one answered and Miriam's heart sank - here we go, she thought. She knew this was going to happen.

'It must be Chloe's,' said George, 'she thinks that eating carrot cake makes her a veggie.' He and Joe sniggered while Chloe insisted that she hadn't asked for it, hers was the chocolate fudge cake which was on the table and which she now took possession of before anyone else claimed it.

Jilly was getting exasperated and Miriam was getting impatient, holding the plate of cake aloft.

Glen looked up from reading a local newspaper and suddenly realised what all the fuss was about and amidst a lot of tutting and sighing from the women, he admitted that the carrot cake was his.

Chapter Twenty-Eight

Abbie waited anxiously at the train station. She'd been dashing around all morning, putting finishing touches to the cottage to make it look as nice as possible and welcoming. She'd put out a couple of vases of fresh flowers and lit some vanilla scented candles just that morning to infuse the place with a homely scent. Because of her last-minute tweaking, she'd left a little late and had to put her foot down to get to the station on time. But now, as she looked up at the arrivals information board, she saw that Luisa's train would be coming in fifteen minutes late.

She waited like an impatient child, watching the minutes tick away on the digital clock, longing to see her familiar friendly face. It felt like an age since she'd seen Luisa, and Abbie couldn't help feeling a little sad to think that their friendship might suffer because of her moving so far away. But she resolved, there and then while she fidgeted on the spot, to make sure they met up more often; they could make it work she decided with determination. Just a few minutes later and they were hugging as if they'd not seen each other for years.

'It's so lovely to have you here. And I've got lots to tell you,' said Abbie.

'Me too.' Luisa looked happy and upbeat and obviously full of news of her own. Abbie was looking forward to talking about Eva and Lilleth and Jed, the unwelcome advances of Alistair Walker and yesterday's argument with Jilly, but she had the distinct impression that Luisa's news was a whole lot more exciting.

'It's great to be here. You know, I can't believe you've been here two months already, it's gone so quick. I've had a mad-crazy time myself - I'll fill you in with all the details, we've so much to catch up on.' Abbie suddenly felt a little flat as they linked arms and walked to the car.

Once they'd arrived back and Abbie was making tea, Luisa wandered around the downstairs rooms. She could see that Abbie had worked hard on bringing her gran's old cottage back to life.

'It's truly beautiful Abbie. I am impressed. I can see you've worked really hard; it looks clean and bright but cosy and homely too. Wow! Well done to you!'

'Ah thanks Luisa. It was hard work, especially rubbing down all that horrible black gloss-work. But worth it in the end I think.'

'Definitely. It looks gorgeous. Have you had any more thoughts on whether it's feasible to do what you originally planned? The gallery I mean. You were adamant at first that it wasn't possible. Now that you've been here a while - I wonder if you've come up with any other ideas?'

'No, not really,' said Abbie, trying not to sound too despondent. 'Well, yes and no actually. Maybe.'

201

'Well that's clear!' laughed Luisa, following Abbie into the living room and sitting down on the new sofa. Abbie placed a tray on the table with mugs of tea and a plate of biscuits.

'The cottage is definitely too small; you can see that. But there's so much land outside, big gardens front and back, I got to thinking that maybe I could extend. So, I got a quote from a local builder. Oh my God, builders, that's a whole other story.'

Luisa gave her a funny look, having just taken a bite of her biscuit.

'I'll tell you later,' said Abbie, waving her hand dismissively. 'Anyway, the quote came through and as I kind of expected, it's pretty hefty. Not doable at the moment anyway. I suppose maybe in the future I could take out a small mortgage, but I'd need to be in permanent work - so we'll just have to see.'

'It sounds like you've got some exciting plans in the pipeline. That's great – you're really making a go of it.'

'Yeah, I'm doing my best,' said Abbie. She hadn't even thought about an extension to the cottage for ages; had virtually written it off for the foreseeable future. Perhaps she ought to look at it again, she thought.

'Have you spoken to Jack recently?' asked Luisa, a little sheepishly.

'Yeah, he phoned a few weeks ago – just about the house really, nothing much.'

'He phones me quite often – asking after you and wanting to know that you're OK.'

Abbie didn't know what to say. She was only up here in Cumbria in Winnifred Cottage because of him. What if she'd made a stupid hasty mistake? They finished their tea in silence and then Abbie led the way upstairs.

'I remember coming up here for the first time – do you remember that Abbie? Finding the stairs in this little cupboard and not knowing what to expect up here.'

Abbie smiled. 'Yes, I was so disheartened with everything then.' As she led the way into what would be Luisa's bedroom for the next few days, she realised with quite a surprise how different she now felt towards Winnifred Cottage. She'd hated it back then, couldn't bear the thought of having to live there and make it her home. And she'd felt uncomfortable with the conflict of her feelings for the place with her love for her gran. But now, having worked tirelessly for so long, and most importantly, having gleaned a few snippets of information from Jed and Mrs Gilbert on her gran's attachment to the cottage, she'd developed a real affection for the place.

'Abbie this is gorgeous. You've done a fantastic job up here.'

Abbie felt pleased to hear all that. This was the first feedback she'd had on her decorating skills and she was delighted to know she'd got it right.

'I'm not going to want to go home,' Luisa smiled and then her expression changed. Abbie just caught it but couldn't decipher its meaning. It wasn't often that she ever saw Luisa looking awkward and uncomfortable.

Luisa was over by the window looking out. 'You're so lucky Abbie, to have this gorgeous view, every day. People travel hundreds of miles to see this for a few days and for you, it's just here, always.'

Abbie walked over to Luisa's side and looked out, seeing for herself the beautiful view over the hills and dales, stretching out for miles. As if seeing it for the first time, she realised, rather shamefully how little time she spent standing here, simply enjoying it.

'What do you fancy doing tomorrow? Do you fancy a walk into the hills?'

'Yeah, that sounds great. I bet you're out and about all the time, in this gorgeous countryside, you probably know it all like the back of your hand. You're so lucky, aren't you?'

'Yes, I am,' replied Abbie, very sheepishly, suddenly a little ashamed to admit that she didn't know the surrounding area at all. She hadn't actually been out walking much, not beyond the confines of the village anyway. The hope was that she and Luisa would go out and about together and explore the place, but it seemed that Luisa was expecting her to be the tour guide.

'So, did Jilly and co arrive OK?'

'Yes, like I told you, they were supposed to be coming in a few days which would have been perfect and then we could have had some time together before she got here. But then everything changed, and they got here yesterday.'

'Oh, it doesn't matter does it? They'll probably be doing their own thing mostly and anyway it'll be OK if we all get together occasionally – it's no big deal.'

'No,' said Abbie, feebly, feeling quite suffocated by all Luisa's good bonhomie. It was becoming quite overwhelming. The thought of her and Luisa getting together for a day out with Jilly and her family was almost unthinkable. She couldn't do that to her best friend. She attempted to explain.

'I had a bit of a ding-dong with Jilly earlier.'

'Oh no, really, when?'

'Friday - just after she got here.'

'Oh no. What was it about?'

'I don't know really. It all started from nothing. I met them all for lunch and it was really awful.'

She looked over at Luisa for understanding and encouragement but there didn't appear to be either on her face. She sighed deeply before continuing.

'Jilly seemed really stressed. And Glen too. And the kids were bored I think. I got talking to Chloe - she's sixteen and has a boyfriend but Jilly doesn't approve of him. So, I tried sympathising with Chloe, which turned out to be a huge mistake, and then Jilly gave me a right mouthful. So that was our first holiday get-together. Good job no-one videoed it!'

Luisa frowned in what Abbie hoped was sympathy, but she couldn't be absolutely sure. 'What is it about the boyfriend that Jilly doesn't approve of?' asked Luisa.

'He's twenty-two and a bit of a yob apparently. He's been in quite a lot of trouble and she told me I had no idea of what had been going on and had no right to interfere or encourage Chloe against her advice.' Abbie dragged her hand through her hair and sighed.

'It seems fair enough,' said Luisa simply. 'She's her mother, doing her best to steer her daughter in the right direction and then all of a sudden Aunty

Abbie thinks she knows best! I think I'd be annoyed too.'

'It wasn't like that,' said Abbie defensively. 'I wasn't making out I knew better – just trying to be friendly.' She looked over at Luisa who said nothing, but she gave her a look that said a lot.

'OK, I messed up. And yes, I feel awful. I shouldn't have got involved, not realising how things were between them over this boyfriend. I thought it was just Jilly being, well you know, awkward. Anyway, I'm going to apologise.'

'You mean you haven't already?' asked Luisa abruptly.

'Well, no, I haven't had the chance,' said Abbie on the defence again. Luisa raised her eyebrows and turned away from her. Abbie couldn't believe it; it felt like she now had two difficult sisters to get along with.

In fact, Abbie had phoned Jilly the following morning after the awful family lunch to see if they would be meeting up again that day, but Jilly said they were planning to go out for the day to an activity centre. She'd added that Abbie was welcome to join them, but it sounded like an after-thought, which rankled her, and then the awkward atmosphere between them was back again. Abbie hadn't thought she could produce an apology that would sound genuine or convincing to either of them and so she left it. For her own reasons which she didn't want to examine too deeply, she didn't bother explaining all of this to Luisa.

'You could make more effort with your sister, you know,' said Luisa, attempting a friendly smile.

Abbie flicked on the kettle switch and began fussing with rinsing out the mugs. Luisa continued.

'She's not so bad - I think she's alright. I don't really know why you two don't get on. I'd like to have a sister, especially one with kids and everything, happy to include you in their lives. You don't know how lucky you are Abbie.'

'So you keep telling me! And anyway, she doesn't include me in her life. We hardly ever do anything together. And when we do it's a disaster.'

'Oh come on, she's often inviting you over, and it's always you who cries off. You always turn down her invitations at Christmas. I mean, for Heaven's sake, she even asked you to be Molly's Godmother, but you declined the offer! That sort of thing is an honour.'

'Hardly! She waited until her third child to ask me,' mumbled Abbie, knowing how pathetic she sounded, and how unfair that comment was. Jilly was Godmother to her best friend's eldest child and had promised to return the invite when she had a child, which turned out to be Chloe. Freda's Godmother was Glen's sister, Sarah, who adored children but who had been told that she was unable to have any of her own - it was typically thoughtful of Jilly to ask her. And Sarah had been absolutely thrilled.

Abbie was beginning to get a headache. The sound of her sulky silence was plain for them both to hear. She smiled, keen to change the tone of the conversation - and the subject. 'Anyway, I've got you for a friend - the best kind. You're all the friend I need and I tell you what, in future we're going to make sure we get together more often. It's been awful being apart all this time. I'll come down to you in a few weeks, if you like.'

At first Luisa didn't respond, she just looked at Abbie with a big silly grin on her face.

'What is it Luisa?'

'Well, like I said, I do have some news.'

'Oh no! What is it?'

'It's OK, it's nothing bad. It's very exciting actually. It's just that, well, we won't be seeing each other for quite a while I'm afraid.'

'Why? What's happening?'

'Well, you see, the thing is, I'm moving to Finland – with Aaron of course. His company has extended his contract for another three years and I'm going with him. How exciting is that?'

Abbie's face dropped. She couldn't believe this was happening.

'Right. This is a bit of a shock. You're leaving.'

'Don't sound too pleased for me,' said Luisa laughing, more to cover her annoyance than anything else. 'This is a fantastic opportunity for me Abbie. I've already got an interview at Aaron's company as an international legal advisor and as you know I've been learning Finnish for over a year now - what did you think I was learning it for?'

'I don't know. I hadn't really thought about it – probably just thought you were doing it for fun.'

'No, it wasn't for fun. I've been studying it seriously for some time.'

'Oh, right. I should have realised that. Sorry.' Yet again Abbie felt humbled - she'd got it all wrong, again. 'Crikey, how will I manage without you, my one true friend?'

Luisa looked directly at her friend. 'That was kind of my point earlier, that you could make more effort with Jilly. She'd be a good friend to you.'

Abbie made tea, avoiding looking at Luisa and not knowing what to say.

'Do you know Jilly often phoned me? To make sure you were OK up here all by yourself. She had a feeling things weren't quite right but she could never get any real information out of you.'

Abbie finally turned and faced Luisa. 'Did she really phone you? About me? I didn't know that. I really didn't think she cared that much. She's always so consumed with everything – Glen and his precious job and her kids.'

'Well, we all get a bit absorbed with our own lives, don't we?' Luisa was smiling kindly. 'We all have our own stuff to deal with, it's easy to get caught up and lose sight of what's happening with others.'

Chapter Twenty-Nine

The following day Abbie woke early, leaving Luisa to have a lie-in and phoned Jilly's hotel and asked to be put through to her room. The phone had rung a few times already and Abbie wasn't sure whether she really wanted someone to answer or whether she'd prefer it if they were all out.

'Hello?'

'Hi Glen, is Jilly there?'

'Yep, just a sec.'

Abbie could hear a mix of chatter in the background.

'Hello Abbie. How are you?' The sound of Jilly's calm voice surprised her – she expected her to still be angry about the other day, but it seemed to be all forgotten. Of course, thought Abbie, Jilly wasn't the sort of person to bear a grudge.

'Hi Jilly. I'm fine. How was your trip to the activity centre?'

'It was fantastic. We had a great time. The weather wasn't brilliant but it didn't matter. We couldn't get the boys off the zip wire and Molly and Freda did a bit of pony trekking – I don't think Chloe is into activities – but at least everyone else seemed happy enough. Oh, and on the way back we found a lovely tearoom, Blossoms, or something like that.'

'Oh yes, I know the one.'

'It's a shame you couldn't make it.' Jilly paused and then added, 'Chloe would have liked you to be there, I think.'

Abbie was touched by the gracious compliment. 'We'll meet up soon, won't we? What are your plans for today?'

'Glen's taking the kids to the pictures.' Jilly laughed. 'It's been difficult finding a movie all the kids are happy with, so the poor boys drew the short straw and are having to suffer a Disney cartoon. They're all going for pizza afterwards so that should make up for it.'

'So, you have the day to yourself?'

'Pretty much. I didn't bother bringing a book along, that would just be too ambitious, but I have a couple of magazines I'm going to relax with. Look at the pictures of all those beautiful homes and kid myself that I can get mine to look that cosy and welcoming.

Abbie was surprised; she thought Jilly's home was wonderful, cosy and very welcoming. She wished she'd said so, but the moment had gone already.

'Oh, OK. Well, enjoy your quiet day.'

'Unless – did you have something else in mind?'

'Well, yes, I was just thinking – do you fancy a drive out to meet Great Aunts Eva and Lilleth. They're both looking forward to meeting you and your family.' This wasn't exactly true; Eva hadn't said anything of the sort but of course Lilleth was longing to meet her other great niece and all her children. 'It might be nice for you to meet them first.'

'Mm, before landing my lot on them all in one go you mean,' Jilly laughed.

'Well, yes, you might be right.'

'OK, let's do it. But what about Luisa? Did she arrive OK? Will she be coming along?'

'Yes, she's here, she's fine.' Abbie felt a little uncomfortable that Luisa and Jilly had formed a sort of bond and had been discussing her. But she put it out of her mind; it was because they cared, she reminded herself. 'I said we might go out for a couple of hours this morning and she was fine with that. hall I come along now to pick you up?'

'Perfect. I'll be waiting outside at the front of the hotel.'

Abbie was ready in minutes. She was really looking forward to this, keen to build some bridges with her sister. She drove steadily through the fine drizzly rain, the windscreen wipers thudding comfortingly and rhythmically. Abbie turned the heater up a notch, it felt more like winter than late spring.

Jilly was waiting, as she said, outside the hotel under an uncharacteristically bright red umbrella with black poodles on it.

'Love the brolly,' laughed Abbie as Jilly quickly got in the car.

Jilly grinned. 'Mm, Chloe bought it for me for Christmas.'

They drove on in silence for a while; Abbie concentrating on the drive – the fine misty rain was making visibility very poor while Jilly was totally

212

over-whelmed by the beauty of the surrounding countryside.

'You're so lucky Abbie, to have all this right on your doorstep. It's breath-taking. Better than the new superstore and its huge car park that I now have to look at.'

Abbie thought she would scream if one more person tried telling her how lucky she was. Did they think she was lucky that her home had nearly burnt down and lucky that her boyfriend had been so pre-occupied he didn't even know how it started? Funny how she didn't feel very lucky these days, but she managed to keep her thoughts to herself. Maybe it was just best to say nothing at all.

The rain was coming down harder now and Abbie's mood was descending too. Jilly made an effort to break the chilly silence.

'So, what's the story with Eva and Lilleth? They live together you said, did they never marry?'

'Lilleth was married but her husband died years ago. It's her cottage and she offered to take Eva in a few years ago, I think it was, after she'd had a bad fall or something. Eva's never been married.'

'Oh?' said Jilly, sounding surprised. 'I wonder why. Maybe she was too picky.'

Abbie laughed. 'She'd be hard pushed to find someone to put up with her, I think.' The comment hung in the air as both women were conscious of the fact that at the grand old age of thirty-four, Abbie was still very much without a partner.

They drove the rest of the journey in silence, both looking forward to getting to Eva and Lilleth's home where conversation might be easier when they didn't have to be alone with each other.

As Abbie pulled up outside the cottage, she had an awful thought that Eva and Lilleth might not be home. How stupid of her, she thought, with a sinking heart, she should have telephoned first. And then she saw, with huge relief, the kitchen light switch on.

Just as they got out of the car the rain came down even harder. Abbie parked right next to the garden gate but even so, by the time they'd run the length of the garden path, they were both soaking. Both women hovered miserably in the porch as Abbie knocked on the door.

'Oh my goodness!' exclaimed Lilleth opening the door wide, beckoning them to come inside. 'Where have you two trekked all the way from?'

'Just the other side of the garden,' said Abbie, smiling wryly and giving her aunt a kiss on the cheek as Lilleth helped her off with her jacket. Abbie was conscious of Jilly watching her, wondering probably at this display of affection for such a little-known family member.

'Lilleth, this is my sister Jilly.'

'Lovely to meet you Jilly,' Lilleth sensed her reserve and smiled warmly, hugs and kisses would hopefully come along later.

'Hello,' Jilly said simply.

'I understand you're up here with your family for a holiday.'

'Yes, that's right,' said Jilly trying to take it all in. 'My husband has taken the children out for the day.'

'Ah, giving Mum a break are they? That's nice. I look forward to meeting them at some point,' said

Lilleth, genuinely looking forward to meeting more members of her suddenly extended family.

Abbie sat at the kitchen table and Jilly did the same wondering where the other sister was. It was as if Lilleth had read her mind.

'Eva should be out in just a moment,' she said, putting on the kettle and bustling about with cups and saucers, plates and biscuits, wondering what on earth Eva was doing and why she hadn't appeared to greet their guests.

Lilleth took the pot of tea over to the table, still thinking about Eva but still managing to notice that her two nieces hadn't said a word to each other since they arrived. Eva was evidently making a point by keeping everyone waiting – she wasn't very hospitable to visitors who turned up unannounced and Lilleth had to admit, on this occasion, it would have been nice to have had some warning. Eva had been in a foul mood all morning and unusually Lilleth had been unable to ignore it. They had been snapping at each other to the point where they had ceased talking at all and there was now an icy silence between them. Neither of them was in the mood for entertaining.

The tea had been brewing for several minutes and Jilly gave Abbie a bemused look as Lilleth opened yet another box of jam tarts.

'Lilleth, I think we've got plenty of cakes and biscuits,' said Abbie as diplomatically as she could.

Lilleth looked at the table and took in the abundance of food and laughed at herself.

'Oh yes, I see what you mean. I was getting carried away there. But please, help yourselves. Eva will be out shortly - there's no need to wait. You carry on - I'll see what's keeping her.' Lilleth opened the door to the lounge and pushed it closed behind her but it didn't shut completely.

Abbie and Jilly were embarrassed at being able to hear Lilleth despite her lowering her voice.

'What are you doing in here? How can you be so rude?' Lilleth demanded to know.

'Shall I pour?' said Jilly, purposely diverting their attention. Abbie pushed her cup and saucer towards Jilly and nodded.

'What's going on?' asked Jilly, noticing the tension on Abbie's face.

'I don't know. I mean, they're not the best of friends, that's true, but it's not normally this bad.' Abbie looked over towards the open door and lowered her voice. 'Eva always moans and groans about everything but Lilleth usually just smiles and tolerates it.'

Jilly sipped her tea and Abbie nibbled a biscuit - both wondering which one of them could be considered the moaner and which one the more tolerant. They avoided each other's gaze. Jilly dabbed some stray crumbs from the tablecloth with her finger while Abbie fidgeted restlessly.

The silence and their thoughts were broken by the sound of Eva's raised voice. Jilly and Abbie instinctively froze, eyes locked to each other, both straining to hear. This was obviously not some petty squabble over whose turn it was to make the tea.

'There are things I could tell you, Miss High-and-Mighty that would shut you up, once and for all.'

'Oh, are there?' responded Lilleth, in an almost teasing tone which seemed to infuriate Eva all the more.

'Oh, you can smile, all you want. But I'm going to wipe that smile off your face. It's about time someone did.'

'Come on then Eva, you've waited long enough,' said Lilleth with such control, the sound of her voice was almost more menacing than Eva's raging threats.

Jilly and Abbie stared wide-eyed at each other. There was silence for a few seconds, Jilly and Abbie hardly daring to breathe for fear of what was to come next. They could just about make out Lilleth's mumbling voice as if she couldn't stop herself from having the last word.

'You haven't got the sense to know when you're well off, you never did have.'

'Well off? To be taken in by you? And to be reminded of it everyday?'

'Don't be ridiculous. That's just nonsense. You've got a chip on your shoulder because you're living in my house. You've always had a chip on your shoulder, because I had a –.'

'What? A husband? Is that what you were going to say? Well, let me tell you – I had my chances.'

'Exactly. You had chances Eva and you let them go. It's your own fault. What about Albert, Albert Atkins – he adored you.' Lilleth took a deep breath to continue but Eva interrupted.

'It didn't mean I had to marry the first man that asked me did it?' she shouted.

'But you didn't marry any of them,' snapped back Lilleth. 'And look at you now, you're alone and getting more and more bitter by the day.' She stopped herself from going too far. Unfortunately, Eva didn't have the same control. She laughed callously.

'What are you saying? That I could have been happy – like you?' she said sarcastically.

'Yes, me and Harry were very happy – for over forty years. And he was the first man to propose to me. Your trouble is, you're afraid of missing something, always on the lookout for something better.'

'Ah yes but were you the first person Harry asked to marry him? What do you think Lilleth? Do you think you were Harry's one and only true love?'

Eva and Lilleth stood facing each other across the room, eye to eye, daring the other to look away first.

'You have something to say Eva. You'd better say it.' It was Lilleth's unbearable self-composure that ignited every nerve in Eva's body. Did this woman never feel any passion for anything? The way Eva felt passionately now that life had cheated her, passed her by unfulfilled and unloved. She was in a rage, unable to stop.

'He asked me first,' shouted Eva, staring wide-eyed, shocked at the sound of her words. Words that she'd kept to herself for so many years. She'd always promised herself she would never speak them but over the last couple of years, living with Lilleth, she'd come to despise her sister's easy-going contentment with the memories of her happy life with Harry. Eva could see, feel, hear, everyday, at first hand, what a loving and companionable

relationship she and her husband had shared –
emphasising her own emptiness all the more.

'He asked me to marry him – before you! I was
his first choice, his first love.' What was wrong with
Lilleth, thought Eva. Why was she just standing
there? Why didn't she say something, shout or throw
something? Eva sat down heavily in the armchair,
exhausted, and rested her head on her hand. The
continuing silence from Lilleth made her look up
into her sister's expressionless face. The lack of
emotion was infuriating but she had no energy left
and she was also a little worried now that maybe
she'd sent Lilleth into a sort of traumatised shock.

Lilleth walked swiftly to the door leading back to
the kitchen, turning back to face Eva. 'I know what it
was with you; you had your eyes on someone you
thought was better. But you never got him, did you?
And I'll tell you this – you never will. Jed Tobin lost
his heart to another Delaney sister a long time ago.'

Eva shifted herself in the armchair, turning away
from Lilleth and staring into the empty fire grate.

Lilleth went through to the kitchen, closing the
door gently behind her. She took her wax jacket off
the hook on the back door and put it on, at the same
time flicking off her slippers and slipping her feet
into her Wellington boots. 'I'm terribly sorry,' she
said jerkily towards the kitchen table, without
actually looking at Jilly and Abbie. 'Please forgive
us.'

Abbie and Jilly looked at each other, maintaining
their shocked silence, wanting desperately to help
but wishing also that they could instantaneously
disappear. Lilleth calmly opened the door, stepped

outside and closed it quietly behind her. They weren't sure what to do next and began half-heartedly clearing the tea things from the table. From the kitchen window they could see the tiny figure of Lilleth already far in the distance, her hood pulled down tight as she trudged in the pouring rain towards the hills.

'Come on, let's go,' whispered Abbie, not wanting to face Eva if she emerged from the other room. She took her jacket from the back of the chair and even though it was still damp, she put it on. They were about to get soaked again going back out to the car but neither of them minded that, they just wanted to get out of there.

As Abbie drove off and along the narrow country lanes, both women instinctively scanned the countryside for a sight of Lilleth, but she was not to be seen.

'I hope she knows where she's going,' said Jilly thinking that there didn't appear to be any obvious place that she might be heading for.

'She's lived here all her life, I'm sure she knows the place inside and out.' Abbie was concentrating hard, even with the wipers on full speed cascades of water tumbled down the windscreen. They were silent for a few moments, both deep in thought.

'Imagine that,' said Jilly finally. 'Holding on to that secret for all those years.'

'Yeah, that's bad enough. And then for it to come out like that – in front of us. It was awful.'

'What did she mean about Jed losing his heart to another Delaney sister? Did she mean Gran do you think?'

'Yes, I think she did. Poor Jed – Grannaliese broke his heart by the sound of it.'

'Well, it just goes to show, you shouldn't keep things bottled up like that. They'll come out eventually and probably in the ugliest of ways.'

They were silent again, both aware that they each harboured various resentments towards each other that had never been voiced and which were increasing in power over the years. They were thinking the same sad thoughts that they too might end up like their aunts Eva and Lilleth, and maybe they weren't that far from it already.

Chapter Thirty

Abbie dropped Jilly back at her hotel before heading home. She went upstairs to change and from her bedroom window looked out at the rivulets of water running in channels down the road. She craned her neck to see clearer, wondering if perhaps some of the drains were blocked - there seemed to be an awful lot of surface water and still the rain was coming down heavy.

Luisa had left a note on the kitchen counter to say she'd popped over to the B & B; she'd left her earrings behind last time she stayed and wanted to ask if they'd been found. She wrote that she'd only be out for a short while and would be back by lunchtime. Abbie glanced up at the clock - she should be back anytime soon. A pretty pot plant of miniature pink roses had been placed to the side of the note. Abbie smiled, happy that normal friendly relations had been resumed between them.

Luisa had been with Aaron for about three years - her first long-term relationship for ages. Abbie remembered how happy she was when she'd first started seeing him and she also remembered, rather shamefully, feeling slightly peeved when this meant she didn't get to see quite as much of her friend as she used to. That was pretty selfish, she thought, squirming at the realisation. Abbie sighed and put the kettle on to boil, perhaps she should apologise for her behaviour although it was a long time ago now. And then, she was reminded that she still owed Jilly an apology over the whole Chloe and her boyfriend thing. There just hadn't been the opportunity to say anything that morning. Abbie made herself a mug of tea and with a heavy heart recognised that she had a lot of making up to do.

For starters she wanted to make a special lunch for her and Luisa so they could enjoy some time together. She picked up her mobile and phoned her friend but there was no answer. After a few minutes she tried again and left a message asking her to call back. Half an hour later and still with no reply from Luisa, Abbie began to feel uneasy. Luisa was constantly checking her phone; it was very unlike her not to return a call as soon as she could. Abbie looked out of the window and frowned; the rain was unrelenting and she wondered if it was affecting the mobile phone signal. Amongst some paperwork collecting on the kitchen counter was the B & B business card. Abbie flicked through the papers, found the card and dialled the number. It rang and rang and eventually Abbie gave up, surprised that the ever-efficient Mrs Gilbert would allow her business phone to ring unanswered.

Abbie left it a few more minutes and tried again but there was still no answer. She couldn't bear this; there was obviously something wrong. She grabbed her Wellingtons from beside the back door, tucked her jeans into them and threw on her mac. Taking her umbrella, she ran down the hill towards the B &

B, letting herself in through the front door. There was no-one at the reception area although Abbie was pleased to hear the phone ringing, so there was no problem this end. She walked around to the side of the reception desk to an office marked 'Private'.

'Hello?' she called out and when there was no answer she knocked on the door, opening it just a fraction but there was no-one there. She then went into the dining room which was eerily empty and from there quickly went through the swing door into the kitchen. It too looked empty but then Abbie heard voices although they were muffled and distant. Going further into the room, she could see an open door leading down to the cellar and on going nearer the voices became clearer and she recognised Mrs Gilbert's and then Luisa's too.

'Luisa? What are you doing down there?'

'Abbie? Is that you? Come down and give us a hand, will you?'

'What's happened?'

'It's flooded down here. Loads of food and stock are getting ruined. Grab a mop and bucket, we need to get this cleaned up.'

'In the corner behind the back door,' shouted up Mrs Gilbert.

Abbie turned and saw a collection of mops and buckets, she grabbed one of each and carefully descended the steep narrow steps down to the cellar. At the bottom her Wellingtons splashed through several inches of water.

'I'm not sure we're doing any good,' said Luisa quietly to Abbie, hoping Mrs Gilbert didn't hear.

The old lady was tirelessly and methodically mopping and squeezing water into a bucket. Abbie and Luisa set to in helping her. It was over an hour later when Mrs Gilbert carried a tea tray into the sitting room. Everyone felt cold and damp and after Mrs Gilbert placed the tray on the table she poked the fire, adding another log to it.

Luisa poured the tea as Mrs Gilbert sank her tiny frame into a large armchair. She looked smaller and more frail than ever - and completely exhausted too.

'Thank-you both for all your help,' she said weakly. Luisa handed her a cup of tea, worried for a second that Mrs Gilbert didn't have the strength left to actually hold it. She and Abbie glanced across at each other wondering what Mrs Gilbert would have done if they hadn't been around to help - she would probably still be in the cellar, tackling it on her own. And they also wondered if in fact all their efforts had been in vain. If the rain continued, the cellar would be flooded again by the morning.

'Shall we get back home?' asked Abbie.

Luisa looked over at Mrs Gilbert and pulled an anxious face. The old lady was falling asleep where she sat, her cup and saucer about to fall from her lap at any moment. Abbie reached over and gently removed them, placing them on the table.

'Do you think it's OK to leave her? There are no guests here at the moment - she's on her own,' said Luisa.

'I think she'll be fine. In fact, she won't like it if she thinks we're babysitting her - she'd probably hate to know she fell asleep while we were here. Tom will be along later, and she has my phone

225

number and I'm sure she's not short of friends around here looking out for her.'

'Yeah, you're right. I forget you have a real community spirit in places like this. You're very lucky.'

Abbie grinned to herself. She was beginning to acknowledge that she was indeed very lucky. She took her brolly from the hallway and they stepped outside, huddling close together, despairing at the continuing heavy rain - was it Abbie's imagination or was it coming down even harder.

As they walked hurriedly along the street, an overwhelming aroma reached them from the fish and chip shop. They glanced knowingly at each other.

'Fish and chips for lunch?' asked Luisa.

Abbie nodded eagerly. It was much too late to start cooking and now she had a craving, it would have to be satisfied. They attempted to run, jostling into each other clumsily and as they reached the shop doorway, they stopped. Two men were laying sandbags either side of the door and just in front of the small step. They stood aside to let the women in.

'It if carries on, these won't stop it,' said one of the men, nodding at the sandbags. 'But they might stop the worst of it.'

Abbie smiled in acknowledgement. She couldn't think of anything useful to say and couldn't help thinking of Mrs Gilbert's flooded cellar and the damage that had already been done there.

'It's getting serious,' said Abbie quietly to Luisa, as if she didn't want to be overheard stating the obvious. They stepped inside the shop which was warm and steamy, the mouth-watering smells of fish and chips and vinegar and the noise of the fryers were all very ordinary, but the bright artificial light was a sharp contrast to the increasing darkness outside, very odd for a mid-afternoon in spring. A quick flick of lightening preceded a low, menacing rumble of thunder. Abbie was keen to get back to the cottage. She placed their order and waited, constantly turning to look out of the window.

With their hot food in a plastic carrier bag, they attempted to run up the hill, virtually abandoning the umbrella by the time they got home, they were so wet anyway. Once inside they left their wellies by the back door and hung their coats up to drip small puddles beneath them on the floor.

Luisa searched the cupboards looking for plates as Abbie began unwrapping the steaming food.

'Crikey, you have enough tinned food here to fill the ark,' said Luisa, worrying slightly that her joke might have been in bad taste. Some of Abbie's neighbours were in serious danger of being flooded.

Abbie came to look in the cupboards. 'Mm, I did get a bit carried away. When I first got here, I didn't know what else to do for a while so I tended to go shopping a lot. Stocked up. No Mother Hubbard cupboards here you see.'

'Well, you've got enough tinned soup to feed an army anyway. Where are the plates?'

'In the end cupboard.'

As they sat side by side on stools at the counter eating the crispy battered fish and soggy, soaked in vinegar chips, Abbie picked up her mobile phone to check for messages. Someone had rung while she'd been out. The caller was Jilly – and she had rung five

227

times. Abbie looked at the display, noting that the last call had only been a couple of minutes ago. She was puzzled as to what would cause Jilly to make so much effort to contact her, especially as they'd only been together that morning. It was probably nothing. She put the phone down and smiled across at Luisa who was obviously enjoying her food, grinning with her mouth full of pickled onion.

'I keep meaning to ask,' said Luisa, 'what are all those tables for, stacked up in there? They weren't here before, were they? Oh, and I love the paint colour, by the way, creamy-vanilla – you've done a good job.'

'Thank-you. The tables – I've borrowed them. I was planning to cook a nice meal for you all, invite Eva and Lilleth and Jed over although it's a bit of a scary thought now. I'll make some tea,' said Abbie, jumping down off her stool and putting the kettle on to boil. She took another chip from her plate while she waited and then picked up her phone again, unable to shake an uneasy feeling about Jilly's calls. She pushed the return call button and surprisingly, Jilly answered immediately.

'Hello, Abbie?'

Abbie could tell straight away that something was wrong.

'I've been calling you for ages, why didn't you answer?'

Jilly's tone would have been irritating to Abbie at another time but at this moment she could tell that Jilly was frantic about something.

'I'm sorry, I left my phone at home. I've been helping at the B & B, they've been flooded, but I'm here now – what's happened?'

'It's Chloe. She's gone missing. She went off in a huff this morning – before we went out. And she's not come back. She's not answering her mobile and,' Jilly's voice trembled as she tried to steady herself. 'We've had to call out the mountain rescue people – oh my God, Abbie, where is she?'

Jilly's voice tailed off and Abbie knew from the following silence that she was crying.

'Don't worry Jilly, they'll find her. They're experts – they do this all the time. Look, I'm on my way over. You just sit tight.'

'OK,' mumbled a very timid sounding Jilly, relief sounding in her voice.

Luisa had stopped eating and was looking anxiously at Abbie trying to work out the context of her conversation.

'It's Chloe, she's gone missing. She went out early this morning. They've called the mountain rescue.'

The kettle came to a boil and clicked off like a full stop. The two women looked at each other trying desperately not to think the worst.

'I have to go,' said Abbie dragging on her boots again. 'I have to get to Jilly. I'm sorry Luisa – for abandoning you.'

'Don't be daft. Do you want me to come with you?'

'No, it's OK.' For some reason, Abbie preferred to go alone. She wanted to do this; she wanted to comfort and help her sister.

'Just let me know if there's anything you need me to do. Keep in touch, let me know what's happening.'

'Yes, I will,' said Abbie as she yanked the door open and ran out into the driving rain to her car. For once, she drove as fast as she dared, all she cared about was getting to Jilly as quickly as she could.

At the hotel it seemed to take an age for the lift to appear and when it did, it drifted up to the sixth floor so slowly, Abbie felt she could have run up the six flights of stairs quicker. Finally, the doors opened, the corridor was empty and she ran to the far end, at last knocking frantically on Jilly's room.

Glen opened the door, a grim expression on his weary face. Jilly was over at the window looking out, but she turned round immediately as she heard Abbie's voice and in the next moment threw herself into Abbie's arms. She held her, instinctively expecting her to pull away but she didn't, she stayed there resting against her, her face buried in her shoulder. Abbie held her tight; it felt strange. Finally, they released their hold and gently pulled apart, smiling at each other with real understanding. In this instance, words weren't necessary.

The room had two double beds and a cot for Molly. Chloe and Freda were sharing a bed and the two boys had a twin room next door. But at the moment everyone was in this room, close by – everyone, that is, except Chloe.

Abbie and Jilly sat down on the bed. Jilly looked pale and tired and her eyes were red and sore. Abbie wanted to know everything, but she could sense how shaky Jilly was and that she was also trying to keep

230

it together and not get upset in front of the other children. It felt oppressive in the room, everyone was self-conscious and watching each other's every move.

'Do you want to go downstairs for a coffee?' asked Abbie.

For a fraction of a second Jilly looked panic stricken. She looked around as if she couldn't possibly leave the room and her family - what if some news came through? She caught Glen's eye; he was quiet, trying to maintain a sense of controlled calm. Inside he was going mad – he wanted his teenage girl back with them right now. He nodded encouragingly and without speaking a word, Glen managed to convey to Jilly that they would all be fine if she went off with Abbie for a while and of course he would come and find her immediately if there was any news of Chloe.

Abbie located a couple of comfy armchairs in a quiet corner spot just aside from the reception area. She left Jilly for a moment to order some coffee and biscuits. Jilly took a deep breath; it felt good to get out of the room for a while.

They sat and looked out the window which gave them a full view of the hotel car park. A small group of business men and women were walking towards the hotel; they were laughing and Jilly thought wryly that they didn't look like they were psyching up for a heavy day of hard business - it was more likely to be a day of silly exercises and role-playing, summed up as a Team Building Day. What a different world, thought Jilly.

Another car drove in and parked. A middle-aged couple got out and they looked to Jilly like the sort of people she and Glen would make friends with. Then the back door opened, and a young girl got out – for a split second Jilly thought it was Chloe; her breath caught in her throat and her stomach leapt painfully. The girl wore the same style clothes; black leggings and a flowery flowing smock top and flat ditsy shoes that were definitely not going to keep her otherwise bare feet dry. The fear and frustration hit Jilly again, desperate to know where Chloe was. She couldn't bear to think of her daughter lost and frightened somewhere and probably wet through in this awful weather.

Another young girl arrived with a tray of coffee and a plate of biscuits – it seemed the world was full of teenage girls. The couple and their daughter were standing at reception now and Jilly sent out a silent plea to them to look after each other. As if Abbie was reading her thoughts, she jolted her back to the present.

'What time did Chloe go out?' she asked gently.

'This morning. Just before you phoned me - we'd had a huge row and she stormed off.'

Abbie was just about to ask why she hadn't mentioned it to her while they'd been together all morning but as she looked at Jilly, she bit her tongue and said nothing. The look that went between the two sisters said there was an awful lot that went on in their lives that they never spoke about.

Abbie poured a little cream in Jilly's coffee – just how she liked it, gave it a stir and handed her the cup. 'What did you argue about?'

Jilly half-smiled. 'Something stupid, of course. She'd been a bit stroppy all morning. There was a lot of texting going on over breakfast – I can guess it was to Dexter and that she wasn't happy with whatever he was saying – she was in a terrible mood afterwards. Being awkward and unhelpful, you know what I mean.'

'We've all been there,' said Abbie encouragingly. Jilly smiled again in agreement.

'Well, Glen was going to take them all out and I was going to stay at the hotel and just have some quiet time. And then Chloe decided she wanted to go for a family hike up some mountain – I mean, what was she thinking? You can't take Molly up a mountain. And the weather! She insisted there was no way she was going to watch a Disney move. For goodness sake, George and Joe didn't mind going and they're three years older than her.' Jilly paused for breath, and then continued more calmly. 'The boys are great; they don't mind things like that. They're so laid back and they love taking Freda and Molly out.'

'So, what happened then?'

'I told her we weren't going climbing in this weather, it would be madness. And I said that it was a family holiday and she should make an effort to join in with what other people wanted to do – she couldn't always have her own way.' Jilly paused, as if not sure she wanted to reveal the next bit, but then she took a deep breath and continued. 'She started shouting about what a joke of a family we were – how George and Joe were only with us because their mother ran away. And how careless I'd been having

Molly at such an old age and how I doted on her and didn't have time for anyone else.' Jilly stopped abruptly and looked down at the tissue she'd been fiddling with in her hands. A single teardrop fell onto her thumb and she wiped it away.

Abbie remained silent. She knew instinctively there was more to come. Jilly whispered something, barely audible, still staring down. 'I hated her. In that moment, I hated her – for saying all those things about our family. I didn't care when she grabbed her coat and slammed out of the room. I wasn't worried about her; she had a key to the room. I just thought that as soon as she gets cold and a bit wet, she'd come back. And then when you phoned, suggesting we go to Aunt Lilleth's, I was glad to get out of there. Freda was crying because of all the shouting and that started Molly off too. Glen and the boys rounded them up and took them off to the pictures and I just came down here to wait for you.' Jilly started to really cry now, trying to speak between her sobs. 'I didn't care about her.'

'Of course you did,' said Abbie, struggling to control her own tears, hating to see her strong, capable sister so stricken with guilt.

'No, I didn't want to be there when she came back. With her foul mood and temper. I wanted us all to be out, enjoying ourselves, so she would realise what she was missing out on. I wanted her to be sorry.'

Abbie leant over and held Jilly's hands tight in her own. 'Of course, you did. Of course, you wanted her to be sorry. She should be sorry for saying those things. But that's all Jilly, you wanted her to be sorry, you weren't wishing anything bad on her.'

Jilly shook her head. 'No, I know. It's just that, you know, her walking out like that, with us all arguing. What if?'

Abbie knew exactly what her sister was saying. What if it were the last time she saw her daughter alive? How would she ever forgive herself?

'Well, we've flounced out on each other often enough after an argument,' she joked, realising immediately that it wasn't really funny.

Jilly looked at her through red and blotchy eyes, a sombre, reproachful look that said they should both be ashamed of that.

'She's a bright, intelligent girl, Jilly. She'll know what to do to keep herself safe. And she'll be found soon, you'll see, and she'll be back here before you know it.'

Chapter Thirty-One

Miriam poured herself a big mug of tea. She was
sitting at one of the tables in the tearoom, looking
out onto the sodden garden. The rain was torrential.
She wondered if this was what a monsoon was like.
Tropical downpours could cause serious damage
although it was doing a fair bit of it here. Heavy
raindrops were bouncing off the flowerbeds,
churning up the soil and depositing it on the path.
The tubs and hanging baskets were flooded and
water was pouring out of them, cascading down.

It was nearing five o'clock, but it was as dark as
an autumn evening. Miriam took her mug in both
hands, resting her elbows on the table and sipping as
she continued to stare, mesmerised by the
unrelenting sound of the rain drumming on the
windows. It wasn't surprising that hardly anyone had
been in today. Anyone would be mad to set out in
this weather unless they absolutely had to. Surely it
would stop soon, thought Miriam, not allowing
herself to consider the consequences of what might
happen if it didn't. People were already talking about
the river level being dangerously high and when
she'd taken Honey and Blossom to school that
morning, she'd overheard some of the mothers

talking about sandbags and moving precious items upstairs just in case.

The main road into this side of the village was already impassable and her friend Ellen had phoned earlier offering to pick the girls up and have them stay overnight with her which Miriam agreed to. It would be a very long journey all round the country lanes to pick them up from school and no guarantee that she would be able to get there even, or back again. Honey and Blossom would love a mid-week sleepover.

Miriam sipped her tea – she had no idea what time Alistair would be home, and she didn't care either. It was unlikely there would be any more customers now and she was enjoying some rare quiet time to herself – just to sit and think for a change.

She looked around at the empty tearoom, her stomach churning at the thought of having to pack everything up for good. She remembered back just over four years ago when they'd moved in. It was supposed to be a fresh start; a new place, a new home and two new baby girls on the way. The tearoom had been her idea a couple of years later. She missed being able to contribute financially and she liked the idea of working from home, just in the daytime hours. The tearoom had always been a secret dream of hers. She was a social person and loved the idea of being right in the heart of her local community. The pretty village of Kirkby Bridge in the Lake District was the perfect place for all these things. But it hadn't worked out quite like that.

Alistair had agreed with Miriam's suggestion that they build an extension to the house for the tearoom.

Being in the trade, it was obvious that he would carry out the work and Miriam went to great lengths to explain what she wanted. Their home, The White House, was late Victorian and she imagined a small, cosy and intimate tearoom in keeping with the style of the house, perhaps with a small fireplace and tiled floor. But as was typical of Alistair, he stopped listening, thinking he knew better. Once the building works started, Miriam was dismayed to see a huge square block of a room being built, stark and characterless. And at that point it was too late to do anything about it.

Even the naming of the tearoom had gone wrong. Miriam had had many ideas for it from the simple 'Kirkby Bridge Café' to what she considered might be too simplistic 'The Tea Room' and had even toyed with 'Miriam's Parlour' but as Alistair suggested, that one might give out the wrong idea. Miriam smiled now, remembering that they had actually laughed at that together. But her smile disappeared as she also remembered what had happened next.

It was the girls' second birthday and Miriam had taken them to the local swimming pool, partly as a treat and also to get them all out of the way while the tearoom was having its final coat of paint inside. She was planning to open in a couple of weeks. When she returned home, her heart sank at the sight that met her. Alistair had wanted to surprise her, but it was much more of a shock and she wished he'd just left things alone. She'd got out of the car and looked up at the sign that ran along the top of the new building, painted in yellow and white, it read 'The

Honey-Blossom Tearoom.' Alistair was so pleased with himself. He was convinced that their daughters would love to see their names painted up like that - as soon as they were able to read, of course, and Miriam didn't have the heart to tell him that actually she thought it was rather crass. And while Honey and Blossom may well love it when they were toddlers, at the ages of six and seven, she was pretty sure they wouldn't by the time they got to be teenagers.

What a strange thought - her twin baby girls becoming teenagers. It was a lifetime away, a fact that Miriam was extremely grateful for at this moment. And who knew where they would all be by then? She sighed now, brought back to the present by a strange creaking noise coming from the trees in the front garden. The wind was picking up and Miriam stood close to the window, looking out. The strength of the wind was swaying the old solid oaks, flipping them about like a group of daffodils in the breeze. The largest and probably the oldest one was leaning and cracking rather worryingly.

The idea of selling the family home still saddened her and she inwardly hoped it might not come to that but if it did, one thing she was absolutely sure of, was that she would not be returning to London. She was determined to keep her girls in the Lake District for their childhood; they were thriving here. And if Alistair dug his heels in then he would have to go alone. Perhaps she ought to be braver and just sell up and have done with. Alistair was never going to change.

Much further away from the village, Eva was looking out the window too. She stood at the kitchen sink, peering out to the distant hills, their outlines hazy and distorted by the rain. Eva thought, a number of times that she'd seen Lilleth emerging out of the misty landscape, but it was only her eyes playing tricks on her, or maybe wishful thinking. Where on earth could she have got to? And in weather like this.

Eva thought back to their terrible argument that morning and fingered the loose skin at her neck, a nervous habit of hers. But then she snapped the curtains shut on the darkening sky outside, thinking bitterly that Lilleth was most likely perfectly fine, cosy and warm by a friend's fireplace enjoying the fact that she was causing Eva to worry. Yes, that would be typical of her, concluded Eva, determined not to give any further thought to it this evening. If Lilleth wanted to play games – let her, she wasn't going to give her the satisfaction of joining in.

Eva sat in front of the fire and turned the television up loud; something that always annoyed Lilleth. And she thought, with definitive satisfaction, that she probably wouldn't even hear the phone if it rang for whatever reason.

Chapter Thirty-Two

Jilly's two stepsons had taken themselves off to their room some time ago so that she could try to settle Freda and Molly in their beds. She guessed they were probably a little relieved to be able to escape the tense atmosphere of the family room although they both said they wouldn't be able to sleep until they heard that Chloe had been found.

Jilly moved the cot over to the corner of the room and turned off the nearby lights, leaving the room in almost darkness apart from one bedside wall-light. It was Glen's turn for a break. He said he wanted to go for a walk and the look of alarmed concern on Jilly's face had caused him to snap.

'I am capable of looking after myself!' He regretted his words immediately. With their eldest daughter lost somewhere in the vast countryside, in such treacherous weather and the night closing in, of course Jilly would want to keep the rest of her family close by. He bent down and kissed her gently on the forehead. 'I'll be fine, I'm just going to have a walk around outside. I'm not going far. Don't worry.' He squeezed Jilly's shoulder and let himself quietly out of the room.

Abbie and Jilly were sitting on the bed, the dim light of the wall-lamp casting a deceptive cosy glow over them.

'He'd probably love to down half a bottle of brandy,' said Jilly. 'Come to think of it, so would I.'

Abbie smiled reassuringly. 'You'll be enjoying a celebratory drink soon, you'll see.'

Jilly nodded and looked down, her hand smoothed the duvet cover, back and forth as she swallowed hard, forcing back the tears. Abbie sensed her sister's need to have her there and was very glad of it. She was surprised to realise how well tuned-in she was to her elder sister's emotions, and it felt reassuringly good. She shifted a little further onto the bed and tucked her legs underneath her and Jilly took this to mean that she was content to stay for a while longer and also made herself more comfortable.

'This isn't the first time, you know,' she said. Abbie nodded for her to continue.

'She's run away before. The first time was a couple of years ago. She wanted to go to some party with some older girl friends. She was only fourteen and obviously there was going to be alcohol there and she could only say that she 'thought' the parents would be there.'

'Which meant they wouldn't be?'

'Mm.' Jilly nodded.

'So, what happened? You didn't let her go, I take it?'

'No, we didn't. We just said no and thought that was it. I peeked my head around her bedroom door just before I went to bed and she wasn't there. I knew instantly where she'd gone. She was furious at

242

not being allowed to go but I didn't, for one second, think she would dare leave the house. She was just fourteen. I didn't expect to have to deal with things like that back then.'

'What did you do? Go and fetch her home, pronto?'

'No, we couldn't. We didn't know where the party was for a start. I just about remembered the girl's name but not her surname – I didn't even know who to ask, she wasn't from Chloe's school. So, I phoned some of Chloe's friends - even though it was the middle of the night.' Jilly cringed with guilt. 'No-one knew anything of any help. We called the police and left messages on her mobile – everything from telling her to get herself home to pleading with her to let us know she was OK.'

Abbie listened, shocked. She was shocked that her niece at only fourteen could have put her parents through such an ordeal but shocked too that this had all happened over two years ago and she had never known anything about it.

'How did you find her?'

'She made a call, in the early hours. Cocky as anything she was.' Abbie was amazed to see her sister smiling, amused almost.

'She said she was having a great time and might just pop home at some point to collect some of her things.'

'Do you think she'd been drinking?'

'Definitely. That was what had given her the courage to phone and speak to me like that. Anyway, the police traced her mobile phone signal and found her, thank God.'

'Crikey, Jilly! You must have been going mad with worry. What am I saying, I'm sorry; you're going mad with worry now.'

'It's OK.' Jilly reached out and squeezed Abbie's hand. 'Yes, I was going mad. And I was so angry with her for putting us all through that and then at the same time, so happy to have her home safe. Such a mixture of emotions; it's a wonder I didn't lose it completely.'

'And you said there've been other times too?'

'Yes, similar sorts of things. When she can't do what she wants – she gets frustrated and just takes off.'

Abbie suddenly had an insight into what it might be like as a mother in Jilly's shoes. She felt an almighty anger towards Chloe for the terrible anguish she was bringing to her whole family; spoiling their holiday, calling the mountain rescue team out. But at the same time, she couldn't even allow her mind to go anywhere near the awful thoughts of what might have happened to her and where she might be now.

'Why didn't you tell me any of this before?' Abbie asked gently.

Jilly smiled. She knew this question was coming and she was ready to explain. They both knew it was much more than just not being very close, or not having the time to talk properly. They realised, in that moment, without needing to actually say it, that they hardly knew anything about each other's lives at all. They also realised that they wanted to. Jilly took a deep breath.

'You always thought I had a perfect life, didn't you?'

Abbie bristled. Already she'd reverted back to taking Jilly's comments as criticism. It was true; she'd always thought that Jilly had a perfect life but she said nothing now and let her sister continue.

'It's OK. I wanted you to think that. Not just you. A lot of other people too, but particularly you, I suppose.'

'But why?'

Jilly sighed deeply. 'Oh, I don't know. You want everyone to think you've got it all together, living a successful, happy life. I didn't want to admit that I didn't.'

'But don't you?' Said Abbie, finally feeling OK to say what she felt without being defensive or provocative. 'I can see you've had some tough times with Chloe but from the outside looking in, it looks like you have an ideal life; the big family and your lovely home.'

'It's not quite how it was supposed to be.' Jilly looked thoughtful as if she was trying to decide how far to go back. 'One minute life was easy, me and Glen and the two girls. I was kind of getting broody for another baby and then suddenly I was expecting – at the same time George and Joe came to us. Suddenly, we have five children to look after – in a three-bedroom house.'

'That can't be easy,' said Abbie, a little embarrassed that until now, she had never even considered the logistics of how Jilly's large family all fitted into their home.

245

'No, we need to move to somewhere bigger. We were looking a while ago.' Jilly broke off mid-sentence and Abbie guessed the reason immediately.

'Until I changed my mind about selling Gran's place?'

Jilly nodded, feeling a little embarrassed. She hadn't meant to bring that up.

'You were *relying* on that money to move?' Abbie was stunned. She was struggling to find a polite way of saying that she thought her sister was rolling in it. But Jilly must have sensed what she was thinking.

'Glen's work isn't doing too well. All the execs have taken a pay cut and that was two years ago. With seven of us to feed, the two boys at university and so it goes on.'

Abbie sighed. 'Jilly, I had no idea you were struggling.' Abbie looked totally distraught and now Jilly felt guilty.

'Oh, don't look at me like that. Our problems are the same as hundreds of others. We'll be alright. And anyway, you're the same; keeping everything to yourself, pretending to think nothing of upping yourself and moving hundreds of miles away.'

'Oh, here we go,' said Abbie. 'You're going to start on me now.' They both laughed, trying not to be too loud in case they woke Freda and Molly. It was a surreal moment; to be laughing at such a time. And to be able to joke together, tease each other and not feel defensive about it. Jilly held her hand out and Abbie reached out to hold it tight. They stared at their entwined fingers for several silent moments.

'Do you miss Jack?' Jilly asked suddenly.

'Yeah. Every day. I still love him.' Abbie was surprised by her words but knew them to be true although the tone of her voice declared she felt she'd lost her chance with him.

'You never know – you could get back together,' said Jilly hopefully. 'Have you spoken with him?'

'He phoned a few weeks ago and we had a nice talk but it's a funny thing; I keep thinking I see him – around here. That's just weird, isn't it? I think I'm losing my mind.'

'Hm, he's obviously *on* your mind a lot. He wouldn't come all the way up here without letting you know, surely?'

'No. It couldn't be him. It's just me, being stupid.'

They both jumped as the door opened and Glen walked in. Jilly almost fell off the bed to get to him.

'Have you heard anything?' she asked, speaking quietly as Freda stirred and fidgeted a little. Glen shook his head, dragging his fingers through his hair. He refused to be defeated.

'I want to be out there, looking for her with them.'

'We have to take their advice,' said Jilly trying to calm her husband and leading him into the room, away from the sleeping girls. 'They say it's best for us to wait here. I know it's hard, but we have to trust in them.'

Abbie didn't imagine that Jilly or Glen would get a wink of sleep that night, but she thought they might need some time alone.

'I'm going to head off,' she whispered, picking up her bag and mac and tiptoeing across the room. Jilly followed her to the door, hugged her and kissed her on the cheek, tears trickling down her own once again.

'I know I don't need to say it but call me when....'

'I will. As soon as we hear.'

Abbie stepped outside the room into the hotel corridor and put on her mac, feeling suddenly exhausted and dreading the drive home in the dark and awful weather. She shivered as she ran across the car park, the wind driving the rain at all angles, thinking of poor Chloe. Abbie threw herself inside the car, impatient to get to the safety of her own home but despite her impatience she drove slowly, struggling to see in the dark with the rain still lashing down relentlessly.

Finally, back in her own kitchen, she was relieved to be home, removing her wet things yet again. It was the first time she'd thought of it as home. She looked around the small cosy room scattered with items she'd bought including a glass light-shade to cover the starkness of the bare bulb which sent rays of soft light about the room. Luisa came down the stairs into the kitchen.

'Hi, I'm sorry, did I wake you?' asked Abbie.

'No, I was just reading. I take it there's no news?'

'No, nothing. The rescue team's out on the hills looking for her.'

'How is she, and Glen?'

Abbie shrugged. 'You know, living on their nerves. Trying to keep calm for the children's sake

248

but going frantic with worry. The weather's so awful; I can't believe the rain out there.'

'I know. I don't think I'd be able to sleep even if I wanted to. Are you hungry Abbie?'

'No, I'm fine thanks. I'd love a huge glass of wine but I'd better not in case I'm needed for something.'

'Settle for hot chocolate?'

'Lovely.' Abbie reached down into the fridge for milk and saw two wrapped packages inside. 'What's this in here?'

'Oh, I didn't feel like eating after you left so I wrapped the fish and chips up – thought perhaps we could re-heat them later.'

'That sounds disgusting. And most unlike you. Although they'll probably taste delicious.' They smiled and made hot chocolate together.

It felt weird, thought Abbie, to carry on with normal activities but what else could they do?

They sat in the living room, sipping their drinks. The sound of rain was everywhere; on the roof, the windows, the garden path and the road. It wasn't cosy and comforting like it could be sometimes – it was deafening in its relentless monotony, scary even. When would it ever stop?

Chapter Thirty-Three

Abbie's mobile jolted her awake in the early hours; the melodious harp music of the ringtone belying the terrible news she might be about to hear. It was Jilly calling and her mind was frantic as she fumbled with the buttons.

'Hello?' she spoke quietly, with dread.

'Abbie, it's me! They've found her! She's OK, safe and back with us.'

Abbie could have wept with relief. Jilly was out of breath with laughing and crying all at the same time, jubilant that the nightmare was over.

'Thank God, Jilly, thank God. Where are you?'

'We're at the hospital, me and Glen. They're just checking Chloe over to be on the safe side but she's fine. She just wants to come home.' At this Jilly completely broke down. Abbie could hear her muffled sobbing and then Glen came to the phone.

'Hi Abbie, it's OK. Jilly's OK; she's crying happy tears.'

'I'm sure they are – thank goodness she's back safe.'

'Yep, she's just getting checked by the doctors and then we should be able to head back to the hotel.'

'That's great. If you need anything, Glen, just let me know.'

'I will. Cheers, Abbie. We'll see you tomorrow.'

Abbie rang off. They didn't need to speak any more tonight. Chloe was safe, that was all that mattered. There was a timid knock on her door and Luisa popped her head inside.

'I heard your phone go. I'm thinking it's good news?'

Abbie was in tears now, only able to nod confirmation as Luisa went over to the bed and gave her friend a big tight hug. After a few moments, Abbie pulled away, smiling through her tears.

'Blimey, what a night!'

'What a day. I'm looking forward to getting back home for a rest!'

'Yeah, you're right. I think I'll come with you. I know what – I'm not going to be able to get back to sleep.'

'How about micro-waved fish and chips and a bottle of white to celebrate?'

'Brilliant idea.'

Back down in the kitchen, Luisa heated the food while Abbie filled glasses with chilled white wine. She was deliriously happy; for herself, for Jilly and her family. Taking a sip of wine, she sent up a silent prayer of thanks and a promise too that she would never take her family or friends for granted again.

Jilly and Glen with Chloe let themselves into their hotel room. The twins were playing cards under a solitary table lamp. Silently they both got up, going over to their step-sister and giving her a quick hug.

251

Chloe was barely able to look at them, she kept her tear-stained eyes averted grateful for the silence, knowing the time would come for talking. George and Joe went back to their own room and Glen almost fell down into the armchair, resting his head back against the wall. Jilly didn't think she'd ever seen him so worn out. She took a couple of miniature bottles of brandy out of the mini bar and poured them both into a glass for him. Chloe took herself off to change in the bathroom.

Glen leaned forward in the chair, cradling the glass in his hands. Jilly was kneeling at his feet, her head raised to his. He kissed her on the forehead, the nose, and the lips. She could taste his brandy and helped herself to a sip from the glass he was holding. They smiled; no words were necessary. It was all going to be OK.

Chloe came back into the room in her t-shirt nightdress and sat on the end of the empty bed awaiting instructions. She was still there when Jilly re-appeared from the bathroom ready for bed.

'Dad's fallen asleep,' Chloe whispered, looking over to her father in the armchair. Jilly took a blanket from the cupboard and gently draped it over him, tucking in the sides making sure he would be warm. Chloe moved over towards her bed with Freda in it, but Jilly called her back.

'Come here, young lady,' she whispered. 'I'm not letting you out of my sight tonight,' she smiled widely to make sure Chloe understood that she wasn't reprimanding her. Not tonight anyway.

Jilly got into bed and pulled the covers back for Chloe to climb in beside her. She snuggled up close to her mother and Jilly wrapped her arms tight around her daughter, almost unable to believe she was back safe and sound with them. They lay awake for some time, taking comfort in each other's steady breathing and familiar scent and although neither of them was aware, they both cried silent tears, in the darkness, of both relief and happiness.

Chapter Thirty-Four

Luisa was still fast asleep on the settee with a fleecy throw over her. She and Abbie had talked over reheated fish and chips and a bottle of wine until it had started to get light outside and then they had both fallen asleep where they were. Abbie unfolded her stiff limbs from the armchair. Instinctively she could tell it was early and a glance at the clock confirmed it was almost seven o'clock.

But something wasn't right. Abbie held her fuddled head in her hands. After the dramatic events of the last twenty-four hours together with a weird night of joyous good news and not much sleep, not to mention the dodgy fish and chips and drinking wine at four o'clock in the morning, Abbie could understand that she didn't feel quite with it, but there was something else. Noises from outside; voices she couldn't identify, and what was that - running water?

She ran upstairs to look from her bedroom window and pulled the curtains apart, immediately drawn to a commotion at the bottom of the hill down by the B & B. Something didn't look right, something was missing. The bridge! The little humped bridge that crossed the river had completely disappeared. It was as if it had never been there. The boundary of the river itself was no longer visible, everywhere was flooding. Abbie pulled the lacy curtain right back for a better view, she squinted into the distance unable to make sense of what was before her.

The whole area directly outside the B & B and the car park outside The Green Man Pub was submerged in several feet of water. The chip shop owners, husband and wife, were half-heartedly baling water from their property. Sandbags were stacked up several feet high across their doorway and every now and then they would stop and look out hopelessly on the scene before them.

People were wading around as quickly as they could manage but it was evident to see that it wasn't possible to work quickly when thigh deep in water. Abbie could see Mrs Kelly from the bakery and Tony the pub landlord; they were banging frantically on the door of the B & B. Immediately Abbie had visions of Mrs Gilbert in her flooded cellar trying to bale it out on her own – she wouldn't be able to cope with things on this scale.

It was only then that Abbie noticed the torrent of water rushing down the road right in front of the cottage garden, taking branches and even small trees with it and what looked like pieces of fence panels among other debris that she couldn't identify. She gasped, staring at the dirty sludge of water surging forcefully downhill, unable to take it in, and looked back again to the bottom of the hill, wondering if the people there had any idea of what was coming their way.

Abbie dashed from the window; she needed to get out and help. But all of a sudden, she caught sight of

Miriam's house, far enough up the hill to be out of danger of being flooded but – Abbie clapped her hand to her mouth – the huge oak tree that had stood, pride of place, in the front garden had crashed through the tearoom roof and was leaning precariously against the house. It had smashed through the name sign which was lying in splinters all over the ground. Abbie thought of Miriam and the little girls inside. She ran from the window, calling out as she flew down the stairs.

'Luisa! Luisa, we need to go and help.'

As she ran into the living room, she was amazed to see Luisa, still groggy from sleep, lift her head questioningly from the cushion.

'What's with all the noise?' she muttered, obviously oblivious to everything going on outside.

Abbie glanced at the clock, realising that she'd awoken only minutes before but how long had her neighbours and friends been struggling in the storm while they'd been sleeping? The scene at Miriam's house came into her mind and with it the terrible thought that she and her family could be trapped inside.

'Come on,' she called across the room to Luisa. 'We have to get dressed and get outside to help.'

Luisa hauled herself upright. 'What's going on? What's happened?' The last she remembered was that Chloe had been found, safe and well, and a few hours ago, she and Abbie had been celebrating.

Abbie was about to run back upstairs but turned now in the doorway, impatient for Luisa to get a move on.

'The village is flooding.' She pointed at the window. 'Down there, at the bottom of the hill, it's all flooded. The river's burst its banks, the bridge has been swept away and everyone's up to their knees in water. Come on, we have to go and help.'

Abbie disappeared into the kitchen and upstairs and Luisa scrambled to her feet to follow. The rain was hammering incessantly against the windows and she pulled back the curtain to look. It was coming down so heavy, it appeared as a fog of water. The front lawn was sodden, more mud now than grass. The flowers that Abbie had planted in tubs looked as if they'd been trampled and water was cascading down from the hanging baskets. Luisa dashed from the room and ran upstairs to get dressed as quickly as she could, her thoughts turning to tiny Mrs Gilbert and her flooded cellar. If it had rained like this all night, it wouldn't only be the cellar that was flooded.

Chapter Thirty-Five

Eva lay in bed in her room at the back of the cottage. She'd been awake for a while but lay there waiting for the familiar noises of her sister brewing their first cup of tea of the day, before making breakfast. Eva could hear the rain hammering the window; on a day like today it would probably be porridge. She looked at the bedside clock – seven fifteen. Lilleth was usually up by now. Was she still angry after yesterday, Eva wondered? Perhaps she was making a point by not making the tea.

Muttering under her breath and feeling slightly outraged by the inconvenience, she flung the bedclothes back and carefully swung her long rickety legs off the side of the bed to sit up. She took her dressing gown from the end of the bed and put it on, feeling a damp chill in the air, so unusual for this time of year. She stepped into her slippers and went through the living room into the kitchen. It looked like nothing had been moved since last night and it felt eerie being there on her own at that time of day. She banged the kettle on the cooker just to cover up the uncomfortable silence, and made a big fuss of lighting the gas, talking to herself and then humming a silly tune to try to create a semblance of normality.

Lilleth's bedroom was along a short narrow hallway off the back of the kitchen and Eva spoke a little louder now, hoping for some sort of response. 'I'm making tea Lilleth,' she said. There was no reply, but Eva ignored the moment and continued setting the table with cups and saucers and for some reason she took the best china teapot from the dresser and placed it on the table. She was blocking her thoughts, refusing to think further than a few seconds ahead, concentrating only on what she was doing at that particular moment. 'Porridge? Or eggs?' she called out, knowing instinctively that there would be no answer. Eva continued making the tea; meticulously warming the pot just the way Lilleth did, spooning in the loose leaves, pouring on the hot water, stirring, lid on, tea-cosy on and leave for two minutes.

Only when she had poured two cups, added sugar and milk and set them at either side of the table, did she look towards the little hallway that lead to Lilleth's bedroom. She just stood there, and the thought occurred to her that in the two years she has lived there, she has never been the first to get up and make breakfast for them both.

It all started when she had a nasty fall a couple of winters ago. She slipped on ice, her legs all over the place like Bambi and bruised her hip badly. It was incredibly painful and took an awful long time to heal. Lilleth had taken her in and cared for her. Eva had been bed-ridden for the first couple of weeks and then she managed to get herself to the sofa each day but not much further than that. She thought back, feeling a little guilty now, that perhaps she hadn't helped her own recovery as much as she could have. Lilleth had done everything for her; the cooking, washing, the housework and gardening and Eva had just let her.

She could feel the heat in her red, shamed cheeks. She held her face in her hands; aware that she hadn't even *said* thank-you let alone attempted to return Lilleth's kindness in any way. She lowered her hands and took a deep steadying breath before marching towards Lilleth's bedroom, telling herself on the way that she was probably just enjoying a rare lie-in.

She knocked gently and slowly pushed the door open. The curtains were drawn, and the bed was made. Instinctively Eva tried to reassure herself that Lilleth might have gone out extra early that morning. But then she saw her handbag on the chair by the door; she rarely went anywhere without it and then she looked out the window – who would choose to go out in treacherous weather like that? Eva closed the bedroom door gently, trying to arrange her wild thoughts into some sort of sensible order that would allow her to keep calm.

But the overwhelming thought was that Lilleth had indeed gone out in yesterday's storm and hadn't come home all night. Lilleth had walked out of her home after having been pushed beyond her limit by the terrible things she'd said to her. Of course, Lilleth could have stayed with friends overnight – they knew plenty of people who would have put her up. But Eva knew in her heart that Lilleth wouldn't want to do that. She wouldn't choose to stay away without fresh clothes and the like. She would want to get back to her own bed. Eva paced the kitchen and then went through to the living room, looking around as if expecting to find a clue as to what she should do next.

The silence was unbearable. The cottage was often quiet; peaceful with the two of them doing their own thing; reading or sewing, baking or doing a crossword. But this was a different silence; loaded with worry and foreboding. Eva flicked the television on, just for the company of voices and went back into the kitchen. She would drink her cup of tea and think of a plan of action. Jed would be the first person to contact, she decided, he would know what to do, and this thought lifted her spirits slightly. But then a voice from the television paralysed her. It was the local news and she heard the reporter speak of atrocious weather in the village of Kirkby Bridge, serious local flooding and at least one fatality – an elderly lady had been found drowned.

Eva stumbled through to the living room, her shaking legs threatening to give way completely. She fell into the armchair and stared at the TV desperate for more information, and yet too scared to listen.

'Mrs Gilbert, seventy-six years old, proprietor of the local Bed and Breakfast drowned in the cellar which had been completely flooded,' said the news reporter, brisk and efficient, standing in the rain under a huge umbrella with the rain lashing sideways at her.

Eva crumpled in her seat, her face in her hands. 'Thank God, thank God,' she whispered, aware that her relief was due to someone else's terrible loss. And poor Mrs Gilbert – Eva acknowledged her guilt at being relieved that it was Mrs Gilbert who had died and not her own sister. She also acknowledged the complete devastation she'd felt, in that moment, when she'd thought she had lost her Lilleth. And now she must find her.

The news bulletin ended, with shocking images of Kirkby Bridge, its high street a mass of swirling water, the river having burst its banks. They even had footage of the little bridge crumbling and being swept away as if it was made of cardboard. Eva stood, on still wobbly legs, and went into the kitchen. She stood at the table and quickly drank her tea, praying that Lilleth had made it to Jed's place and stayed there, safe and sound, for the night.

Back in the living room she picked up the telephone receiver but there was no dialling tone. She tapped the connection button several times but still nothing. As Eva replaced the phone, she breathed a gentle sigh trying to remain calm in the face of the knowledge that she was completely cut off in a very remote part of the countryside. She closed her eyes remembering conversations with Lilleth who'd suggested many times that they get a mobile phone each. Just for emergencies. Eva had stomped all over the idea as utter nonsense but now how she wished she hadn't been so stubbornly argumentative.

Eva dragged a chair out and sat down heavily. At this moment she wished she'd done a lot of things very differently.

Chapter Thirty-Six

Abbie dressed in minutes and met Luisa in the kitchen where they were pulling on their boots and waterproofs. She unlocked the door, pulling up her hood as she stepped outside, realising immediately that her outdoor wear wasn't going to do much to protect her from the atrocious weather. Running down the garden path with Luisa close behind, they were aware of the sound of their footsteps slapping on the surface water. Visibility was good for only a few feet ahead, but they knew where they were going, turning left out of the garden and running as fast as they dared down the hill.

As they got closer, they could make out the glow of fluorescent jackets belonging to various rescue and emergency service workers. They were calling out, guiding residents and helpers away from the area, encouraging them back up the hill towards safety. But people were milling around, dazed and unsure where to go.

They were level now with Miriam's house on the opposite side of the road and looked across at the huge oak tree leaning precariously against the tearoom roof. There was no sign of anyone around and Abbie had a sudden terrible vision of Miriam injured inside and her little daughters unable to summon help.

She turned to Luisa who was close behind and called out. 'Invite these people back up to the cottage. Get the stack of tables out and make them some tea or something. Do you mind?'

'Of course not. Where are you going?'

'Across the road here, this is Miriam's house, she's got two young children. I want to make sure they're all OK.'

Luisa nodded in agreement. Already she was speaking to people who were trudging up the hill towards her, directing them up to Winnifred Cottage offering shelter, warmth and a cup of tea. She walked on ahead, encouraging them to follow.

Abbie ran across the road and into the garden of The Honey-Blossom Tearoom or what was left of it. Two sets of French doors were smashed; woodwork and glass were splintered everywhere. She made her way carefully around to the front of the house, looking in the windows as she went for signs of life. At the front door, she knocked loudly already thinking ahead to what her next move should be if there was no answer. But there was no need; Miriam opened the door wide and beckoned her inside.

'Come in, come in. My goodness, you look half drowned.'

'Miriam, thank God you're alright.' In contrast to the panic and mayhem that was going on outside, Miriam was perfectly composed. Abbie paused for a moment, wondering if it could be possible that Miriam was unaware that a huge oak tree had fallen on her house. 'I was worried someone might have been hurt - by the tree?'

'No, no, we're all fine,' said Miriam as Abbie breathed a sigh of relief that she didn't have to break the awful news, although Miriam did sound a little odd, resigned, complacent even.

'Thank goodness for that.'

'Yes, thank goodness. So many roads were flooded yesterday, I wasn't sure if I'd be able to pick the girls up from school yesterday and then a friend offered to take them back with her for the night.'

Abbie nodded. 'But your poor tearoom, it's been destroyed.'

Miriam shrugged her shoulders as she turned and walked across the hall to the doorway leading into the tearoom. Abbie followed, conscious of her dripping clothes but sensing that this, together with the tree in the roof, was not something of concern to Miriam. They stood in the doorway looking in and actually it didn't look so bad from this side. The French doors were broken but ironically the tree was sheltering the openings from the worst of the rain.

'The structure looks to be sound,' said Abbie questioning herself for coming out with such gibberish nonsense. What did she know about building structures? Probably not as much as a builder's wife. 'I mean, it might not be too much of a big job to put it right.'

Miriam shrugged again. 'It doesn't matter now anyway. I've just found out Alistair's sold the house. We're going to have to move out.'

'Oh Miriam, I'm so sorry. But, can he do that? Without your permission?'

Miriam sighed. 'No, not entirely. But he'd had the house valued without my knowledge and even put it on the market, and now someone's interested in looking around. We can't afford to keep it apparently, and so there's no point in me fighting it. We'll just have to get somewhere smaller.'

'Will anyone want to buy it like that?' said Abbie, indicating the wrecked tearoom.

'I don't think it's as bad as it looks. I'm not sure if it's covered under the insurance, and if not, Alistair will just have to put it right. He's arranged for a builder friend of his to come here later today; he's got professional lifting gear to remove the tree and then secure the building. And I don't think anyone will be dropping by for a cup of tea today, do you?' said Miriam putting on a brave smile.

Abbie shook her head and smiled back. She wondered if Alistair was somewhere in the house and avoiding her although she was getting the impression Miriam was dealing with most of this on her own.

'Well, I just came by to see if you needed any help, but I've really got to get back.' Abbie led the way through the hall to the front door. She turned to Miriam. 'You are lucky, you know, that no-one was hurt, and we're both lucky living further up here. It's chaos at the bottom, the river's burst and people's homes have been flooded.'

Miriam was shocked. 'I had no idea. The rain, it's been terrible. The ground was so sodden, and I was worried about the trees but after that one came down, I looked around and everyone else seemed to be OK. Where are you going now? Back down the hill to help?' They had the front door open and Miriam was craning her neck, concerned to see what was happening.

'No, I'm going back to the cottage. We're making cups of tea for people who've been flooded, just to give them a breather. I've left Luisa on her own, I really must get back.'

'Let me come, let me help,' said Miriam immediately. She didn't wait for an answer but grabbed her raincoat from the cupboard and putting it on, she dashed into the tearoom, collecting giant bags of bread rolls and a catering size box of tea bags. 'Let's load up the car with this stuff, there's no point in leaving it here,' she said.

Abbie and Miriam made several quick trips from the tearoom to the car, filling it with home-made cakes, scones, a huge tub of butter, jams and cream. And at the last minute, Miriam thought to bring a box of mugs. Soaked through, they flung themselves onto the front seats and Miriam drove away from The White House up to Winnifred Cottage.

Chapter Thirty-Seven

Eva put her heavy old Wellingtons on, her wax jacket and rain hat. She quickly put some things in the car for Lilleth; her warm winter coat, a couple of blankets and her handbag. They looked a crazy random mixture on the back seat, but she couldn't think straight. She couldn't even remember what Lilleth had been wearing yesterday.

She sat in the driver's seat and tentatively turned the key, relieved that it started straight away. Eva hadn't driven for years; neither she nor Lilleth enjoyed driving. Mostly they took the bus but when it couldn't be avoided, she always insisted that Lilleth do the driving because of her stiff hips but she had no choice now and it wasn't really a surprise to discover that she was absolutely fine. She was aiming for Jed's place – he would know what to do. Taking it slowly she drove along the narrow country lanes, praying all the way that Jed would be home and please God, let Lilleth be there too.

Eva bargained that if only Lilleth could be safe and unharmed, things would be different from now on. She'd be a better sister and show her gratitude to Lilleth for taking her in. She'd help out around the house much more, and financially too. And hopefully Lilleth would forgive her for all the terrible things she'd said yesterday. But could she ever be forgiven for hoarding a secret all those years, waiting for the moment when she could cause maximum hurt and damage. What on earth had she been thinking?

Jed stood in the living room of his cottage looking out the window at the rain. He couldn't recall ever seeing anything like it – except for 1958, of course. It had been the wettest summer he'd ever known, and it had actually prompted him to follow his dream of travelling around Europe. Jed smiled remembering how, as a young man, he'd anticipated gaining valuable life experiences as he basked in the warm climates of Italy and France, musing around the art galleries. He swiftly put plans in place and set off for his adventure. Would he have gone if he'd known what he would lose in exchange? He knew now that you didn't need to travel to find life experiences – they would always be right on your doorstep whether you wanted them or not.

He sighed deeply, looking out onto the muddy lane. The rain always reminded him of Annaliese. It had poured when they'd said good-bye at the train station. Raindrops had trickled down her pretty face and mingled with her tears as he assured her he'd only be gone a few weeks, that is if he could bear to be apart from her for that long.

Jed huffed another sigh and turned away from the window, cross with himself for getting melancholy about the past. He needed company or at least to get out of the cottage. What he really wanted to do was to go up to his studio and paint but even if he was able to run fast he'd be soaked by the time he got up there.

The swishing of car tyres on the muddy road brought him straight back to the window. He recognised immediately that it was Lilleth's car and was surprised and concerned that she was out in such terrible weather. He was also surprised when the door opened, and Eva climbed out. He didn't even know that she could drive. Instinctively he knew something was wrong and went to the front door, opening it ready for Eva to dash inside.

'Eva, what is it? What's wrong?' he asked, not even bothering to say 'hello'.

Eva's heart sank. She knew immediately that Lilleth wasn't there.

'Oh Jed. It's Lilleth. I don't suppose… have you seen her or heard from her today or yesterday? I'm so worried.'

'No, I haven't. What's happened?' Jed couldn't help his abruptness; he was worried about his dear friend.

'She went out yesterday, in the afternoon, into the storm. And she hasn't been back since. And there's been this terrible flooding everywhere, people drowning.'

'Now, now, slow down. Take it easy. Come on through Eva, let's get you settled, and you can tell me everything.'

Jed led the way into the kitchen with the intention of making tea but once he was there, he found he didn't have the patience. He pulled out a chair for Eva and sat down himself, giving her the cue to continue. 'She left yesterday afternoon, you say?'

'Yes, early afternoon it was.' Eva paused but knew she couldn't conceal anything. She had to be honest, now of all times. She took a deep breath. 'We'd had a terrible argument. About the past.' She paused, looking down at her hands, squeezed tightly together on the table. 'I said some terrible things,' she whispered. And then she covered her face with her hands. 'Dear God, forgive me,' she sobbed. 'What have I done?'

Jed stood and patted Eva on the shoulder. 'Come on now, this isn't going to help,' he said. Not being particularly familiar with female emotions, he was surprised at his ability to deal with the situation. And he'd always suspected there was a softness buried deep somewhere within Eva's hard as nails exterior. He placed the kettle on the stove; Eva needed time to compose herself and when she was a little calmer they could talk some more and plan where best to start looking.

Jed pottered about making the tea with his back to Eva as if to give her some privacy. She pulled a tissue from her pocket and dried her face, wiping her eyes roughly and blowing her nose. She felt much better and smiled weakly at Jed as he brought two mugs of tea to the table.

Jed was impatient to get out and start searching. He drank his tea standing up, pleased that Eva hadn't removed her coat – he didn't want her to get too settled. He paced the kitchen and was surprised when Eva stood, having hardly drunk any of her tea.

'We ought to get going Jed. Every minute that passes – well, I can't bear to think about it.'

'Yes, you're absolutely right.' Jed banged his mug down sloshing tea onto the old pine table. He'd never seen such concern from Eva for her sister, and now she was getting tearful again. He stroked her arm as gently as he could.

'Come on now, we need to be strong otherwise we're going to be of no use to anyone. Let me get my things on and you tell me all the places you think she might be.'

'I don't really know. I was hoping so much that she'd be here. I mean, we know everyone around – she could've maybe waited out the storm with anyone, I suppose.'

'Yes, that's probably it. That's what she's done and she's probably back home right now – wondering where you are.' Jed smiled, not terribly convinced by his effort to be positive.

'The thing is, Lilleth is a strong woman, she can look after herself. The only reason she'd be out this long is if something has happened. And what with all this terrible flooding. And I haven't even told you – poor Mrs Gilbert, she's been found dead. Drowned, she did, in her own home.'

Jed had pulled on his waterproof coat and looked up in shock.

'Kirkby Bridge is flooded?'

'Yes, it was on the local news. The river's burst its banks, even the old bridge has been totally swept away.'

'Abbie. Good Lord, I hope she's safe.'

'I'm sure she's fine Jed,' snapped Eva, the old irritation and impatience surfacing again, baffled as to why he was worrying about her long-distant great niece while Lilleth was out in the wilds somewhere.

Jed nodded but he remained resolute. 'We have to get over there – make sure she's safe. And you never know, maybe Lilleth has made her way over there too.' There were things he needed to explain to Eva but not right now. He suspected that Lilleth already knew but as always she could be relied on to be discreet.

'Yes OK, if you think so,' said Eva, buoyed up by Jed taking charge and relieved to be actually doing something constructive.

'We'll go in my Land Rover; it'll cope better if we come across any flooded roads.'

Chapter Thirty-Eight

Miriam was in Abbie's tiny kitchen opening tins of soup and pouring them into a large saucepan. She caught Abbie's eye. 'You like soup then?' she said, smirking.

Abbie shook her head non-commitally. 'We all do funny things at times.' She went to stand next to Miriam at the cooker. 'And what flavour is that one going to be?'

'It's mushroom with tomato and oxtail, spring and winter vegetables and a dash of mulligatawny for a bit of a kick!'

'Hmm.' Abbie peered over the saucepan, wrinkling her nose and pretending to disapprove. Actually, it smelled delicious.

'It'll taste fine,' confirmed Miriam. 'And it'll go further this way. At the end of the day everyone will just be grateful for something hot and tasty.'

Abbie smiled. 'I'll butter some more rolls.'

Luisa came into the kitchen. 'Crikey, it's filling up fast out there. I need to make more tea.'

Miriam moved aside so that Luisa could fill the kettle. 'I'll go back out to the car and bring the rest of the stuff in – looks like we're going to need it all.'

Jed drove slowly into the village of Kirkby Bridge. The rain had eased but water was still cascading down the road and just passed Winnifred Cottage the emergency services had completely blocked the way, as it wasn't safe for cars beyond that point.

'Perhaps we should call the police,' suggested Eva, hoping Jed would reassure her that it wasn't necessary yet.

'Let's ask around a bit, see if anyone's heard from her. We'll just give it a little more time, eh?'

Eva nodded but remained silent. They were both puzzled by the number of people trudging up the hill, heads down and pulling their coats tight to them, and heading up the path to Winnifred Cottage. They looked at each other with the same questioning look and shook their heads in unison. Jed parked his Land Rover up the little lane, close to the cottage.

'That's Miriam Walker's car,' said Eva as Jed switched off the engine. They climbed out to see Miriam at the back of her car, stacking boxes precariously in her arms.

'Are you both OK?' called out Miriam above the wind. 'Are you coming in for tea, it'll be a bit of a tight squeeze I'm afraid.'

'Yes, we're fine,' said Jed rather bewildered; the enormity of the devastation sinking in. 'Do you want a hand with those?'

'Oh yes please, thank-you. Go on get inside, I can manage with this last load.'

Eva and Jed let themselves inside. Eva was amazed at the transformation; the previously dull and dingy cottage had been transformed into a bright but cosy home. Jed was speechless; he hadn't been inside Winnifred Cottage for over fifty years and although it looked completely different, he was still overwhelmed with emotion and memories. He led the way through to the kitchen with Eva following mutely behind. They nodded in recognition of their neighbours and politely smiled at those they didn't know. A friendly atmosphere of togetherness permeated the cottage as people shuffled around to make room for others, listening for the first time to each other's stories and experiences that would no doubt be re-told again and again over the years.

Abbie came back into the kitchen with a tray of empty mugs and bowls to be washed up. News was gradually filtering through of what was happening further down the hill, of devastating damage to properties and people being rescued. On seeing Jed's familiar rugged face Abbie flung herself into his arms. Perhaps it was the emotion of the day but whatever it was, she felt an inexplicable sense of joy and relief that he was safe. Jed hugged her in return, albeit a little tentatively and awkwardly.

'Oh Jed, I've just heard about Mrs Gilbert. I can't believe it. It's just so awful.'

'I know, I know,' comforted Jed, patting her back.

Abbie pulled away, looking at Eva and then back to Jed. 'Where's Lilleth?'

Jed sighed and dragged his hand through his ruffled hair. 'We were hoping she'd be here with you. Have you heard from her?'

'No, nothing,' said Abbie, confused initially at how Eva could have lost her sister. And then she remembered. 'Oh my goodness, don't tell me she hasn't been back? Since yesterday?' Abbie clapped her hand to her mouth, gasping in shock. She looked at her aunt for answers, but Eva averted her eyes, which was all the confirmation Abbie needed to know that Lilleth had walked out into yesterday's terrible storm and was still out there somewhere.

'We need to call the police, or someone,' said Abbie frantically.

'I think all the emergency services will be stretched to the limit at the moment,' said Jed calmly, trying to think straight and plan what to do next. 'We don't know that she's in any trouble, she might just be sheltering with friends. The phone lines are down so she has no way of letting us know if she's OK.'

'I hope you're right,' said Abbie, staring at the dirty soup bowls and trying to bring her focus back to the task in hand. 'Would you both like a cup of tea or we have hot soup if you'd prefer?'

'No, no, thank-you. We are going to get out of your way, young lady. You're doing a grand job here helping all these people but we're fine and we're very lucky to have safe, dry homes to get to. We're going to drive around for a while, stop at some friends and find out if anyone's seen anything of Lilleth.'

'OK that's a good idea. Let me know as soon as you hear anything, won't you?'

'I will my dear. Now don't you worry. It'll all be fine.'

Miriam had been in and out and now returned with the last of the supplies from the car, weaving her way between groups of people standing around cradling hot mugs of tea in their hands.

'There's a white van just pulled up outside,' she called out to everyone. 'A white van waiting outside, is anyone expecting a lift?'

In the kitchen Abbie and Luisa locked eyes, speechless. They were washing and drying mugs and plates and soup bowls ready to be used again as Miriam appeared with a stack of boxes in her arms, unloading them onto the worktop.

'What sort of van Miriam?' asked Abbie as casually as she could.

Miriam shrugged. 'Sorry I don't know. Just a boxy white van. Oh, but with lots of dents in the side. Bit of a wreck actually.'

Abbie gaped at Luisa, her eyes agog. 'Do you think?' she whispered.

'Only one way to find out.'

Abbie pulled off her rubber gloves and almost jumped into her Wellingtons as she grabbed her mac and went out the kitchen door into the back garden. From there she ran around to the side of the cottage where she had a view of the lane. And right there parked behind Miriam's car was Jack's old van. He got out and stood there for a moment looking up at the cottage as if deliberating whether or not to go and knock on the door. And then he caught sight of her peeking at him from a distance. She ran towards him, smiling and tearful both at the same time.

'Jack, I'm so happy to see you. How comes you're here?'

He wrapped his arms around her tightly, enveloping her completely in his hug. 'I saw what was happening on the news. I had to come – make sure you were alright.'

'You came all this way just to make sure I was OK?'

'Of course, I did. I'd drive all the way up to Scotland if I had to.'

Abbie looked up into Jack's face, her own beaming a wide smile. He stroked her hair back and kissed her for a long time, in the rain. 'Listen, there's a couple of things I have to tell you,' he said.

Abbie laughed. 'Later, let's go inside before we get soaked through.'

'OK, but just one thing first. I have to say this, it's important for you to know. The fire report says that it was probably started by a faulty appliance; a bedside lamp.'

Abbie looked sheepish. 'The one with the dodgy switch you were always telling me to replace?'

'Yep, could be the same one,' said Jack smiling.

'What about the cigarette theory?'

'No idea. There's no mention of it in the report. I've got a copy of it here with me – you can read it yourself.'

Abbie was shaking her head. 'No, it's OK,' she said, although she was still rather confused.

'You know what, I reckon it was that stupid copper's fault. He probably heard something, someone guessing at what started the fire and thought he was being clever by repeating it. Stupid bastard.'

Abbie took Jack's hand in both of hers. 'I shouldn't have been so ready to doubt you. I had no reason to.'

279

'No, you didn't,' said Jack abruptly, but when Abbie looked into his face, he was grinning like a cheeky monkey. 'Don't do it again!'

'I won't. I promise,' she said, standing on tip-toe to kiss him on the cheek. 'Come on, let's go inside.' Abbie led him around to the back of the cottage. 'Are you staying up here tonight?'

'Is that an invitation?'

Abbie looked over her shoulder at him and smirked.

'Actually,' continued Jack, 'that leads me to the second thing I have to tell you.'

Chapter Thirty-Nine

Jed and Eva drove back out of the village. The rain was easing making visibility clearer as they both scanned the narrow lanes and wide, open countryside beyond. Not that either of them expected to see Lilleth wandering aimlessly around in the middle of nowhere but what else could they do but look?

Jed switched on the local radio station. They were providing regular news updates, keeping everyone informed of the latest weather and travel conditions. It had just been announced that the phones were back in service in Kirkby Bridge and the surrounding areas.

Back over in Flanders Way, they drove around for a couple of hours, calling in on neighbours and friends but no-one had seen anything of Lilleth.

'It's no good Jed. With just the two of us looking, we could be driving around all day and still only cover a tiny bit of this area.'

Jed drove on in silent agreement.

'Take me back home please Jed. I'm going to call the police. She's been gone for over twenty-four hours. I don't know if that counts as a missing person but I have to do something more than this.'

Jed nodded and drove on in the direction of Gordon Cottage. He parked close to the garden gate and unbuckled his seat belt.

'No Jed, there's no need. I'll be fine on my own. Thank-you for all your help. I'll phone you in a little while.'

Jed acknowledged Eva's request with a slight nod. He understood her need to be alone for a while. He turned in his seat and squeezed her shoulder. 'I'll wait for your call,' was all he said.

It was mid-afternoon, and Winnifred Cottage was emptying out. People who needed to had made arrangements to stay with family or friends. Others, more fortunate, had been given the all clear to return to their homes to start the clean-up process. Gradually they left, gathering their boots and waterproofs at the door, thanking Abbie and Luisa and Miriam for their hospitality. Only two elderly couples remained; they were neighbours who lived in the bungalows a little further down the hill. Their homes weren't in any real danger, but they'd been evacuated as a precaution. They seemed to be having a good chat together.

Miriam took them over the last of the scones and Abbie watched as she chatted patiently, relaxed and smiling. She was puzzled; this looked to be a completely different Miriam from the frosty lady she'd met when she first arrived. She had been on the go non-stop since arriving from The White House that morning and was still flitting around with endless energy.

'Come on you two,' called Miriam to Abbie and Luisa. 'The soup's all gone so we'll have to survive on apple strudel cake.'

The three women gathered together at the kitchen worktop, eating cake and drinking tea. 'Where's Jack, has he left already?' asked Luisa.

'No, he's outside. He said the van was making a strange noise on the way up and now that the rain's almost stopped, he's having a tinker under the bonnet.'

'So, what's the story?' asked Luisa cheekily. 'Is he staying here the night?'

'Well, actually he'd booked into the B & B.' All three fell silent as their thoughts turned to dear Mrs Gilbert and the tragedy that had happened only that morning, but which already seemed like ages ago. 'I'll ask him if he wants to stay,' confirmed Abbie although the fun had gone from the conversation.

They finished their tea and cake and then Luisa collected the plates and filled the sink for yet another round of washing up. Abbie was grateful, at last, for the opportunity of a quiet word with Miriam.

'We all did a good job this morning. Thanks so much for bringing all the food and everything from the tearoom.'

'It would all have gone to waste anyway. The tearoom won't be open for some time, if at all, and not by me anyway. And besides I was happy to help. It was good of you to open the door on your home.'

Abbie shrugged. 'It just seemed like the right thing to do at the time. Listen, if you want to get off, if you need to collect your girls – it's fine, we can finish up here.'

'Thanks, I'll help you clear up a little and then I will need to go; see if the tree man has arrived. And then I'm off to my friend Ellen's to stay there with the girls for the night. My poor parents phoned earlier when they saw what was happening on the news. They've offered to look after the girls for a few days, which will be a great help.'

Abbie had to ask. 'Is Alistair not around at the moment?'

Miriam smiled, paused and took a deep breath. 'We've decided to separate,' she announced, a little shocked at the sound of her words; it was the first time she'd spoken them out loud. But now Abbie didn't know what to say. It wasn't the moment to pipe up with the cliché that she'd be better off without him, and maybe she already knew that anyway. Miriam was a lovely lady whereas the little experience she'd had of Alistair Walker proved that he was hardly deserving of her. For a second she thought of telling Miriam about Alistair's behaviour towards her but decided that it would serve no helpful purpose.

'I'm sorry Miriam, that things haven't worked out for you.'

'Thanks Abbie,' she sighed deeply. 'I'm sure we'll be fine. Alistair is going back to London, but I'm determined to stay here with the girls. We'll work it out. Like I said, I'm staying at my friend's tonight and Mum and Dad have the girls for a few days so that'll give us the chance to talk things through. Anyway, I'm out of here. You've been listening to people's problems all day – the last thing you want is to have to listen to mine.'

Abbie grabbed her shoulder and gave it a squeeze. 'I'm happy to listen Miriam – anytime. I mean it. That's what friends are for. Just call me or pop over, if you need a chat, OK?'

Miriam was pulling on her coat. Watery eyed and struggling not to break down completely, she managed to whisper her thanks before leaving the cottage to go back home.

As Miriam went out, Jack came in. He went through to the kitchen where Abbie and Luisa were collecting the last of the crockery to be washed. The bungalow couples had finally gone and the place was eerily quiet and empty.

'Any chance of a cup of tea?' asked Jack. The two women gave him a look; a look they hoped conveyed the words 'You'll be lucky!'

'Right. I get it. You've both been making tea all day – I'll do it.'

They all laughed. And then Abbie turned to Luisa and sighed wearily. 'Oh Luisa, I'm sorry for all this. Your visit has been a disaster.'

'It's hardly your fault,' said Luisa, smiling, as she stacked the washing up next to the sink.

'No, but you know what I mean. We've hardly had any time together and you're going home tomorrow.'

'We've still got today,' said Luisa, conscious that neither of them had the energy or enthusiasm for doing much. 'Jack, are you heading back tomorrow? Could I catch a lift with you?'

'Afraid not; I'm planning to stay up here for a couple of days at least. Sorry.' Jack finished making

285

the tea as Abbie pulled a face at Luisa which said that this was news to her, albeit not unpleasant news.

'Not to worry,' said Luisa, giving Abbie a knowing look.

Jack placed two mugs of tea in front of them. 'You could come back with me Abbie, visit Luisa before she heads off to Finland. We'll have stuff to sort out anyway – with the house.'

'That's a great idea,' said Luisa. Abbie nodded in agreement although she was thinking more about what Jack had just said. What did they need to sort out?

Chapter Forty

Eva walked slowly and wearily up the garden path. She heard Jed turn his vehicle and drive away but didn't turn to wave to him. She walked into the kitchen, head down, turning to close the door, overwhelmed by her burden of guilt and shame. And possible loss but she wouldn't allow herself to think about that yet.

As Eva turned into the room, such was the shock, she had to grab the back of a chair to steady herself. Lilleth was standing at the stove, box of matches in one hand and the kettle in the other.

'Cup of tea?' she asked, pleasantly enough but unsmiling and sharing no emotion.

'Lilleth! My God, where have you been?' Eva rushed towards Lilleth but stopped abruptly, not knowing what to do. Lilleth turned away to place the kettle on the hob and light the gas.

'I got caught in the storm and found somewhere to shelter,' she said, knowing that wasn't really the answer to the question.

Eva dropped back and wearily removed her raincoat, flopping it over a chair. She'd imagined finding Lilleth would be a joyous relief; that they would both be happy to see each other. But Lilleth was obviously still angry and she had every right to be. 'I was worried about you.'

Her unusually quiet voice sounded sincere and Lilleth looked up in surprise. She nodded in acknowledgement. 'I was angry with you.'

'Yes, I know.' Eva didn't apologise. She knew there was plenty of time for that, but not at this moment. 'Are you hungry? You must be starving, let me make you something to eat.'

Lilleth smiled, amused. This was a turn up, being fussed over by her sister. 'I'm fine. I'm not hungry, just fancy a nice cup of tea.'

'Well, you sit down here.' Eva pulled out a chair. 'And I'll make it and I'll put a little extra something in, shall I?'

'Yes, OK.'

Eva flitted around, making tea and putting some of the special biscuits onto a plate. Lilleth sat there silently and finally Eva joined her, sitting opposite at the table.

'Where did you go?'

Lilleth smiled again. 'I was in the hay barn. Over at Granger's farm.'

'Oh Lilleth, that's awful.'

'No, it wasn't. It was heavenly. Better than being here with your constant moodiness.'

Eva looked down at the untouched biscuits. She didn't know what to say, and so avoided the comment. 'It can't have been very comfortable.'

'Actually, it was perfectly comfortable.' Lilleth relaxed a little; it was tiring giving Eva a hard time. 'At first, I just popped inside to shelter from the rain but then it just kept coming down, heavier and

288

heavier. I made myself comfy to sit it out, snuggled into some loose hay and before I knew it, I'd fallen asleep. The rain had eased by the time I awoke but do you know what Eva? I didn't want to come home. I wanted to stay in that little barn. Anyway, I walked the little way over to the farm shop, bought myself some milk and cheese and bread. It's lucky I have an account with them as I didn't have my handbag with me. And then I snuck back into their barn and decided to stay there the night. It was quite an adventure.'

Eva couldn't look her sister in the eye. 'You didn't want to come home. Because of me?'

Lilleth was silent.

'Oh Lilleth, I'm so very sorry for all those things I said. I wish to God that I could take them back.'

Lilleth nodded, as if to accept her apology.

'I thought I'd driven you into shock,' continued Eva. 'You just went quiet, you didn't say anything.'

'Eva, I already knew. Harry told me he was going to ask you to marry him and he told me when you refused him. He was very upset.'

Eva looked up now and almost gasped out loud.

'Of course, I would have preferred it if Harry had not asked my younger sister to marry him first, but we were so happy in the end, it didn't matter. I often wondered, over the years, if you regretted your decision and that's why I never said anything – and I never would have done – to spare your feelings. Neither of us mentioned it and I thought it was better that way.'

'I wanted to hurt you. I was so angry with you.'

'I know you were. What I don't understand is, why?'

Eva shook her head. 'I don't really know. Yes, I do. It was jealousy I suppose.'

Lilleth laughed. 'Of what?'

'You're always smiling, everybody loves you and they all think I'm the grouchy, bad-tempered sister.'

'Well, that's because you are!'

They both smiled now, Eva's watery, tear-filled eyes meeting Lilleth's smiling ones. Eva placed her hand over Lilleth's on the table; it was as near a loving physical gesture as she'd ever made. 'I was so worried I'd lost you,' she whispered.

Lilleth squeezed her sister's hand in return. 'There now, you don't get rid of me that easily. Come on, this isn't like you.'

'Good. I don't want to be like me. Lilleth, I'm so sorry for the way I've behaved. Not just yesterday. But for all the times.' Eva sniffed and took a tissue out of her skirt pocket, wiping her nose and taking a deep breath to continue. But Lilleth stopped her.

'Alright now,' she said gently, patting Eva's hand. 'This is over now. Let's put all this behind us.'

'Do you want me to move out?' asked Eva, alarmed.

'No, of course I don't. I'd miss you – maybe.' They both laughed. 'Let's start afresh shall we? No more of any nonsense.'

'Yes, we'll start afresh.'

'And meanwhile I'll make another cup of tea, with less tea this time and more of the extra something!' Lilleth got up and put the kettle on to boil. 'By the way, where's my car?'

'I drove it to Jed's, it's still at his place. We went out looking for you.'

'You drove it to Jed's? My goodness, things are already changing around here.'

'Oh Lord! That reminds me, I must phone him and let him know you're safe. And Abbie too – she was very concerned for you.'

'Well, you go and make your phone calls while I finish making this tea and then you can tell me if I've missed anything while I've been away.'

Chapter Forty-One

Jack and Abbie had just returned from taking Luisa to the train station. As Abbie glumly waved her friend good-bye, Jack had given her a big squeezy hug. 'Don't be sad, you'll see each other again in a few days,' he'd said.

Winnifred Cottage seemed incredibly empty after yesterday and with Luisa gone too, Abbie was very glad to have Jack there. She was pushing Miriam's borrowed tables together and placing the chairs around it. 'Do you fancy helping me cook a meal, the day after tomorrow?' she asked Jack.

'Yes, I think so,' he said doubtfully, knowing Abbie and sensing it wasn't going to be that simple.

'There'll be fifteen of us.'

'What!'

'Well, I can't leave anyone out. There's Jilly's lot, Eva and Lilleth and lovely Jed. And I'd really like to invite Miriam and her little girls, me and you. It'll be fine.'

'OK, if you say so.'

'I do. And it'll be fun. What's wrong - what are you hovering about for? You're all fidgety. And anyway, why exactly are you staying up here? Not that it isn't lovely having you here, of course.'

Jack took a deep breath. 'I have got something to tell you actually. Sit down for a sec.' They sat at the end of the row of tables; Abbie was very curious and Jack was feeling quite anxious now. 'OK, I know you love it up here. I do too. And after everything that's happened, I can understand you wanting to escape and make a fresh start. I'd like that too.'

'You want to escape? From me you mean?'

'No. Not from you. I mean generally; do the things we've always said we wanted to do. I've always wanted my own studio, push my own work more.' Abbie nodded. They'd spent many hours discussing their shared dreams.

'OK, so I've been looking at property up here. I was just looking at first and then I saw the perfect place for a studio – it just happens to have a house attached. I've put in an offer for it and I can't believe it, but it's been accepted.'

'Wow, I can't believe it. That's fantastic.' Abbie was having difficulty taking it all in. She was delighted that Jack would be nearer although she couldn't quite get to grips with the idea of him living close by but apart from her. She wondered how things were going to work out. Jack continued.

'I was planning on showing you the place – on our way back from the station.'

'Yes, I'd love to see it. Is it fairly near here?'

'Yeah, really close. Just a little further on down the hill. The problem is, yesterday's storm caused some damage. What I mean is, a tree fell on it. The house is fine but the extension that I'm planning to use as a studio is a bit smashed.'

293

'I don't believe it! You've gone and bought The White House.'

'Yeah, that's the one. What do you think? Have you been inside?'

'Yes, I have. It's a lovely house, rather big though. But I know what you mean about the business side of it – it really would be perfect as a studio. I've thought that myself.'

'Ah, you see, great minds think alike!'

Jack's mobile rang, and Abbie got up and left him to the call, wandering into the kitchen. This was huge; Jack buying The White House and moving up here, but she still wasn't sure what was on his mind. Did he want her to move in with him? What about Winnifred Cottage? She'd already bemoaned to him that it wasn't suitable for what she originally wanted. Did he expect her to sell it? She wasn't sure how she felt about that. They had a lot to talk about.

Chapter Forty-Two

Jed walked up the garden path to Lilleth's cottage, marvelling at the gorgeous weather; picture perfect blue skies and melting warm sunshine that soothed his old bones. He could hardly believe that only two days ago the brutal forces of the same Mother Nature could have caused so much havoc.

He gave his cursory tap-tap on the door and let himself in. The two sisters were huddled together over the stove, the scent of blackberries and sugar filling the air. Jed paused and stared for a second; was it his imagination or did Eva appear to have her hand gently resting on the shoulder of her sister as they gazed into the huge preserving pan, laughing at a shared joke.

'Good morning ladies,' he said, reluctant to intrude on their moment although they both turned and greeted him warmly in return.

Eva took over the jam stirring as Lilleth went towards Jed for a brief hug as he kissed her on the cheek. 'Good to see you back home,' he said, attempting to give her a stern look; chastising her for wandering off and making them all worry. But immediately his face unfolded into a wide smile conveying much more than words could, that he was very relieved to have her back safe and sound.

Lilleth smiled back. 'Time for tea, I think.' She filled the kettle and Eva took it from her, placing it on the stove and lighting the gas. Soon after they were sitting around the table, a big pot of tea brewing in the middle.

'I'm not stopping too long,' said Jed before anyone could suggest adding a little something 'extra' to the tea. 'I'm taking Abbie out, just on my way to pick her up now.'

'Lovely,' said Lilleth as she poured. 'Anywhere nice?'

'We've got a bit of business to attend to,' he said vaguely.

Instinctively Eva was about to prod for more information, but she bit her tongue; she was a reformed character, she reminded herself, in all ways, and stayed silent. She was pleased that Lilleth took up the cause.

'Sounds mysterious Jed,' she teased. She had an inkling where this was going. It had taken a while for Jed to get to this point but obviously he was ready now. 'Are you going to confide in us?'

'Not just yet,' he said adamantly. He grinned at her. He knew she knew. He'd always suspected but had never been absolutely sure. He was grateful for her discretion.

Eva looked from one to the other. She knew nothing and felt very much the odd one out; like the person who doesn't understand the joke but doesn't want to ask for it to be explained to them. She waited patiently which in itself was a new experience for her, hopeful that someone would put her out of her misery. Jed noticed the lost look on her face and continued.

Diplomatically he said, 'I will tell you both one thing and it's this; Abbie is my grand-daughter.'

Lilleth smiled, looking down and stirring her tea. Eva gasped and was wide-eyed but speechless.

'Your sister Annaliese and me, well, let's just say we had a liaison. Many years ago. I knew that she had a daughter and I knew that the little girl was mine.' Jed took a deep breath and sighed as if the effort of the conversation was wearing him out.

Lilleth patted his hand. 'That'll do Jed, we can talk another time.'

He was grateful for her understanding and drank his tea. Eva, still trying to take it all in, as well as the fact that Lilleth didn't seem to be too surprised by this enormous revelation, desperately wanted him to continue with his story. And this time she couldn't stop herself.

'So, does Abbie know? That you're her grandfather?'

'No, she doesn't. That's why I'm taking her out; it's one of the things I need to talk to her about.'

Eva wanted to know what else he was going to talk to her about but Lilleth got up and interrupted the moment by collecting the empty cups and putting them in the sink. Jed gratefully took his cue and got up to leave.

'Thank-you for the tea. Lovely to see you home Lilleth; lovely to see the both of you.'

Abbie was putting bread into the toaster as Jack appeared behind her, circling her waist with one hand as he pulled back her hair with the other, kissing her on the cheek. 'Good morning sleepy head. I was hoping to keep you in bed all day.'

Abbie turned and leaned against the counter, looking directly into his smiling eyes. 'Mm, a nice thought but some of us have things to do.'

The first night Jack had stayed at Winnifred Cottage, he'd slept on the sofa but once Luisa had left and it was just the two of them – well, neither of them wanted to sleep apart. It was just like old times, thought Abbie, as she lifted her arms around his neck, reaching up to be kissed. Better in fact, she decided, as the toast popped up making them jump.

'And what's keeping you so busy today?' asked Jack, as Abbie took a couple of plates from the cupboard and started buttering the toast. 'And what's with the toast? I was going to make us a slap-up breakfast.'

'Nope, I haven't got time for that. Do you want marmalade or marmite?'

'Marmalade.'

'I was hoping to go to the supermarket and pick up all the things I need for tomorrow's family meal and I was going to rope you into coming with me. But Jed has invited me out with him for the morning – all a bit of a mystery actually. And he'll be here pretty soon so I need to get myself ready.'

'I haven't met this Jed character yet. I can trust him with you, can I?'

'Perfectly. He's lovely,' said Abbie smiling. 'It's funny, perhaps it's because he's a friend of my aunts', but I can't help thinking of him as an uncle. You'll love him.'

298

'I'm not sure that I will but I am looking forward to meeting him.'

Abbie continued eating her toast and took it with her upstairs to get dressed.

Abbie heard Jed's Land Rover pull up exactly on time and went out to meet him.

'So, am I to know where we're actually going yet?' she asked cheekily.

'Not just yet. Be patient,' said Jed, his eyes twinkling, he was obviously enjoying this. He drove out of the village and carefully along the narrow lanes that were caked with mud from the recent storm. As he drove they talked about all sorts; the tragedy of Mrs Gilbert and the damage to the village that would take some considerable time and money to put right. Jed was particularly interested when Abbie told him about Chloe going missing and he seemed genuinely relieved to know that all was well. And then he proceeded to fill her in on Lilleth's return home – a heart-warming story that left them both in no doubt that the whole experience had brought the two sisters closer together. Although she didn't say anything, Abbie was very much aware that it was in fact two sets of sisters who'd become much closer over the last few days.

As Jed took a turn into a very muddy lane, little more than a dirt track, Abbie realised she'd been here before. 'I know where we are,' she said. 'There's a gorgeous little gallery just down here.' She was just about to explain that she'd brought a painting in to be re-framed, but Jed stopped her short.

299

'I know,' was all he said but he was smiling, secretively. Curiosity was bubbling up inside Abbie, but she knew from the look on Jed's face that she would have to sit tight and wait to see where this mystery tour was really going.

Jed parked to the side of the gallery and got out. Silently he led the way up the wooden stairs and into his workroom. Once inside, still trying to figure out what was going on, Abbie began to look around the room. It was an artist's paradise; the quality of light coming in at all angles and something extra, a peaceful, comforting atmosphere that made you not want to leave. Abbie was soon in her own little world, examining a few rough sketches left on the workbench and the artist's materials looking to be left randomly about but which were probably carefully placed exactly where he wanted them. Her attention was drawn to the furthest wall. The blind was down on the window sheltering a small collection of watercolours. She stood and studied them. They looked familiar. She turned back to Jed who in turn was studying her; wondering if the penny had dropped yet.

'These remind me of something,' she said.

'Is it this?' asked Jed, handing her a gift-wrapped package.

'What's this?' Abbie laughed and as she tore off the paper, suddenly she knew what was inside. She lifted out her gran's painting with its new frame. 'Oh, it's beautiful. It's perfect.' She looked at Jed, still confused. He realised he would have to spell it all out. He sat down wearily on a wooden stool with his back to his easel and gestured for her to hand him the painting. Taking a deep breath, he turned it over, indicating the inscription. 'That's me there. G.T.'

'Is it? But you're Jed.'

'Gerald. Gerald Tobin. And this is my gallery.'

'Oh. Oh, I see.' Jed watched as the jigsaw puzzle of thoughts tumbled through Abbie's mind, finally making a complete picture. 'You painted this for Gran?'

'Yes, that's right.'

Abbie looked whimsically down at the painting. 'She was your inspiration?' she asked, pretty much working out what that meant but nevertheless wanting to hear it from Jed himself.

'Yes, she was.' Jed smiled. 'Me and your gran; we were courting, as we used to say. We had a dream to be married. It was your gran's dream to make Winnifred Cottage our home. And being the strong-willed woman that she was – she bought it.'

'On her own?'

'Yes, she wanted to surprise me. She had some money her father left her, and she'd always saved hard but even so it was unusual for a young single woman to buy property.' Jed looked across the workroom and out the window. 'Even more unusual to keep it and leave it empty for the next fifty years,' he added sadly.

'What happened? Why did you never marry?'

Jed shifted uncomfortably on his seat. 'I went off to Europe to look around the galleries and taste the life in a foreign country; it was something I'd always wanted to do. It was just supposed to be for a few weeks; me and your gran had a tearful good-bye. Well, the few weeks turned into a couple of months

301

and before I knew it, I'd been away from home for six months. We wrote to each other and Anna encouraged me to stay, she said that I should follow my love of art if that's what I really wanted. And I foolishly thought that I could do what I wanted, and she would simply be waiting for me to return.'

'When did you come back? And why didn't she wait?'

'I returned shortly after six months of being away. And Anna was married and living miles away on the other side of The Lakes. We met up just the once, a couple of years later and she explained that she thought I might be away for years – she didn't want to tie me down or make me feel that she'd trapped me.'

'Trapped you? Oh, my goodness!' Abbie sat down heavily on a stool next to Jed, the final pieces of the puzzle finally falling into place. 'She was expecting a baby. My mother. Oh my God – you're my grandfather.' Abbie laughed, not quite able to take it all in. They looked at each other and smiled in silence for a few moments. Abbie looked down at the painting still in her hand. 'And you're an artist. Of course, you are.'

'And that's a beautiful frame you chose – perfect for it.'

'I can't take all the credit. Your assistant helped me choose it.'

'Ah yes, Rhona. She's leaving me in a few months.' Jed stood up stiffly and walked over to his collection of paintings on the wall. Abbie followed.

'These are all yours? They're amazing. I love them.'

'Thank-you,' Jed nodded in appreciation. He didn't bother to explain at this point that they sold for tens of thousands of pounds. He sold one occasionally by word of mouth, but he knew with the right marketing and selling techniques he could sell a lot more. And this was only one collection, he had many others stored around the place.

Jed took a deep breath. Now that he was at the crucial part of his plan, he didn't know how to broach the subject and so he just dived in. 'How would you feel about working here?' he asked rather abruptly.

Abbie smiled in surprise. She definitely needed another job, something more than working in the pub. 'I'd love to.' She wasn't entirely sure what Jed had in mind. 'Do you mean until you find someone to replace Rhona?'

'No, I mean for you to replace Rhona,' he said, more gently now. 'In fact, I'd like you to have the gallery, run the place, manage it properly, work in it, paint in it, whatever you want.'

'Oh Jed. I can't believe it.' Abbie put her hands to her face, stunned and unable to take it all in. Her thoughts were in turmoil; what with Jack returning and buying The White House with the intention of creating his own studio and now this.

'And you're not to worry about your sister – that is, my other grand-daughter, I'll see her right too, one day. But you need a job and an income if I'm to keep you up here with me.'

Abbie was tearful and could hardly speak.

'I take it that's a 'yes' then?'

303

Abbie nodded, that's all she could manage at the moment.

After a celebratory cup of coffee which they drank as Jed gave Abbie a tour of his workroom and the gallery below, he drove her back home.

'Would you like to come in for a while Jed? For a cup of tea?'

'Yes, lovely.'

As Abbie made tea, she noticed Jed looking around him.

'Does it feel a little odd to be here after all this time, and with all your memories?'

'Yes. Yes, it does. And a little sad too, I have to say.'

Abbie didn't push the point; Jed seemed very subdued all of a sudden, although he seemed to snap himself out of it just as quickly. 'Was that your young man earlier, in the white van pulling out when I came to pick you up?'

'Yes, it would've been. That's Jack, he's staying here for a few days.'

'Ah, that explains the rosy cheeks then. And the twinkle in your eye.'

'Or that could be because of you and what you've just done for me!'

Abbie handed him a cup of tea.

'So, what does Jack do?'

'He's a professional photographer and an artist too. He's just bought The White House – or very nearly anyway, from Miriam and Alistair Walker. He's planning to set up his own studio there.'

Jed nodded, deep in thought. 'Does that put you in a bit of quandary? With him living there and you wanting to live here?'

Abbie was relieved Jed had raised this point. 'Well yes, it does actually. Gran was obviously so sentimental about this place. And she left it to me to look after.'

Jed gave her a dubious look.

'Don't you think?'

Jed sighed. 'I think dear Anna, your grandmother, was indeed very sentimental about this place. And she was also a daft woman to hang on to it for the next fifty years, leaving it empty and letting it almost fall down. I don't know why she left the cottage in her will; she could have sold it and shared the money, I don't know. But I do know, from the way she encouraged me, that she would hate for this place to be a burden for you. We missed out on our opportunity to be together and she would want you to grab your opportunities with both hands and be happy and if Winnifred Cottage helped you along that path, she would be very happy indeed.'

Abbie thought for a few seconds. 'Do you mean selling Winnifred Cottage?'

'If that's what you want. If that's what you need to do, then do it.'

Jed smiled, satisfied. All was well in his world. He put his cup and saucer in the sink and turned to face Abbie, holding her shoulders and giving her a quick kiss on the cheek. 'That's allowed, I think, as I am your grandfather! And I look forward to seeing you tomorrow evening for what I'm sure will be a very interesting soiree.'

305

Chapter Forty-Three

There was a knock at the door. 'Aaarghh – I'm not ready! Jack can you get it?'

'Yep.'

That was one of the things she loved about Jack – he was so laid back. He was never flustered. Even when he was stressed, he put his energies into getting the problem solved. Abbie momentarily thought back to the fire and how anxious he'd been for her to believe him. She felt ashamed at how quickly she'd mistrusted him. But not anymore, this was a new start.

She could hear voices downstairs. It was Jed and Eva and Lilleth, the first people to arrive. Abbie just needed a couple more minutes and she would be ready. She'd put a flowery cotton summer dress on in honour of the glorious warm sunny evening. It was so nice not to have to wear warm waterproofs. She imagined Eva would be moaning about how rude her hostess was to keep them waiting and hurried herself, not bothering to put her earrings on. She was hoping that Jilly would arrive first so that she could have a quick word with her about Jed and the gallery. She didn't want to explain things over the phone and now she just hoped Jed didn't say anything before she got a chance to.

'Hello everyone.' Jack had done a perfect job; everyone was seated in the living room with drinks in hand. Abbie was surprised to see Eva and Lilleth sitting cosy together on the settee, Eva fussing her sister, putting a cushion behind her back and making sure she was comfortable. She looked questioningly at Jed who gave her a conspiratorial wink.

Jack handed her a glass of red wine. 'Cheers everybody,' she said, raising her glass. 'Ooh, I see you've brought more supplies.' Several bottles of home-made wine had been placed on the coffee table. 'No doubt, we'll start on those later,' said Abbie, wondering what effect the lethal brew would have on everyone. Perhaps they'd all be dancing merrily by then.

'Just a few of last year's tried and tested efforts; these are definitely some of the best,' said Lilleth with a wicked grin.

There was another knock at the door; Jilly and her family and Miriam and her two girls all arrived at once.

'I can't believe this weather,' said Miriam.

'I know,' agreed Jilly. 'It's typical, we're going home tomorrow.'

'You'll be back,' said Abbie sincerely hoping that it wouldn't be too long before she saw her again. 'Come in everyone.'

Honey and Blossom wanted to play in what to them was a huge garden, but the grass was still water-logged and muddy, and Miriam had a hard time persuading them that they had to come inside.

'Oh, this is lovely Abbie,' said Jilly looking around. 'It's so pretty.' Abbie had forgotten this was the first time Jilly had been to the cottage – it had been such a chaotic week.

'I'll show you around properly a bit later,' Abbie whispered. 'I need to talk to you.'

The living room was getting crowded and so Abbie ushered everyone into the next room, the makeshift dining room, where she'd pushed three of Miriam's tearoom tables together. Miriam had also lent her white linen tablecloths and half a dozen small vases which Abbie had filled with bunches of Sweet William. Cutlery and glasses had been laid out and it all looked very stylish. One thing Abbie hadn't thought to do was to set out place cards and now there was a lot of fussing and organising getting everyone into their seats.

Abbie had spent ages deliberating over what to cook. In the end she'd decided to keep it simple in the hope that it would satisfy everyone, even the children. She'd opted for a traditional Roast Chicken with lots of different vegetables, a choice of potatoes, stuffing and gravy. She decided against a starter; too many plates and too much fussing about. But for dessert she'd really gone to town. There was a choice of ice-creams which she thought the children would like and she had wafers and cornets and chocolate flakes to help keep them occupied. For the adults there was a boozy trifle or berry cheesecake.

The food was served, and the room became momentarily quiet as everyone tucked in. Eventually small groups of conversation got under way as everyone relaxed and enjoyed themselves. The surprise of the day was watching Eva and Lilleth natter away to each other with a different kind of ease, even chuckling occasionally at their own private jokes. Jilly and Abbie caught each other's eye; the observation hadn't been wasted on them.

The other personality change was evident in Chloe who seemed somewhat humbled by recent events. She was quiet and pleasant and helpful to Miriam, especially with her younger sisters.

Jack was seated at the head of the table and Abbie was next to him. Jilly called across, 'I was thinking we should make a toast. You should do it Abbie.'

'Yes, you're right, but I'm not doing it. You do it Jack.'

Jack shook his head, smiling as he picked up his glass. 'Attention everyone,' he called playfully. 'Thank-you all for coming today. Can you please get on with the washing up now and then go home!'

Everyone laughed except the teenagers who gave him derisive looks berating the way adults always thought they were so funny.

'OK, only joking. Seriously, thanks to Abbie for this gorgeous meal. It's been a crazy week but I'm very happy that we're all here, safe and sound to enjoy this. And like it or not, I'll be sticking around for quite a while longer. As most of you know, I'm hoping to move into The White House.' Jack raised his glass in acknowledgement to Miriam who smiled back. 'And Abbie's moving in with me.'

Abbie smiled, hoping that Jack wouldn't say too much. He knew that she wanted to speak to Jilly first. He continued.

'We're planning to convert the old tearoom into a studio – what shall we call it? Jack and Abigail's?' he suggested teasingly.

'Or Abigail and Jack's?' Abbie responded, laughing.

More seriously now, Jack looked directly at her and lowered his voice just a little. 'I was hoping for the Mr and Mrs Jack Matthews Photographic Studio. What do you say?'

Abbie placed her hand over his, gazing directly back at him. 'Well, this wasn't on the menu,' she said laughing.

'You said you wanted a surprise for dessert! Do I get my 'yes' or have I got to wait for cheese and biscuits?'

'You most definitely get your 'yes',' said Abbie, leaning over for a kiss at which point everyone clapped and cheered and chinked glasses in celebration.

Some time later while the elder children were looking after the younger ones in the garden but with strict instructions to keep off the grass, Miriam and Abbie shooshed everyone else into the living room while they cleared away.

Abbie noticed that Miriam was unusually subdued. 'Everything OK Miriam?'

'Yes, I'm fine, thanks,' she said unconvincingly as she finished the drying up. She folded the tea towel neatly and placed it on the worktop, deep in thought.

'Actually Abbie, I was wondering. What do you plan to do with the cottage? I mean, now that you're moving in with Jack?'

Abbie was placing the crockery up in the cupboard. 'I'm putting it on the market. It's the sensible thing to do. And then we can put the money into the studio and, oh, it's going to be brilliant.' Suddenly the penny dropped, and she spun around. 'Miriam!'

Miriam smiled. 'I should come away with quite a substantial sum from the sale of The White House and I have a few savings of my own. And I know my parents would help me out. Winnifred Cottage would be perfect.'

'It would! You and the girls could live above....'

'I know, I know. I've thought it all out. The two main rooms here would make perfect tearooms and the kitchen just off them is ideal. And the garden is fan-tas-tic. I have so many plans for that.'

'Miriam, it's a brilliant idea. Come and have a look at the rest of the place. You haven't even been upstairs have you?'

Suddenly Miriam had a serious look on her face. 'It seems too good to be true and I am a little worried about the timing and everything. It's going to take a while for me to get finances in place and you know what it's like, these things always take longer than you think.'

'No problem,' said Abbie dismissively. 'I won't even put it on the market. I'm sure we can agree everything between us. And anyway, it's going to take a while before Jack moves into your place and

I've got to go back and sell my house down south –
it'll all work out fine. We'll make sure it does.'

Miriam was beaming and gave Abbie a hug, not
able to convey a fraction of the happiness she felt.
Just at that moment Jilly walked into the kitchen
feeling immediately that she was intruding on
something.

Abbie really needed to talk to her; there was so
much going on and she didn't want Jilly thinking she
was keeping her in the dark. 'Actually Miriam, do
you mind if we do the tour another time?'

'Of course not,' said Miriam, diplomatically
leaving the room to see what her children were up to
and to make more plans in the garden.

'I wouldn't mind a tour,' said Jilly. 'Oh, and by
the way, congratulations.' Jilly gave her sister a
squeeze and a kiss on the cheek. 'You kept that
quiet.'

'I had no idea he was going to ask me. Honestly.'

'Well, I think it's brilliant.'

'Thank-you. Come on, upstairs before anyone
else interrupts; I've got lots to tell you.'

'There's more?'

'You wouldn't believe.'

Abbie was about to lead Jilly into her own
bedroom but when she looked behind, Jilly had
disappeared into the spare room, the one decorated
for Luisa. 'This is lovely; you've done it really nice.'

'Thanks,' said Abbie, as she shut the door behind
her. 'Look we'll do the tour another time. Sit down,
I need to talk to you.'

Jilly sat on the edge of the bed feeling slightly
anxious now.

'Is something wrong?'

'No, absolutely not. Nothing wrong at all.' Abbie was impatient to get this over and done with before something else happened to distract them and then Jilly might end up finding out from someone else. 'OK, gosh I don't know where to start. Right, first of all, what do you think of Jed?'

'Well, I've only just met him, but he seems like a lovely man, I suppose.'

'He is. That's good, that you like him. Because, well, he's your grandfather – and mine too, obviously.'

'What? Are you sure?'

'Yes, definitely sure. He and Gran were, sort of, betrothed to each other I suppose. It's a long story - he went away travelling and then she discovered she was pregnant but ended marrying someone else. I'll tell you properly another time.'

'When did you find this out?'

'Only yesterday. I suspected Jed had a thing for Gran but honestly I had no idea of anything like this.'

Jilly looked confused; this was too much to take in, and Abbie wasn't giving her a moment to think.

'OK, the next thing; Jed or should I say grand-dad has asked me…..'

There was a tap on the door and Chloe peeked her head around the door. 'Sorry Mum, Molly's fallen over, and she won't stop crying. She wants you.'

'Can't Dad deal with it?'

Chloe shrugged her shoulders and grimaced. 'She just wants you.'

Jilly sighed and got up off the bed. 'Sorry Abbie, back in a sec.'

After about ten minutes Abbie deduced that Jilly had got waylaid with another family drama and went back downstairs.

'Ah, there you are,' said Jack. 'We were just talking about going down to The Green Man – do you fancy it?'

'Yeah, why not?' It seemed a nice way to end the evening and it was a little cramped with all of them in the cottage.

As they were getting organised, Abbie noticed Jilly and Jed having a quiet word together just outside the front door. They were smiling and then Jilly reached up and gently kissed him on his bearded cheek. Poor Jed, he was a little overcome, but very proud too.

'Come on then, let's get going,' he said, taking charge. Everyone followed Jed as he led the way, strolling down the hill on a beautiful summer's evening.

Inside the pub, Jed ordered drinks for everyone and they made their way outside and spread themselves between three picnic tables on the patio area.

The children had grouped themselves around one table; the elder ones keeping the younger ones entertained. Honey was sitting on Chloe's lap and then, of course, Blossom wanted to climb up too but there was hardly room for the both of them at once and they were having to take turns.

Abbie sat next to Jack with Jed opposite. She was jittery in case he spontaneously made a toast to her as the new gallery owner. She was desperate to speak to Jilly and drank her wine quickly in the futile hope that everyone else would do the same.

'More drinks everyone?' she said, standing up.

'Wow, you're thirsty!' said Jack. 'OK, I'll come with you.'

'No, no. It's OK. Well actually, Jilly, give me a hand, will you?' She nodded surreptitiously towards the pub, hoping to indicate that this was an opportunity for them to grab a couple of minutes alone together. All of a sudden Jilly understood and followed Abbie inside. It was busy, and they waited at the bar.

'You were going to tell me something else?' remembered Jilly. 'I'm not sure I can take much more today.'

'It's OK, this is more good news.'

'Oh, I don't mind that. I'm always open to good news,' said Jilly, quickly looking around to see if it was their turn to order yet. There was one other person before them.

'Jed, or should I say Grandfather – although I can't get used to calling him that yet – well, he's given me his gallery.'

Jilly looked completely blank. 'What gallery? I didn't know he had a gallery.'

'Oh no, of course you didn't. And nor did I until yesterday. Oh crikey, this is another long story but look, we don't have time right now. All you need to know is that Jed has an art gallery right here in the village and he's gifted it to me to run however I please.' Abbie stopped abruptly. Jilly's face had clouded over; she was trying bravely to smile, as if it was the right thing to do but she was obviously struggling.

'Wait, I haven't finished yet,' said Abbie, falling over her words, desperate to get them out. 'I want us to be partners, you and me.'

'I don't know anything about how to run an art gallery.'

'You don't need to, I do.'

'And how can I be involved, living three hundred miles away in Dorset?'

'You can't. And I don't want you to be involved as such. You've already got enough on your plate.'

Jilly sighed, exasperated.

'I want you to be a silent partner. That is, I run it, get in more artists, schedule different exhibitions.' Abbie moved in a little closer and whispered, 'Jed's work sells for a small fortune. Can you believe that we have a semi-famous artist in the family? There's masses of his works already there, stored away that just needs proper promotion.'

'And why do you want me involved then?'

'For the simple reason that we can share the profits, fifty/fifty which is only right and fair.'

'Not really, not if you're doing all the work.'

'OK, we can come to some agreement. But what we are definitely splitting down the middle is from the sale of Winnifred Cottage.'

'You're selling the cottage? But why?'

'Because I'm moving in with Jack, of course. I don't need two homes and then we can put some of the money into setting up the studio at The White House and the gallery.'

'Will you be able to manage, working in two places?'

'I'll give it a damn good try. This has always been my dream and now it's finally come true – double true, in fact.'

Jilly placed a steadying hand on the bar. Her legs felt slightly wobbly and she wished she was sitting down. She was totally speechless, and Abbie continued.

'You know what this means? It means you and Glen can start looking for a bigger house again, doesn't it?'

'Yes,' said Jilly nodding, her eyes filling with tears, so touched by Abbie's obvious delight at being able to help. 'Thank-you,' she whispered. Abbie placed her hand over Jilly's, still resting on the bar, and smiled.

The barman loomed towards them, unaware that he was interrupting a special moment. 'What can I get you ladies?'

Abbie looked across at Jilly. 'A bottle of champagne, I think. And lots of glasses, actually you'd better make that two bottles.'

The barman said he would send it out and Abbie and Jilly returned to the garden to bewildered looks from everyone.

'It's coming,' said Abbie. Eva and Lilleth were on their own at a table and Abbie and Jilly sat down opposite them, just as two waitresses appeared with the champagne in ice buckets and trays of glasses, setting them down carefully.

'Ooh champagne, how lovely,' said Lilleth. 'What are we celebrating?'

317

'Everything,' said Abbie. 'Family, love, art,' she laughed. 'What about you Jilly?'

Jilly thought for just a second and raised her glass. 'My family, my children and my very wonderful sister.' She nudged Abbie playfully and linked arms with her.

'And Lilleth?' said Abbie.

Lilleth wrinkled her nose at the champagne bubbles. 'All of those things,' she said, smiling widely and taking another sip.

All eyes were on Eva who needed no prompting. 'And my wonderful sister too.'

They chinked glasses and Abbie looked across to the other table where Jack raised his glass and winked at her and then Jed did the same. Miriam was gazing into her glass, seemingly lost in her own world.

They all had many things to be thankful for and to celebrate. Abbie sent up a silent thank-you to her gran. Whether they realised it or not, they all shared a gratitude to Annaliese Delaney and Winnifred Cottage.

I hope you enjoyed reading Winnifred Cottage and if you did, I would be very grateful if you could leave me a review on Amazon to let me and other readers know what you think.

Thank-you,
Jennie Alexander

www.JennieAlexander.biz

JennieAlexander@hotmail.co.uk

Other books by Jennie Alexander

The Beach Hut

Ella Peters hides behind a tree to watch her ex-husband marry his new young bride. Now she wants to run away and hide for good.

And where better to go than England's beautiful Hampshire coast and to Ella's family beach hut?

Inside is a cosy home from home, a love nest and a place to shelter from the elements.

The beach hut soon plays witness to events that bring tragedy as well as joy - a welcome retreat for those who seek solace there.

Libby Pinkney thinks she has life under control; with two well-behaved teenagers, the biggest house with the best sea view and an increasingly impressive presence within the local community.

But when a new neighbour moves into the old cottage next door, her well-ordered life threatens to tumble around her like a house of cards.

Tied with a Ribbon (A Christmas Story)

It's only four weeks until Christmas but Alice has had a tough year and is struggling to get into the Christmas spirit.

As the owner of a gift-wrapping shop 'Ribbons and Bows', this is her busiest time of year and as much as she'd like to, Alice cannot possibly escape all the seasonal festivities.

Dena has worries of her own, not least of all, financial ones which are threatening to put a dampener on Christmas for her and her family.

These two life-long friends do their best to help each other out at this particularly poignant time of year when it's all too easy to feel alone.

The Renion Party

Five young women become the best of friends at The Ashford Chef Academy where they've signed up for three years of intensive training.

Talented and passionate, they are also wildly ambitious - determined to succeed in their chosen profession.

Imogen Ravenscroft isn't allowed to join their tight-knit group. She's the one born with a silver spoon in her mouth; the girl who has everything. But ten years after graduation, it's Imogen who's holding a reunion party.

That summer Ellen and Janey, Alicia, Fran and Mel reflect on the last ten years, reconciling their hopes and dreams of the past with what has become their reality.

Inevitably, they contemplate how they might compare to their former friends, and who might be found lacking.

The reunion party is a huge success. Good friends reunite, and inspirational stories bounce around the room like champagne corks. True to form, Imogen has spared no expense; her generosity and kindness still a mystery, but on that balmy summer evening all is soon to be revealed.

Live Laugh Love

In a pretty village in the Surrey countryside, life is good for neighbours Hope Clements and Josie Bell. Both are happily married and working hard on their hopes and dreams for the future.

Hope has prepared meticulously for six months and is ready to set off for her dream holiday – six weeks at a well-being retreat in Bali.

But something happens the night before departure which threatens not only her long-awaited holiday but everything she's worked for in life.

Josie is on hand to provide comfort and support. But what starts out as a seemingly harmless favour soon forces her to reassess her own life, threatening to destroy her own happiness in the process.

It seems to Hope that every way she turns, she is met with lies and deceit, even from her daughter who is supposedly away studying at university.

How will she manage to maintain the roles of wife and mother and carer in the face of such dishonesty? And will she ever find the courage to challenge those in question?

A Nice Glass of Red

Winnifred Mayhew has exciting plans. The vineyards of southern France are beckoning, and she is preparing to become an oenology expert.

However, life often has a way of side-stepping even the best laid plans, and a family tragedy shatters her dreams.

Winnie finds solace through her friends and family, and also from the colourful members of The Wine Club - where it soon becomes apparent that everyone is dealing with their own demons.

Gift Wrapped (Non fiction)

Basic Techniques and Exquisite Gift Wrapping

Creative gift-wrapping adds to the joy of both giving and receiving.

You may be surprised to learn that this form of paperwork craft is easy and many of the elaborate effects shown in this book are actually very simple.

It provides step-by-step photo instructions showing how to wrap a gift to make it look both impressive and stylish.

There's advice on the best type of wrapping paper to use for each project and finally a chapter on ribbons and bows to add the final finishing touches to your gift.

The Owl who made Friends with the Moon

Oswald the Owl may be a nocturnal bird, but he keeps getting lost in the wood.

Luckily, he soon makes a friend who helps him find his way back home.

Enjoy the rhyming story in this children's picture book, ideal bedtime reading for young ones.

Made in United States
Orlando, FL
19 April 2022

16982245R00180